Hook, Line,
and
Homicide

Also by Mark Richard Zubro

The Paul Turner Mysteries

Sorry Now?
Political Poison
Another Dead Teenager
The Truth Can Get You Killed
Drop Dead
Sex and Murder.com
Dead Egotistical Morons
Nerds Who Kill

The Tom and Scott Mysteries

A Simple Suburban Murder
Why Isn't Becky Twitchell Dead?
The Only Good Priest
The Principal Cause of Death
An Echo of Death
Rust on the Razor
Are You Nuts?
One Dead Drag Queen
Here Comes the Corpse
File Under Dead
Everyone's Dead but Us

Hook, Line, and Homicide

Mark Richard Zubro

St. Martin's Minotaur
New York

This is a work of fiction. All of the characters, organizations, and events portrayed in this novel are either products of the author's imagination or are used fictitiously.

www.minotaurbooks.com

Library of Congress Cataloging-in-Publication Data

Zubro, Mark Richard.
  Hook, line and homicide / by Mark Richard Zubro. — 1st St. Martin's Minotaur ed.
    p. cm.
  ISBN-13: 978-0-312-33303-4
  ISBN-10: 0-312-33303-X
  1. Turner, Paul (Fictional character)—Fiction. 2. Gay police officers—Fiction. 3. Vacations—Fiction. 4. Canada—Fiction. I. Title.

PS3576.U225H66 2007

813'.54—dc22   2006052542

First Edition: July 2007

10 9 8 7 6 5 4 3 2 1

Acknowledgments

For their kind and gracious help, I wish to thank Barb D'Amato, Jeanne Dams, Mike Kushner, Bob Beran, Joel Michel, and Vinnie.

Hook, Line,
and
Homicide

.1.

"Dad, are we moving to Canada?"

Paul Turner looked up from his fishing tackle box. "We're going fishing like we do every summer," Paul told his eleven-year-old.

"But we're not moving?"

"Why would we move?" Paul asked Jeff.

"Because of all the antigay stuff." Jeff was restringing his fishing reel. He had his Zebco rod teetering on the arm of his wheelchair, the reel in his lap, and he was using both hands to pull on a new line.

Paul knew his son was referring to the antigay amendments in the United States Congress and the prohate amendments and referendums that had passed in many states. "Did somebody say we were going to move?" Paul asked.

"Well, no, but I read the news on the Net. I know some people have left."

Paul was glad his son read so much, but this activity

tended to exacerbate Jeff's seemingly infinite need to have questions answered. Paul did everything he could to reply to the boy's questions patiently.

"Do you want to move?" Paul asked.

"No," the youngster said, "I've got plans with Bertram to go to the aquarium after we get back, and I'm getting Mr. Faneski for a teacher next year. He's a good teacher. He has the honors kids do the coolest science projects. I want to try working with some gravitational anomalies."

"You know what gravitational anomalies are?" Paul asked.

"Yes, and I can spell it," Jeff said. "We aren't moving?" The boy could be relentless in his questions and his need for assurance. He was awfully bright, but he was still a kid.

Paul said, "Ben and I have no plans to move. This is our country. We'll stay here and fight if we have to."

"Are there going to be fights?"

Paul's older son, Brian, thumped down the stairs and breezed into the room. Paul sometimes wondered if the stairs would last until Brian left for college. "Who's fighting?" Brian asked.

"Nobody, right now," Paul said.

Jeff said, "We were talking about moving to Canada."

"With or without you?" Brian asked his younger brother.

Jeff said, "We were thinking of abandoning *you* on an island in the middle of the lake."

"No parents. No rules. What's the downside?"

Paul said, "No fast cars, no junk food, no adoring girlfriends."

"They'd flock to any island I was on."

Paul said, "Jeff wanted to know if we were thinking of moving because of all the latest gay-hate legislation."

Brian sat down next to his younger brother's wheelchair. "You need help with that?"

"I'm almost done. I've got a few hooks left to sharpen." Brian reached into the pile, pulled one up, and picked up a file. Brian looked at his father. "You and Ben don't talk about it much."

"Our roots and our home are here," Paul said.

"How come Ian is going with us this year?" Jeff asked. "Is he thinking of moving?"

Jeff was referring to Ian Hume, Paul's first lover, and still a good friend, and the best reporter for the largest gay paper in Chicago.

Paul said, "He's written a few articles for the *Gay Tribune* about people who have left, but I think he's going this year mostly because he hasn't had a vacation in a long time."

"He's never been fishing," Brian said. "What's he going to do up there?"

"Relax? Read a book?"

Jeff said, "He's gonna look weird if he doesn't have any fishing stuff."

Brian said, "He enjoys being weird."

Jeff said, "And he won't drive with us. He's flying in."

Paul said, "Teenagers and kids make him nervous."

Brian said, "Don't most people make him nervous?"

"Usually I don't," Turner said.

"If people make him nervous, how can he be a reporter?" Jeff asked.

Paul said, "He loves interviewing people, and he enjoys skewering them with their own stupidities. He just doesn't want to socialize with them."

"He's weird," Brian said.

"How often do I make judgments about your friends—"

Brian opened his mouth to answer.

Turner continued, "—and tell you about it?"

"Not often," Brian conceded.

▲ 2 ▲

The Turners and Fenwicks always drove up to Canada in tandem. The Fenwicks had joined the annual Turner family excursion every summer since the two detectives had become partners eight years ago. They always stopped at the Wisconsin Dells on the way up. They spent two days among the crass materialism because the kids enjoyed themselves on the rides and attractions, and Fenwick could fill up on junk food.

Buck Fenwick was a heavyset man who had a ghastly sense of humor. Turner liked him and his wife, Madge, immensely.

They crossed the border into Canada at International Falls. Then they drove west until they picked up Highway 71 going north. The sky was cloudy and fits of rain gusted against the two SUVs as they motored north. Ben, Paul's partner, was riding shotgun. Brian was next to Jeff's specially installed wheelchair access seat. In the far back in regal splendor was

Mrs. Talucci, their next-door neighbor. The ninety-something friend of the family always accompanied them. At the moment she was reading *Beauty Tips from Moose Jaw* by Will Ferguson, a Canadian writer she had been recommending. Paul knew it was a humorous travel book about Canada.

As they drove past Kenora, the sky cleared, and the wind rose from the north.

They arrived in Cathura, a small town of about five thousand, half an hour west of Kenora. It sat right on Lake of the Woods. The harbor they went to was a half a mile east of town. It was still largely an old fifties-style resort with little individual cabins and houseboats that could be rented by the day and week. A newer addition was a gargantuan log-lodge that, when finished, had managed to block the lake view of half a dozen angry lakeside property owners. Trees and small boats crowded together on shore all the way from the lodge to the water. The ramp into the lake had three boats in line waiting to be launched. Leaning against the wall of a jam-packed bait and convenience store was Kevin Yost, their guide.

Turner had come to this same spot with his parents when he was a kid. Back then Turner's father had used an old guide named Peter Yost. Kevin was Peter's grandchild. For years, Turner had seen the boy helping his grandfather. His understanding was that Kevin's parents were less than adequate: distant, indifferent, or gone. He had not pried. The boy knew the best fishing spots on the lake. He was polite, respectful, quiet to the point of taciturnity. Kevin understood fishermen's needs, usually anticipated them. He was only seventeen, but he'd been helping since he was six, been a guide since he was thirteen. After his grandfather retired to

Florida several years ago, Turner had taken a chance on the teenager. For the past three years, he'd worked out magnificently. He always had everything perfectly prepared. He'd discussed food and bait and tactics with Turner before they arrived. The guides were affiliated with the resort but not hired or paid by it. Turner liked the kid. He was also one of the best guides on the lake.

Kevin was only a year older than Brian. They'd been buddies for nearly ten years. Sometimes Kevin slept overnight on the boat. The two boys had become friends back when Kevin's grandfather had still been their guide. Their physical competitions were often amusing, with the two boys competing to show who was strongest. Brian, a star athlete in his high school, was several inches taller than Kevin and far more muscular, but Turner had seen the far slighter, older boy heft much larger fishing tackle boxes than Brian and with far less strain. Kevin had a subtle sense of humor that he mostly kept hidden. Paul wasn't sure he'd seen the boy smile more than a half dozen times. The teenager was able to handle Fenwick's sense of humor, and sometimes even appreciate it, a rarity at any time and place, especially in the North Woods.

Kevin greeted them with a small wave. He and Brian began loading supplies onto both houseboats.

The owner of the marina, Michael Zoll, joined them. Zoll had purchased the marina when Turner was a teenager. Zoll struck Turner as the kind of guy whose cheerfulness was forced, especially after Turner had begun appearing with Ben at the lake. He'd asked Fenwick and Ben and Madge about it. Fenwick had said he hadn't noticed any change. Ben said he had nothing to compare it with, but that he did find the man vaguely off-putting. Ben had said, "That much cheerfulness can't be healthy." Madge had said, "It's all fake. I don't think he likes anybody. He rarely meets anybody's eyes, and never yours, Paul. He's got a fake smile and a damp-greasy handshake. I don't like him." But Zoll had never done anything outwardly unfriendly, so Turner had swallowed his unease. Fenwick liked Zoll's bait and convenience store because it provided the largest variety of beers within fifty miles. At least according to Fenwick this was so. Turner always took Fenwick's word for it on beer. Turner was content with a lite beer. He didn't need designer lite beer.

Precisely at four o'clock a sleek cigarette boat roared up to the dock. Every summer that they'd ever come here, Mrs. Talucci had been met at the dock by this silver racing craft. As a kid, Paul remembered asking his parents where Mrs. Talucci was going. They always said she was visiting a friend. As an adult Paul had asked Mrs. Talucci where she went. She told him, "Visiting."

The person in the cigarette boat was always a man in his middle-to-late twenties. There had been different ones over the years. The man was always dressed in a navy blue blazer, khaki pants, a white polo shirt, and blue deck shoes. He always handed Mrs. Talucci aboard and took her bags below. She donned her life jacket and sat next to the driver's seat. She held a tin as large as a bread box in her lap. She would wave to Paul and his family and be off.

Turner never asked why the driver also carried a gun concealed in a discreet holster under his jacket. Nor why the taut muscles on slender frames seemed to ripple expectantly.

Madge Fenwick had speculated once, "I bet she's off trysting with a secret love."

Fenwick had said, "She's in her nineties."

"Good for her," Madge said. "I hope she keeps going when she's over one hundred."

"Is it safe?" Ben asked.

Madge said, "I'm sure she knows what a condom is."

Fenwick said, "That sounds like something I'd say."

"I wouldn't want to try and stop her," Turner said.

Fenwick said, "We tried to follow her once. That boat can outrun anything we can afford to rent."

Paul said, "And we got a typical Mrs. Talucci response when she got back."

"What did she say?" Ben asked.

Fenwick said, "She laughed in that wonderful way of hers and said, 'Nice try, boys.'"

"Does she bring fishing tackle?" Ben asked.

"Nope," Turner said. "The same boat brings her back on the day we leave. She always has a big smile on her face."

"What's in the tin?" Ben asked.

"Fudge," Turner said.

"Fudge?"

"Yep."

"How do you know?"

"I asked. She told."

Madge said, "I hope it's a hot sexual tryst with a stud who picked her up in a sleazy marina in Kenora."

"I doubt it," Turner said. "We never see her in town. She never talks about spending money up here. Wherever she goes, it's not on her nickel."

They unpacked the SUVs and stowed gear on the two houseboats. Then they began some of the traditional rituals of fishing. Whether they wished to admit it or not, all fishermen were superstitious. Fenwick cheerfully admitted this. Paul smiled and submitted to his own family's superstitions. Before anyone ate, Brian tested the Jet Ski. Paul took Jeff in his wheelchair to Zoll's bait shop, where they had to purchase specific lures and baits from Jeff's list. It was always just the two of them on this minor excursion. Jeff was insistent on taking this short jaunt. Paul guessed it was to make sure the trip began with a little time spent with his younger son. He was glad to acquiesce.

Besides bait, the shop had candy, souvenirs, handmade arts and crafts, and the ubiquitous T-shirts with the "I heart" whatever random thing someone was hearting at the time on the center. The newest thing this year Turner saw was a branch carved into a fish with wind chimes dangling from it. They had brought two cases of beer with them so he didn't need to purchase any. Since it was more expensive in Canada, they often brought their supply of brew.

Fenwick rushed to the nearest Tim Hortons for a supply of Timbits. While they obtained the variety of provender necessary for the duration, Madge rowed with the Fenwick girls around the shoreline. They kept to the thick weed beds where walleye often hid on hot, bright summer days.

3

Turner had begun wondering where Ian was when he heard the engine of a floatplane. A few moments later, one landed out in the harbor and motored to the lodge's dock. Ian emerged. He clutched a backpack and a suitcase. He nodded to the pilot, spotted Turner, and ambled over. Ian gazed continuously over Turner's left shoulder.

Ian said, "I saw that from the air."

Turner didn't follow the look. He knew what Ian was talking about.

Ian said, "That is the biggest goddamn concrete fish I have ever seen. It's got to be the biggest concrete anything anyone has ever seen. With any luck no one has gotten the idea to make concrete representations on such a scale anywhere else on the planet. Why is there a three-story concrete fish that can be seen for miles from anywhere on earth? And it's painted pink. Who would paint a concrete fish pink?"

"You should see the picture we have," Jeff said. "It's Mr. Fenwick standing in its mouth holding a can of Molson's."

"Something to look forward to. How big are those teeth?"

"Three feet," Jeff said. "It's a muskie."

"Tough luck for the muskies. That thing is awful."

"It's kind of a Canadian thing," Paul said. "Big concrete structures, grilled cheese sandwiches, and Timbits."

"What?" Ian asked.

Ben said, "We've seen a bunch of these concrete things over the years."

Jeff said, "Remember the huge moose in Moose Jaw?"

Ian said, "That is not possible."

"Bigger than that fish," Jeff said.

"The moose's name was Mac, wasn't it?" Ben asked.

"MacMoose," Brian said.

"Yeah," Jeff said, "we took a picture of that, too."

"Am I on the same planet I was on earlier?" Ian asked.

"You came a thousand miles to pick on Canadians?" Paul asked.

Ian said, "I'm being objective. Grilled cheese? Timbits?"

Ben said, "Supposedly the local joke is that grilled cheese sandwiches are the national dish of Canada. We'll introduce you to Timbits later."

"Is that a person, place, thing, or idea?" Ian asked.

"Yes," Turner said.

Ian gazed at the concrete monstrosity. "If I were an international terrorist, I'd start with that thing."

"I don't know," Ben said. "It's not so bad. The moose was worse. Of course, you could paint the moose dark red, and you could call it a 'puce moose.'"

Brian said, "If it was made out of wood, it could be a spruce moose."

Ian gaped from Ben to Brian. "The water here has turned you into little Fenwicks. Only he could come up with puns that horrible."

Jeff said, "If you put a hat on his head and a scarf around his neck, you could have a Seuss moose."

Ian said, "I am absolutely and completely opposed to the death penalty, especially among friends. However, I could be tempted to make exceptions. If I got to pick the victims."

Brian added, "If the concrete platform came unstuck, you could call it a 'loose moose.'"

Ian said, "A week this is going to last. A week. And Fenwick hasn't even made his entrance. At least I only have to look at a fish, not a moose." He turned his disdainful stare to the houseboat. "I'm going to live on that?"

Paul said, "You could swim along behind for a week. Or as the old joke goes, 'How long can you tread water?'"

Fenwick emerged from the passenger-side door of his SUV. He wore a pair of sunlight yellow shorts. Turner hoped there wasn't another pair either matching or brighter. If it was brighter, it would make the sun blush. Fenwick called them his "lucky fishing shorts." Madge had less pleasant sobriquets for them. Fenwick had been wearing them while on fishing trips for five years since he'd found them in a thrift ship in International Falls. Turner had regretted that stop. He noticed the fish-cleaning stain on the butt of the pants had faded over the years by about half. The color had not. Fenwick's pullover shirt was an electric blue.

Turner knew that many fishermen wore the same hat or shirt they'd had success with before. One of the things he discovered about Ben was that he wore the same gray boxer shorts out fishing every morning, but changed them to black briefs for night fishing. Turner stopped mentioning this oddity when Ben pointed out a few of Turner's peccadilloes.

Upon catching sight of Fenwick's garish garb, Ian said, "You planning to scare the fish to death?"

Ian wore his slouch fedora, a black T-shirt, khaki shorts. His shins were pale. His muscular calves had a dense covering of hair from the hem of his shorts to the top of his sandals. Fenwick looked him up and down and said, "You're going to be cold."

"It's summer," Ian said.

"This is Canada," Fenwick reminded him. Fenwick claimed the cold never bothered him. Normally, during their trips the temperature was Midwest warm and occasionally Midwest sweltering, but it could get Canada cool in a big hurry, especially after a few thunderstorms and the passing of a cold front.

Turner wore faded blue jeans and a gray pullover sweatshirt with the sleeves cut off. Jeff wore his new black jeans and a T-shirt snug over one of his older brother's much larger flannel shirts. Brian wore a sweatshirt with the sleeves cut off and old baggy khakis. It would cool off as evening neared.

Ian said, "You've come to Canada to kill fish."

"You're the one who wanted to see what a family vacation looked like," Turner said.

"I wanted to see the new gay paradise. So far, it's cold and rainy. With ten minutes of sun since I landed and this wind is cold."

"You'll get used to it."

"Get used to it? I've been on a floatplane. Do you know what the pilot said?"

"You wanted to fly here. You told me you picked him to fly with because, when you saw his picture on the Internet, you thought he was hot."

Ian said, "The last thing the hunky idiot told me after we were airborne was, 'You might want to hold on to your door.' Silly me asked why. He said . . . do you know what he said to me?"

"I'm going out on a limb here, but my guess is that what he said was something that bothered you."

"He said, 'You'll want to hold on to that door because it tends to come open when we're up in the air.' A plane with a door that just pops open. Now you expect me to kill fish, sweet, innocent little fish, who have never harmed anyone?"

"I don't care if you fish or not. Maybe the pilot was kidding." Paul doubted this. He'd been on enough floatplanes to know that more than a few of them flew on even less than the proverbial wing and a prayer.

"I don't even eat fish," Ian said.

Jeff said, "It's good for you."

"Do you eat everything that's good for you?" Ian asked.

"No, but Brian eats everything that's good for him. He does enough for all of us." Going into his second year now on a total health diet, Brian wasn't as sanctimonious about it as he used to be.

Paul said, "What did you expect to do while you were here?"

"Stare at burly lumberjacks and studly Mounties."

"You'll have to catch those for yourself."

Fenwick said, "Ian, you might learn that all the decisions you make don't revolve around your prick."

Madge whacked his upper arm and said, "That is not an appropriate comment in front of children."

"Neither is making decisions that way," Fenwick said.

Madge said, "Not appropriate in the North Woods or in Chicago?"

Ian said, "It's the only criterion I use whether in the North Woods, Chicago, or anywhere else. This is the North Woods?"

Ben said, "There's a lot of woods and it's north of Chicago. How much more north and woodsy do you need?"

Ian said, "Adventures. Vistas. Nature. Puke."

Turner said, "I've got my complaint-index scorecard here somewhere. Let me get it out. I promised all our friends I'd keep track. I've got you in the pool at over seven hundred." He pulled a notebook and pen out of the air and proceeded to thumb through the nonexistent pages. "Let's see, grousing while still on the dock. I think there's extra points for that."

Ben said, "Done while here less than an hour. Don't forget points for that."

Ian glared at Ben. Ben said, "I've got you as good for over eight hundred."

"Less than an hour in Canada or less than an hour on the dock?" Turner asked.

Ben said, "It is also not fair for Fenwick to goad him on. He's got an even higher number in the pool."

"What do you get if you win the pool?" Jeff asked.

"Peace and quiet," Turner said.

Ian said, "I may like fishing after all."

"Why?" Madge asked.

"The fish will like me because I leave them alone, and I will like them because they don't make snarky comments."

4

After purchasing supplies, it was nearly five. For an hour they fished from the side of the boat, or, in Ian's case, napped. Ben and Paul swam in the lake. Brian took a turn on the Jet Ski that had a nest on the back of the houseboat. Paul and Ben took showers after their swim and made quiet love in their room while the boys wrangled on the dock about the best bait to use for catching lake trout.

For the evening the Fenwicks' eldest daughter was taking her younger siblings and Jeff for pizza, a movie, and ice cream in Kenora. Brian was going out with Kevin and some of his local buddies until late. Ian chose to stay on the boat and read. He was halfway through C. A. Tripp's *The Intimate World of Abraham Lincoln*.

This year the adults decided to eat at the Naked Moose, which advertised itself as serving five-star Canadian cuisine. Turner had heard last year that they were planning to erect a gigantic concrete quadruped out front as a tourist lure.

Rumor was it would rival Saskatchewan's gigantic moose. The thing to be built had been nicknamed Mel in a local schoolkid competition. Fenwick had strongly suggested they name it Bullwinkle after his favorite television character of all time. Turner appreciated the show's humor, the few times he'd seen it in old reruns. He also didn't care what they named the soon-to-be-constructed monstrosity. He wasn't about to mention it, however. The moose incident earlier had called forth a plethora of puns. Fenwick would only add to the ghastly word games.

The restaurant's food had turned out to be a perfectly ordinary fusion of Denny's and Cracker Barrel.

After dinner Turner and Ben were near their car waiting for Madge and Fenwick. Madge always teased Fenwick about taking forever in the john after having a meal. Fenwick always just said, "Digestion." Turner was glad he left it at that.

The long Canadian twilight continued to bathe the world about them in gentle hues of green and gray. A few dim lights had begun to attract the first bugs of the evening. If Fenwick took much longer, they'd have to get the bug spray out of the car. You didn't want to be unprotected when the nightly infestation of Canadian insects closed in.

A cluster of First Nations young men huddled near the back of the parking lot. They were as close to the woods and as far away from the meager light as they could be. The tips of lit cigarettes occasionally flared. If there were recreational chemicals connected to the smoking, Turner didn't want to know. It wasn't his city. He wasn't on duty. No cop he knew thought the so-called antidrug wars made sense, nor did they think most of the drug laws or campaigns were remotely close to realistic. He couldn't imagine arresting someone in Chicago for smoking pot, although if they puffed away brazenly, he'd get himself interested. In this parking lot, these looked like young men who didn't have much to do and were doing it quietly here. Most seemed to be in their late teens or early twenties. He sensed no interest in him and Ben, and they were not near his SUV. He wasn't automatically suspicious of clots of idle young people, but he was always careful about his surroundings. He checked every space he entered, noting how many people were present and where anyone was. It was second nature to any seasoned cop.

A second clump of young people drove up in a flame red Mustang. One of the passengers in the backseat favored Ben and Paul with an extended middle finger. A young woman was scrunched with her copious butt on the lap of the shotgun-side passenger, with her enormous tits rubbing against the right arm and chest of the driver. Paul knew her breasts must be of gargantuan proportions for him to pay attention. Mostly he noticed the ass and crotch of hot men. Something on a woman had to be truly extraordinary for him to notice. Paul also thought the gearshift must be digging painfully into unseen tender parts of her anatomy.

The car spurted to the back of the parking lot. Stones flew, several of them thudding into Paul and Ben. The car screeched to a halt with the left front tire an inch from a skinny young man's foot. Obscene gestures and shouts were exchanged. Turner took out his cell phone. They didn't work at a lot of places this far away from large cities, but he'd noted he usually got a signal in and around Cathura. As the doors of the Mustang opened, he called the local police to report a disturbance.

As the call was being answered, the inmates of the

19

Mustang piled out and hunkered down next to the driver's-side door. This new crowd consisted of five men and one woman, their skin much paler than the original crowd's. Muttered words formed a rapid tattoo in the night. Turner couldn't catch what was being said. Moments later shouts began to punctuate the confrontation. Shoves were exchanged. A cop car with CATHURA POLICE printed on the side drove into the parking lot. It had its Mars lights rotating, but the siren was silent.

Turner glanced at his watch. Less than five minutes for the cops to arrive. Not bad. The car crunched gravel as it eased past them.

Fenwick and Madge arrived. Fenwick eyed the Mars lights. "We got good guys and bad guys? Or the local entertainment writ large?"

"Writ large?" Madge asked.

"I'm a poet," Fenwick reminded her, "I can say 'writ large' anytime I want."

"Yes, dear, but try not to do it in public."

"And I read books," Fenwick said.

Madge said, "Blow it out your ass."

Turner said, "The crew nearest the red Mustang came in looking for a fight."

Fenwick peered at the aggregation. He said, "The First Nations guys have been here about half an hour." Fenwick had used the Canadian designation for people who in the United States were often referred to as Native Americans. "You had your backs to them when they drove in. They met some of the employees."

Two cops emerged from their vehicle. One slouched over

to Turner and his companions; the other moseyed toward the incipient problem. Turner thought he recognized several of the young people in both camps from seeing them hanging around town or helping with the tourists at the marinas.

The cop who approached them said, "You call this in?" Turner nodded.

"Kids," the cop said. Turner and Fenwick identified themselves as police officers. The cop didn't seem interested.

They watched the other cop deal with the small group. From what Turner could see, the six from the Mustang seemed to be doing a lot more strutting and swaggering than a chagrined group of youngsters should be doing in the face of a cop.

Turner said, "The five from First Nations were standing there minding their own business. The other kids showed up and started giving them a hard time."

The cop said, "We get this all the time. First Nations kids causing trouble."

Turner said, "They were not causing the slightest bit of trouble."

The cop narrowed his eyes at him. "You from the States?"

Turner's group heard raised voices and turned to the sound. The tallest one from each group was shouting at the other. They must both have been above six feet tall, with the First Nations kid being at least fifty pounds lighter than his opponent. The cop who had been talking to Turner hustled toward his buddy. Turner and Fenwick followed, trailed by Madge and Ben.

The extremely skinny First Nations kid with brush-cut hair looked ready to take on the entire North Woods. The other tall kid was fresh faced with a muscular figure and blond hair but the same brush cut as the other. Both had fists clenched, jaws taut, and lips pursed.

As Turner and his group arrived, the skinny kid was shouting, "We were just standing here! We weren't doing anything! We weren't bothering anybody!"

Before anyone else could speak, Turner said, "That is exactly correct." The assemblage turned to him. The kids from the Mustang gaped. The cops looked annoyed. The First Nations crowd looked astonished. Turner was not about to put up with prejudicial bullshit no matter where he was. The cop who had been talking to him had pissed him off. Plus, he had Ben and the Fenwicks to back him up. "They were chatting peacefully," Turner said.

Ben added, "Absolutely. The kids in the Mustang were the ones who came in looking for trouble." Fenwick added, "We didn't see anyone in the First Nations group do a thing wrong."

The cops looked from them to the young adults. If there was going to be prejudice tonight, now was not the time for it to happen. The First Nations kids had a set of respectable adults to back them up.

The cop who'd been talking to Turner's party said, "Let's break it up. Nobody's hurt. There's no blood or broken bones. Nobody wants to press charges."

The teenagers and twenty-somethings from both sides shook their heads. The Mustang crowd got in their car. At the edge of the parking lot they squealed their tires and then headed on the road out of town. Those of the First Nations got into two trucks and took off in the opposite direction. Their vehicles were late-model Chevies scored with dents and covered in dirt.

The cops got in their car and left. They said nothing to Turner and his party. "That was odd," Madge said.

Fenwick said, "There are articles in the papers sometimes about problems between First Nations people and the police. I wonder what would have happened if we hadn't been here."

They returned to their SUV. The Mustang roared back into the parking lot. The driver sped straight at them. The adults scattered. The driver stopped a layer of paint's distance from Turner's left leg.

The large blond male stuck his head out the driver's-side window and said, "You're the fags who rent the houseboat. Those your little boy toys?"

Turner said nothing. Car doors slammed. Six hulking teenagers stood in front of them, five men and one woman. This time as they got out of their car, two had sawed-off baseball bats in their hands. Two others flicked open switch knives. The woman wore pink-framed glasses on her bulbous head and a stunningly yellow and orange blouse over the epic endowments of her torso.

Turner and Fenwick moved in front of Madge and Ben. Fenwick said, "This could be fun."

Turner said, "Perhaps we have a different definition of fun."

Neither detective was currently armed.

The young men came on silently. Two yards away, the five men formed a semicircle around them. The woman stood to the right of the blond. She snapped her gum, then said, "Who the hell are you fags to interfere?"

Fenwick laughed. "This is going to be way more fun than I could possibly imagine." Turner flashed on the fight scene in the excellent movie *Secondhand Lions*. He smiled at the

23

memory of the Robert Duvall character taking on and defeating four muscular and snarling teenagers at once.

The blond male with the brush cut said, "What are you smiling at?" He feinted at Fenwick, then shoved at Turner. Turner caught his wrist and twisted it back.

"Hey! Ow!" The other four made a move toward Turner, who let the teenager go and faced them. The woman didn't move.

Fenwick stood next to Turner. One teenager waved his knife and said, "Keep out of this, fat man."

Madge said, "You left me out."

"Back off, lady."

Ben stepped to the other side of Paul. They caught each other's eyes. Turner sighed. He loved watching bravado-infested assholes of any age get the shit beat out of them. If they were homophobic bravado-infested teenagers and got the shit kicked out of them, all the better. Madge was maybe half the size of her husband. Without a gun, she was just as lethal. The most heavyset one in the group made a lunge for Madge and attempted to shove, slap, or hit her. Turner was never sure which. Several deft moves and seconds later, she had broken his wrist. He screamed and fell to his knees.

Fenwick said to her, "I've told you to be more gentle with them. How many times have I told you, don't break the wrist first thing? It leaves less time for torture."

The attacker bellowed in agony. He sank to the ground.

Madge said, "I left the rest of them for you."

The most muscular one with one of the baseball bats suddenly swung at Turner. The kid might as well have sent snail mail to let him know the attack was coming. Turner dodged and grabbed the bat, then swung at the hand of the man with the other bat. In seconds Turner had both weapons.

The teenagers backed toward their car. One assisted the kid with the injured arm, who was still howling. They jammed themselves into the car. With another squeal of tires, they roared off.

Fenwick said, "Ben and I didn't get to hit anybody. You guys are supposed to share."

Ben asked, "Should we call the police?"

Fenwick said, "We could chase the Mustang."

Madge said, "We are not going to go up and down the highways of rural Canada in the middle of the night."

Fenwick said, "You always take the fun out of everything."

"Let's not do another round of debate on the meaning of fun," Madge said.

Ben asked, "Did someone get their license plate number?"

Turner said, "I did." He quickly got pen and paper out of the glove compartment and wrote it down. After noting it, Turner said, "I can describe the kid who attacked me. He was the driver. I don't know his name, but I recognized him from around town. They must have known that we might be able to identify them. Why do something so blatant?"

The other three agreed that at least some of them looked familiar.

Fenwick said, "Either they planned to kill us all or somebody's daddy owns half the North Woods. Do we want to press charges? None of us is hurt."

Madge said, "They're not afraid of being recognized and must not be afraid even if they are caught. Even somebody directly related to Mayor Daley can't get away with that in Chicago."

Turner said, "It's puzzling."

Ben added, "If we say something, it could redound back on us."

"How so?" Madge asked.

Ben said, "If they have powerful connections, they may feel an even greater need or even more empowered if nothing comes of our report."

Turner said, "Corrupt Canadian police?" He remembered the scandal he'd read about police misconduct in a murder investigation in the papers the summer before.

Fenwick said, "The cops who showed up earlier seemed willing to take sides in a pretty prejudiced way. We've got to be careful."

They all nodded.

5

Flashing Mars lights and a wildly swaying Maglite flashlight beam met them upon their return to the pier. Ben said, "That's our dock."

Turner pulled into the parking lot and the four of them rushed from the SUV to the edge of the pier. Paul noted that the Fenwicks' SUV wasn't back yet. Had something happened to the kids? On the sand next to the dock was a city of Cathura police car. Ian held the flailing flashlight. The foot-long thing in his hand wavered erratically as he gesticulated wildly.

Paul, Ben, and Madge were the first to arrive, with Fenwick puffing up behind.

Paul could hear Ian's voice. He was addressing an audience of four: two cops, and the resort owner and his wife, Michael and Gertrude Zoll. "Just kids' stuff! Are you out of your mind? I chased the little bastards halfway to the North Pole. They were laughing at me. Laughing. I didn't dare go far in the woods. They were screaming and yelling homophobic slurs."

Zoll said, "Now, now. We get kids doing all kinds of stupid stuff. They call each other gay at the drop of a hat. It doesn't mean anything."

The cops hadn't been among those present at the incident in town. Zoll addressed the police officers. "We get minor vandalism all the time out here. You know that. How often do we call you? Couple times a week in the summer?"

The cop said, "It's hard to patrol every inch of the woods." His name badge read VINCENT SCHREPPEL. The word *Chief* was stitched in yellow underneath it.

Ian said, "This isn't the woods. This is a dock. Are you telling me criminals get to run amok in the North Woods?" His tenor voice echoed through the night.

"What happened?" Turner asked.

Ian said, "These people won't listen."

Schreppel said, "We had a report of a break-in."

"Break-in? Break-in! If I hadn't gotten back when I did they'd have destroyed both boats. There was less destruction on the *Titanic*." Paul had never seen his friend so angry. He looked at the boats. They were still afloat. Nothing looked broken or damaged.

Paul tapped Ian. "What happened?" he asked again.

Ian focused on him. "I went for a walk along the lake. Damn bugs could eat you alive. I came back sooner than I intended. I got here and our boat was swarming with teenagers."

"How many were there?" Paul asked.

"It was dark. There was only that one light at the end of the pier. I hadn't taken a flashlight with me. I know you told me to. I didn't. There were at least four or five. All males. All white. Late teens, early twenties. I surprised them when I came on board. They panicked and ran. They plowed into me and nearly knocked me into the water. I got up and chased them. Once we got into the woods, I nearly got lost. The fuckers were chanting their goddamn slurs from among the trees. A few minutes later, I heard a car roar away. They were on some road I couldn't find in the dark. I really got turned around finding my way back."

"What kind of damage did they do?" Paul asked.

"Take a look."

Ben and Paul climbed aboard. The Fenwicks hurried to check their boat. Ian stood on the deck as the other two entered the main cabin. The Zolls and the cops remained on the dock.

Paul turned on the lights. The kitchen was a mess. Drops of cleansers still leaked from crushed bottles. Liquid from plastic drink containers formed pastel pools on the floor. Hunks of food from the refrigerator swam in the murky mess. Smashed bits of the portable plastic chess set Jeff had not put away made tiny islands in the juices. Dented and scarred pots and pans lay in a mound near the stove. The only bedroom attacked had been Ian's. It was nearest the front.

Ian said, "I think I got to them before they could get to the other rooms."

Paul checked the boys' bedroom. Everything looked fine. In their bedroom Ben checked the Agatha Christie book he always took along. They kept the extra cash and traveler's checks in the Agatha Christie book. Or as Ben put it, he always kept the cash in the Christie. Their funds were untouched.

"What did they get of yours?" Paul asked Ian.

"They got my traveler's checks. I left them on the nightstand. They took my watch. I had my wallet with me. I'll have to call American Express. They ripped up a bunch of the clothes. Tore pages out of every book, ruined most of them."

"You took a chance when you confronted that many of them."

"They were cowards. They ran. If I'd have been a bit quicker, I'd have gotten one of them. It's good I got back when I did. They could have ruined all of our stuff."

Ben said, "They could have all turned on you. Even you might have a hard time with a bunch at once."

The Fenwicks came aboard. "Nothing happened to our boat. Are you okay?"

Paul said, "Yes, some damage. Nothing irreplaceable." The five of them went back on deck. The cops and the Zolls joined them.

Schreppel asked, "Did you want to file a report?"

Ian said, "Of course, I want to file a report. Why wouldn't I?"

Schreppel said, "The resorts have all kinds of problems with this. We do what we can."

"Why don't they hire security?" Ben asked.

Schreppel said, "We patrol as often as we can. It happens. You didn't get a good description. It could have been anyone. I'm sorry."

Ian said, "I lost my watch and my traveler's checks."

Schreppel said, "Better cancel them first thing in the morning."

"I knew that," Ian said.

Zoll said, "I'll do whatever I can to make things right. I'm sorry it happened to you."

Ian said, "It happened to us for very specific reasons. There's other boats here. Nothing happened to them. They made slurs."

Zoll said, "What can I do to help?"

Ian made his report. Ben and Paul cleaned. The Fenwicks helped. Ben said, "At least the kids weren't here for this. They should be back soon." They would have to resupply with groceries after they got back from their morning fishing.

After the cops and Zolls left, Ian groused from the kitchen counter. "They didn't believe me. They wouldn't listen. This was a direct attack on us."

Paul said, "And if it was, how is that going to help us catch them? Or get a new supply of groceries?"

"Is this place safe?" Ian asked. "I don't want to be the next Matthew Shepard."

"Is any place safe?" Ben asked. "You can get hassled by homophobic teens on Clark Street in Chicago as well as far out in the middle of nowhere."

Ian said, "Zoll is a shit. He wanted to placate me. He's trying to save the reputation of his resort. He's a homophobe or a closet case."

Ben asked, "Could this have been done by the crowd from the restaurant?"

"Who's that?" Ian asked.

Ben explained.

Paul asked Ian, "Was one of them kind of a frumpy, heavyset woman?"

Ian shook his head. "It was twilight. I just didn't get a good enough look."

Ben asked, "If it was them, how would the timing work on that?"

Paul said, "We came straight back here after the parking lot. They must have done it before they began hassling the First Nations kids."

"Just before," Ian said.

"If it was the same ones," Paul said.

When Jeff and the Fenwicks' kids returned, Paul and Ben sat with Jeff and talked about what happened.

"Are we leaving?" Jeff asked.

"We're going to be careful," Paul said.

Jeff said, "I don't want to be chased away from our only vacation."

Paul said, "We'll take every precaution."

⟍ 6 ⟋

After playing chess with his dad, Jeff was rereading a Walter R. Brooks *Freddy* book. Ben was tuning the strings of a dented five-string guitar that the last people who'd rented the boat had left. Ian was nestled in a large chair on the screened-in portion of the upper deck with the Tripp book. Paul heard a sharp slap and the reporter groused, "Nobody told me the bugs here were as big as elephants."

Brian would be out with friends until late. Paul wasn't sure his older boy ever did much sleeping on the vacations.

Paul settled into the boat's only easy chair. Ben came over and sat between his legs, rested his left arm on Paul's right leg. "Aren't you going out tonight?" Ben asked.

On the first night of their vacation Paul always took out the small rowboat onto the lake. He did this the first night of every one of their trips.

"I wanted to stay close for a while," Paul said. "It's been a little bit of an unusual night."

Ben said, "It's quiet. Jeff's fine. Ian will never be fine."

"I heard that," Ian called. "Too much truth can ruin a vacation."

Ben whispered, "You should go. You always do. I'll take care of things."

"You sure you're all right?"

"Yes," Ben said. "You enjoy the time alone and you don't get much of that. If you're worried, don't go as far this year or don't stay out as long. We'll be fine." He kissed him. "It's okay."

Paul nodded. The alone moments in an active household and an active job were few and far between. He checked on Jeff and then clambered on deck and untied the rowboat. Ben waved as he rowed away. As Paul glided along the shore, he heard Ian's voice grumbling about the bugs and humidity.

Paul knew these waters. His father had brought him here since he was four. In a very short time, he would be unable to hear any sounds his family might be making.

Paul rowed for twenty minutes and then let the boat drift. He arranged the extra life jackets and seat cushions into a sort of couch on the bottom of the boat. He lay on them, his head resting near the stern. He watched the stars drift overhead. He loved these moments. He didn't have to think about criminals or crime or kids. He forgot everything in the glory of starlight and clouds and moonlight. He felt the tension of city living and responsibility drain from him. For a few minutes he thought of contentment and bliss.

The boat ambled along in the current.

Ten minutes of drifting later, he heard several gusts of raucous laughter echo from the near shore. Noise from campers or trysting lovers was a fairly common occurrence, and normally it did not jangle his nerves. But this time, he was fairly certain it was Brian laughing. The kid's *basso gusto* laugh was hard to mistake. Paul was sure Brian said he was going to a late movie in Kenora. The laughter burst out again, a rumbling lilt in the darkness. Paul lifted his head. He was in a channel between two islands. He was supposed to be running with a light, but this channel was well known to him. Other boats were too large for this narrow byway between two islands. On a shore about thirty feet away was a campfire. He saw a boat about the same size as his pulled onto the beach. In its lee was a small fire. The light could be seen for miles in this wilderness. He saw two people. They were slathering Bug-Be-Gone spray on their naked torsos, arms, and faces. One was Brian. The other was Kevin Yost. He saw Kevin kneel behind Brian and begin applying Bug-Be-Gone to his back. He saw Brian lean into the other boy's arms. Then Kevin leaned his head forward and kissed his son. Brian did not pull away.

Paul slipped his oars into the water. He was a master oarsman and could row silently when he wished. At this moment, he very much wished to leave undetected.

This far north you half expected to meet a bear in the woods or to be startled by or to startle some woodland creature. The intrusion of humans, one of whom was his son, was unexpected. Paul had made love in the woods before. To his knowledge he had never been discovered doing so. Seeing his son gave him an odd chill up his spine.

It wasn't that he didn't think his son was a sexual being. The boy paraded about in his boxers at home and dressed fashionably straight. To this moment, as far as Turner knew, his older son was relentlessly heterosexual. He'd dated a huge number of girls and had given no indication that he was interested in boys. There was no question about what Paul had just seen. He had no intention of discussing it with anyone, least of all Brian. He rowed silently and powerfully away.

Paul rowed for nearly half an hour, sticking carefully close to the shore, farther along which they had docked. It wouldn't do to get lost in the night. If he did, he would have to wait for morning either to find his way or wait to be found, and even that could take a while.

The moon and the stars were gorgeous. He sat on the boat seat and watched the ripple of the water in the streaming moonlight. The stars glittered on the mirrored water.

Upon his return, Paul said nothing to Ben about what he'd seen. Jeff was asleep. Ian was snoring. Brian had not returned. Ben and Paul crawled into bed and cuddled for a while. Paul felt Ben's breathing settle into sleep.

Paul lay staring at the pine ceiling. He felt conflicted about what he'd seen. At the simplest level, his son had lied about where he was going. Obviously he was not at the movies in Kenora. It was possible that they had done something as simple as changing their minds and deciding to do something else. Certainly plans to go make out in the woods, straight or gay, were not announced to one's parents. It was too early for them to have gone to the movies and come back again and gotten as far out as they had. As teenage lies go, it was in the midlevel range.

Paul knew he didn't care if his kid was gay. And was he gay? A kiss in the woods was more than just being friendly. One of the demarcations Paul kept in his head between straight and gay guys was that more straight guys than people expected would hold still for a blow job, but the truly straight ones drew the line at kissing a guy. And had Kevin and Brian done more than kiss?

Paul also didn't know if his son was still a virgin. According to studies he'd read, the average age for someone losing their virginity in this country was sixteen, which Brian was. Paul realized statistics didn't mean much when it came to your own kid.

Who could he talk this over with? And why did he need to talk it over? Ben would understand. Fenwick would be supportive. Mrs. Talucci would be fine with it. Paul realized his hesitancy had little to do with whom he wanted to talk to. It was his own reluctance. He mostly didn't want to think about his kid's sex life. As a kid, you didn't think about your parents'. As a parent, you didn't want to think about your kid's.

He listened to the wilderness for half an hour. Soft waves murmuring against the hull. Loons calling. Mosquitoes whining. Dim mutters of other humans. A far-off train whistle. A logging truck lumbering by on a distant highway. Finally, he heard thumps on the deck. He heard Brian mutter, "I'm home, Dad." His son would know he was awake waiting. He heard the refrigerator door opening. He knew Brian would be drinking from the only unbroken bottle of an esoteric brand of nonsweetened organic juice. His son would not be using a glass.

7

Paul awakened in the dim morning light to the soft murmuring of voices. It was his sons comparing techniques for getting some breakfast without awakening the adults. Ben whispered in Paul's ear, "They never catch on, do they?"

Paul smiled. He arose, threw on jeans, a sweatshirt, socks, and heavy shoes. He saw a light in the galley section of the Fenwicks' boat. Madge appeared briefly at the window. They exchanged waves.

Everyone, except Ian, was up. The reporter had told them to let him sleep. Promptly at five Kevin arrived on the dock.

Neither boy gave any indication that something unusual had happened the night before. Paul didn't notice them giggle in intimate ways or stagger against each other in accidental bumps that might indicate . . . what? Hot sex under the stars? A secret romance? Each boy looked like he could use a lot more sleep, but Brian was used to sleeping until late in the morning in the summers and five in the morning was early for just about anyone. Turner yawned and took a gulp of his coffee. He turned the wheel and guided the boat away from the dock. Mist shrouded the land and water.

Ian staggered out the door of the houseboat and onto the deck. He wore tight white boxer briefs, white socks, and a dark blue hooded sweatshirt. He looked from houseboat to houseboat and from each of the silent anglers preparing lines, sipping coffee, or setting lures.

Ian slipped on the deck and landed on his butt on top of a small heap of rods and reels that Jeff had been sorting.

One of the rods began to tumble off the boat. Turner snatched at it just before it dropped into the water. He began slipping, caught himself on the railing, steadied himself, then turned to Ian. He held up the rod. "This is a specially designed St. Croix Legend Tournament Spinning Rod."

Ian tried to right himself by leaning his weight on one hand. He slipped again. Ian huffed, snorted, then grumbled, "So what?"

"It costs at least half your monthly salary. If it lands in the lake next time, you might want to follow it into the water. Try not to come back without it." Turner placed the rod back in the pile then grinned at Ian and offered him a hand.

Ian grabbed Paul's hand and pulled himself up. Ian said, "Thank you. Once what little dignity I have returns, I shall be most careful." He glared at the dawn light, the lake, the boat, shook himself, then turned to his friend. "Is there a god at this hour of the morning?"

"You don't believe in any kind of god or religion," Turner said.

"Can you blame me?"

"Are you going to get dressed?" Turner asked.

"Will the fish care?" Ian asked.

"Some of the muskies tend to be sensitive."

"Is there coffee? There can't be enough coffee." He peered at Turner's large mug. "You have coffee. If I leave with you all, am I going to be stuck on this godforsaken thing all day?"

"You could swim back to shore anytime you like."

Ian glowered at the receding shoreline. "Big damn lake." He turned and scowled at the currently placid water. "There's mist," he announced.

"Yes, I know," Paul said.

"Is it safe to be out in this?"

"Safe compared to what?" Turner asked.

Ian gazed some more at sky, water, mist, boat, and his friend. "I'm complaining too much."

"Yes."

"You aren't going to get lost in this? How do you know where you are?"

"Global Positioning radar."

"They have that?"

Turner pointed. Ian looked. Turner said, "This one has chips that plot rock outcroppings and sandbars." He pointed at the little black lines that showed where they were going. There was a tiny triangle that followed the line. If the triangle moved off the line, you were off course.

"And you trust this?" Ian asked.

"And we have a guide."

"That kid knows what he's doing?"

"That kid knows more about fishing than most of the guides in Canada."

Off the starboard side of the boat, they passed a large rock protruding ten feet above the surface of the lake.

41

Ian asked, "Are we going to hit any rocks?"

Turner said, "The lake is up this year. There's been a lot of rain. There are marker buoys, but you always have to be careful. A rock that used to be above water could now be concealed. You have to know the lake or at least the parts of it where you are going fishing. If you don't know the waters, you go very carefully."

Ian said, "I think I'm going to die."

Turner said, "Can you do that with less complaining?"

"If I'm going to go, it's going to be noisy." Ian stumbled back inside the houseboat. Turner heard cursing and grumbling for about five minutes.

He did indeed wonder why his friend had decided to come along on the trip.

Kevin came up to him and nodded toward the sound of grumbling. "Do you want me to help him?"

"He's fine," Turner said. "Thanks for offering." Kevin never made comments about Turner being gay. Or about Ben, and now, not about Ian.

Half an hour later, Ian was huddled on a chair next to Paul. By the light from the early-morning fog he was reading. In one hand he had the *Ontario Provincial Police Marine Safety and Cottage Security Awareness Handbook.* In the other he had a large mug of very hot, extra-strength coffee. Paul checked the buoy markers for rocks as they trolled by. On this first day he would be concentrating on making sure he spotted them. While your regular car insurance would cover any collision, he wasn't eager to rip a hole in the bottom of the boat.

They were heading for a new place that Kevin had found for them. On their first day of fishing every year, they followed Kevin's itinerary of new places to fish, listened to him discourse on new techniques and other tips he might have. They would return to the dock that night. Then for the next few days they would be off by themselves much of the time. Turner had learned more from the seventeen-year-old than from any other guide. After anchoring the houseboat, Turner and Fenwick would fish together for several hours. They used a small motorboat, which had been towed along behind.

The weather report had been for patchy fog in the morning, then hot and humid with the possibility of showers later that evening. Turner planned to be back at the pier long before any rough weather could overtake them. He'd been on the lake in a violent thunderstorm. He wasn't worried about it happening, but he was not eager to repeat the ordeal.

Turner said to Ian, "You need to put on your life jacket."

Ian looked up from his reading. "Is there a difference between a personal flotation device and a life jacket?"

Jeff grabbed a life jacket, thumped its orange exterior, and handed it to Ian. Jeff said, "These come in only three colors, red, yellow, or orange, and they're more likely to keep you upright if you wind up in the water."

"Why would I be unconscious in the water?" Ian asked.

Turner said, "Depends on which one of us pushed you in, what we hit you with before pushing you, or what you hit on the way into the water."

Jeff said, "The PFD comes in lots of colors."

Ian said, "I'll put on the life jacket if there's a problem. Do adults really wear them? Kids should, but don't adults know better?"

Jeff said, "I have to wear one because I've got this whole

wheelchair problem. Even the wheelchair's got this special float and ballast."

Turner had insisted that every safety precaution had to be taken for Jeff. Before permitting him on the lake, he'd insisted on a specially designed wheelchair equipped with enough flotation devices to raise the *Titanic*. Paul wasn't taking any chances that his son could be pitched into the lake and drown because some precaution hadn't been taken.

Turner said, "Grabbing for a life jacket when there's danger would be like someone who decides to put on his seat belt when he realizes he's going to have a car accident. Little late by then."

"That's what they say in this booklet. You memorize the booklet?"

"Most of the stuff is common sense."

"But it says you only have to have enough of the life jackets on the boat for each person to have one, but you don't have to be wearing them."

Paul said, "We all wear them. Usually. You don't have to. You can swim?"

"Yeah."

"Good."

Ian asked, "Why is there a Jet Ski on the back of the houseboat?"

Brian said from inside, "It's a sop to teenagers who might get bored. I get to zoom around later."

Ian said, "The phantom speaks." He stuck his nose back in his book. Turner followed the Global Positioning radar.

They occasionally heard other boats. Turner wasn't happy about the fog, but it was early and it should burn off. The Fenwicks' boat stayed near them.

44

After five minutes of silence, Ian asked, "Am I going to get seasick?"

"If you want," Paul said.

Brian and Kevin joined them on deck. Normally, they would have been listening to iPods or MP3 players and getting ready to go fishing. Paul preferred to think that's what they were doing and not indulging in any romantic diversions.

Lying. That was the problem.

Kevin handed Ian a can of Bug-Be-Gone. "Spray this on," the teenager said. "The flies up here are as big as B-29s. Some people refer to them as the national bird of Canada. Trust me, you want this on."

Ian reached for the can. "I almost got eaten alive last night."

Turner said, "The three essentials of North Woods camping." Ben, Brian, Jeff, and Kevin joined Turner in the chorus. "Suntan oil, bug spray, beer."

"Nothing about fishing poles?" Ian asked.

"You don't have one of those," Jeff said.

"Do I put all of them on simultaneously or do I layer it?"

"Not the beer," Brian said. "You drink that. Later in the day usually."

The fog kept all but the Fenwicks' boat hidden. About an hour out, Paul heard a motor that was louder than usual. He didn't like that. He looked to Jeff to make sure he was secure. He glanced at the Fenwicks' boat. Buck was at the wheel. His partner shrugged from across the water. Ben came up next to Paul.

"I can't tell where that's coming from," Paul said.

Ben peered with him into the mists.

Kevin said, "He's too close."

Paul agreed. Paul's father and Kevin's grandfather had been able to tell distance and direction of sounds on the lake with an uncanny accuracy. Kevin had displayed the same gift often in the past.

An instant later a charcoal gray cigarette boat loomed off to the right of the Fenwicks' houseboat. Turner heard Buck cursing. He saw the Fenwicks' houseboat swerve away from theirs. The cigarette boat rushed past the Fenwicks' and bore down on the Turners'. Paul envisioned a crash about amidships. He wrenched the wheel sharply to port. Out of the corner of his eye, he saw Ben grab onto the console. Ian flew out of his chair and hit the deck. His book flew into the water. Jeff, secured in his chair, swayed, but stayed put. Kevin and Brian hung on to the outside rail of the boat.

The cigarette boat swerved at the last second and then turned into the mists. The sight and sound of it quickly faded.

"Who was that asshole?" Ian asked.

"My thoughts exactly," Jeff said.

"Idiot boaters," Kevin said.

"Did you recognize them?" Turner asked.

Kevin shrugged. "I know a lot of boats on the lake. It's too foggy. I didn't get a good enough look at it." No one else had been able to recognize them.

Ben said, "Accidents happen on the lake especially in this fog. Reckless fools."

They slowed and eased close to the Fenwicks' boat.

"You okay?" Paul shouted.

"Yeah," Fenwick yelled back.

Paul didn't bring up his suspicion that they now had this

attack to add to the parking lot incident and the break-in. The kids could hear, and it wasn't the type of discussion he wanted to have shouting from boat to boat. This could also have been a random accident, but for the first time in all these years of trips north, he felt cold fingers of fear race up his spine. Vigilance, constant vigilance.

Just after seven Brian and Jeff along with Kevin took the ten-foot motorboat the Fenwicks had been towing. The two boys always spent time together while they were fishing. Kevin would often join them. Jeff's floating wheelchair apparatus was secured to the spot where a comfy fisherman's chair would have been in the middle of the boat. Paul trusted Brian or Kevin at the controls.

They might be in danger. Should he forbid it? He scanned the horizon. The mists were maybe half of what they had been. He neither heard nor saw any sign of trouble. They would be fishing for northern pike this morning. They would be near shore, where shade, weed, and pad beds provided cover for these fish.

"Be very careful," he said to them just before they left the houseboat. They all nodded, eager to be away fishing.

Turner said to Ian, "You are going to steer our boat."

"I am?"

"You are. You're going to carefully troll around this little cove and wait for us to come back."

"I can do this?"

"Sure."

"Why don't we just anchor the thing here?" Ian asked.

"That would be good, too," Paul said.

Ben and Madge and the Fenwick girls would take one houseboat and motor in the shallows casting lines from the side. Fenwick and Turner would use the powerboat and fish deeper waters off rocky points of several small islands that Kevin had recommended. They were fishing for muskie. Being temperamental helped make them a tough fish to catch. This led to long periods of absolute boredom. Paul enjoyed those rare moments, especially because during them, Fenwick had the gift of silence.

Turner stood near the prow of the boat. Fenwick sat on the swivel seat in the center. Turner's rod was six feet long and thick. It didn't bend much. Muskie could easily be fifty or sixty inches. Turner put his thumb on the spool, pushed the button with his other thumb, engaged the reel, brought the rod back, and then bombed a cast out. The Suick was heavy and landed at least 150 feet out. He started reeling in and giving pulls to the rod, reel again, pull, reel again. He did a figure eight with the line at the end of the retrieve.

Over an hour passed with rare remarks added to the sound of fish surfacing, birds chirping, and waves softly lapping at the hull. Turner experimented with different-colored lures and stuck with baits in the six- to ten-inch size. They trolled at different speeds. The sun broke through the mists. Heat beat down on them and humidity rose from the water. Turner and Fenwick caught several fish but released them because they were too small. They'd just emerged from between two islands. Fenwick was steering. They could see far out over the lake. "Kind of dark along the horizon line," Turner commented.

They both peered carefully in that direction. The lake could get very rough very quickly. Without pause or question Fenwick turned the boat around and headed back toward the houseboats. If it had been the two of them, they might have made a more leisurely return, occasionally casting for fish. With others to be concerned about, they didn't hesitate. Still some distance from the Turners' houseboat, Fenwick asked, "Is that thing riding low in the water?"

Turner examined his houseboat critically. "I'm not sure. We can check it tonight when we get in to port."

As they hurried onto the deck, Ian looked up from his book. He'd replaced his earlier tome with *Harvard's Secret Court* by William Wright.

"Storm's coming," Paul said. "We need to get everyone back on board and get to a sheltered dock."

Ian scanned the horizon. "Where?" he asked.

Turner pointed directly west. "There," he said. Just over the trees on the island, they could see the tops of dark clouds.

8

They tied up the powerboat, weighed anchor, and headed
for the scheduled rendezvous. As they rounded the island
beyond which they assumed they'd find Jeff, Brian, and
Kevin in the other motorboat, Turner thought he heard a
nasty rumble. He looked to the west. While darker, the
clouds were still miles away. Weren't they too far to hear
them?

Once completely beyond the island, he realized the
sound was from a large motor. It wasn't from their boat.
Their engine wasn't that loud. Turner saw a charcoal gray
cigarette boat bearing down on his sons and their guide.
Brian and Kevin, backs to Turner, were standing in the motorboat, waving oars and shouting. Jeff was waving his fists
in the air. Turner didn't see the other houseboat with Ben,
Madge, and the girls.

The cigarette boat was nearly twice as big as the motorboat. Turner could see that the attacking boat could easily

have been the one that passed so close to them earlier that morning. It seemed to be heading straight for his sons' boat. Turner let out a shout and shoved the throttle of the houseboat on full. He had no thought of hidden rocks. He needed speed.

The cigarette boat came within two feet of the smaller craft before veering away. Brian and Kevin clung to the sides. A sluice of water drenched them. The wake from the attacking boat nearly swamped them. Turner saw Brian checking Jeff's flotation devices and the connections of his safety seat. The cigarette boat was making a circle. None of the boys showed signs they were aware of the arrival of Turner and Fenwick.

The two cops were standing next to each other. Turner said, "I'm going to get between them." It would take a great deal to swamp the houseboat. It could ride the waves from the cigarette boat. Turner would insert himself between his sons and danger. And then he'd be sure to catch the sons of bitches who were dangling death in front of his boys. Turner judged where his sons would be when the cigarette boat finished circling. He headed directly for that spot. He watched the driver and passengers in the attacker boat. He couldn't make out faces. It was too far.

Turner watched the cigarette boat turn then swerve in their direction.

"They've seen us," Fenwick said.

"Good," Turner said. He aimed their boat directly at the mad attackers.

The wind whistled past them. He began blaring the horn of the houseboat. One, to tell his kids that help was at hand; two, to give fair warning to the attackers that the shit was about to hit the fan.

"Get the motherfucker," Fenwick said. They were both braced in the wheelhouse. The houseboat was solid, but a collision would certainly hurt it. Turner also knew that their large, clunky craft could sustain a hit and survive more probably than the more fragile cigarette boat. A crash might kill them. Of course, Turner would place himself between his sons and danger.

Fenwick smiled at him. "They don't know that even I would never play chicken with you."

Turner's eyes were fixed on his opponents. They were less than a quarter mile away by now and hurtling toward them.

"Who the hell are these people?" Ian asked.

Paul had glimpsed several figures in the well of the other boat. All wore hooded sweatshirts. Two had on baseball caps.

"He doesn't want to hit us," Paul said.

Ian said, "Sure as hell looked like he did earlier."

"Wrecks his boat at least as much as ours," Turner said.

"We got guns?" Ian asked.

"No," Paul said. He turned their houseboat so it was aimed directly at the other. He pushed the throttle to full. The houseboat wouldn't go as fast as the other, but it could work up a decent speed.

"Are you out of your mind?" Ian asked.

Paul smiled. "You never played chicken?"

Fenwick put his hand on Turner's shoulder and said, "No fear."

"Fuck fear," Turner said. They could certainly be outrun. In such a large lake the faster boat could play games with them all day. Paul was not about to put up with this. He gripped the wheel, checked the GPS for possible shoals and rocks, saw none, gazed at the other boat, kept his hand full on the throttle, and didn't swerve.

Ian said, "He's not going to turn."

"Bets?" Paul said. He and Fenwick grinned at each other for a second, old friends at a supreme moment. Turner hit the houseboat's horn again. The wind blew the cacophony of the blasts back at them.

At the last second the faster and more maneuverable boat turned aside. Paul let go of the throttle. Immediately their houseboat began to slow.

Paul turned the boat toward Jeff, Brian, and Kevin. Turner saw the two boys working quickly with Jeff's wheelchair. When they were next to the motorboat, he jumped aboard and helped them finish getting Jeff unhooked. In minutes they were all safely on board.

"Go, Dad!" Jeff exclaimed.

Paul scanned the horizon. The cigarette boat was circling back. Paul said, "See to your brother." Brian took up a position next to Jeff.

Paul was not so certain now that he wanted another game of chicken. His sons were on this boat. Should they try to anchor and get to shore? That would leave Ben, Madge, and the girls out on the lake facing this menace. He steered the boat at a much lower speed toward the open water of the lake. Turner suspected now that the other boat was toying with him. They weren't going to hit him, but they could keep this up all day, or at least until everybody's fuel ran out.

Once again the enemy was bearing down on them. Ian and Fenwick were at his side. Paul looked back where Kevin and Brian flanked Jeff.

"We gonna hit him?" Jeff asked.

"Probably not," Paul said. He saw the Fenwicks' houseboat, Madge at the wheel, chugging up far behind the cigarette boat. Now the charcoal gray threat was sandwiched in. He saw several people near the wheel of the other boat, but he was still too far away to make out any faces.

The two houseboats began to converge. The cigarette boat picked up speed and was once again heading straight for them. Paul held on steady, sure they would swerve.

They did. Paul tried to see who they were, but the other boat turned half-sideways as it veered off. In the middle of the rush of noise from the other boat, Turner saw several small flashes. There were two booms. He felt his ears ring. A third flash went off in front of his eyes. He staggered back. Brian caught him. He felt someone brush past him. "I've got the wheel." It was Fenwick's voice but coming as if from a far distance.

He felt breath next to his cheek. "Are you okay, Dad?" This was Brian. The voice was dim. Paul realized he had his fists against his eyes.

He felt strong hands cradling him against the deck. "I'm okay," he said. Even to himself his voice sounded disembodied.

"What happened to your eyes?" This was Ian.

Paul opened his eyes behind his fists. They were watering profusely, but he could see. He felt the boat gently swaying in the water. They were almost at a full stop. He heard the hull scraping.

"Did we hit something?" he asked.

He heard Fenwick's voice. "The boat's fine. Is everybody okay?"

Paul pulled his fists away from his face. "Can you see?" Brian asked.

"Yeah," Paul said. "Where's Jeff?"

"I'm here, Dad. Are you okay? Your face is all red."

Paul's eyes were watering. Brian said, "You're bleeding."

Paul sat up. He shook his head. It was painful to open his eyelids. Squinting through his left eye, he saw Ian handing him towels. He realized it was Brian holding him up. Fenwick was at the wheel.

The houseboats bobbed next to each other in the slight swell. Paul heard thumps on the deck. Seconds later Ben was next to him. He saw Kevin and Madge placing the hooks between the boats so the two wouldn't drift apart. Madge hurried over.

"Are they still out there?" Paul asked.

Fenwick said, "I can't hear them."

"They could be hiding," Madge said.

Brian took a washcloth and began dabbing at the left side of Paul's head.

Paul touched his own face then squinted at his fingertips. "Not much blood."

"You can see," Brian said. He sounded very relieved.

Madge brought a water bottle. "You should flush your eyes."

Paul didn't object. He leaned back and let her pour water carefully over his eyes. He blinked, shut them hard, reopened them.

People's voices were beginning to come in more clearly.

Brian said, "Those fuckers are going to die if they ever get near us again." Paul looked at his son. He had never heard such fury in the sixteen-year-old's voice. Obscene language wasn't banned in their home, but it wasn't encouraged. He didn't correct the older boy.

"Who was it?" Ian asked.

Kevin said, "I couldn't see the faces of the people driving it."

Ian said, "You drove straight toward them."

Paul said, "Now is not the time for second guessing." He was trembling as much from the shock of the explosions as from the actual encounter. He was glad Brian was still supporting him.

"What were the explosions?" Jeff asked.

Fenwick said, "Firecrackers. Big damn ones." He held up a bit of paper that had landed on the deck. "Not big enough to kill you on their own, probably. Enough to scare you, maybe cause an accident and get you killed. If they hit close enough, blind you."

Paul was still resting on the deck. Jeff put his hand on his dad's shoulder. Paul hunched himself up so he could hug the younger boy. Jeff clutched him fiercely. "I'm fine," Paul whispered, "I'm fine."

When he felt the boy's arms loosen, Paul eased back. He looked into Madge's and Buck Fenwick's faces. "You should see a doctor," Madge said.

"I can see okay."

Ben said, "You've got some small cuts and abrasions and your left ear is bright red."

Paul said, "My hearing seems to be all right now." He leaned up and looked over the side. "Any sign of them?"

Ian was at the prow. "Nothing."

Paul frowned at the western horizon. Several of them followed his gaze. Half the sky was dark gray. The wind rushed past them and the lake surged and heaved. Paul stood. The time taken up for the chase, rescue, and attack had been nearly an hour. The storm was closer than he would have liked. The wind was up and the waves were lapping at the houseboat. He said, "We need to get everything tied down, and we need to get to shelter. The storm is coming earlier than anyone predicted."

The Fenwicks returned to their boat. The two craft were quickly unhitched. Ben took the wheel. Everyone else set to tying down anything that could be tied down and making sure all the gear was stowed tightly. Then they all returned topside to watch the approaching storm.

Madge called across the way, "Your boat is riding too low. Something is wrong with it."

Waves occasionally sloshed nearly up to the deck. The boat pitched. Ian said, "Are we sinking? Tell me we're not sinking."

"We're not sinking," Paul said.

Kevin said, "We shouldn't be this low in the water."

Turner rushed to the bilge pump and pushed the button to get it working. Back on deck, he searched the shore for a cove to hole up in.

"We can't get under the boat to check out what's wrong," Paul said. "It can't be too bad, or we'd have been sinking sooner. Going fast like this might be making it worse."

"Water is getting in?" Ian asked.

"Yes," Paul said. "We won't sink. Not as long as the bilge pump keeps ahead of the water being taken in. We've got to find a place to tie up." For fifteen minutes they raced northeastward, rounding islands and trying to keep ahead of the storm. The Fenwicks followed close behind the Turners.

Ian said, "I've never been this close to a storm."

Jeff said, "You never went camping as a kid?" He and Brian were playing a game of chess on Game Boy.

"Never," Ian said. "I think I'd rather be in the middle of this storm in my apartment in Chicago."

"We'll be fine," Kevin said. "These are fairly common. There's a marina around the next island."

"You sure?" Ian asked.

Kevin didn't bother to look at him. Ben said, "If the kid says there's a marina, there is one."

Thunder roared. Lightning danced on the lake surface. They watched in awe as the rain shield swept toward them, then overtook the boats. The fat drops thudded and thrummed on the roof. The poor visibility caused them to slow their speed.

No sign of human habitation appeared as they spotted the outline of the island through the downpour. The wind buffeted their boat. Turner did a quick check of everything. The bilge pump chugged away.

9

Five minutes later they rounded the island and saw the sign for Sam's Marina flying in the wind. They hustled into the more sheltered spot. Several other boats had pulled up to the piers leading to the marina. Brian and Kevin leapt out and helped secure the boat. They were immediately soaked. Paul found himself letting out an extended breath. The much lighter swell was a comfort.

The wind still buffeted the boat. Turner did a quick check of the interior. Brian's gear was all over the space he slept in, whether from the storm or teenage negligence. The rest of their gear was safe and solidly stowed. The bilge pump labored at its task. Thunder and lightning crashed almost continuously.

For a while they sat and watched the rain. The sky blackened further. One bolt of lightning hit a tree limb fifty feet from them. The roar was enormous. At times the rain swept by horizontally.

Ben said, "We should try to get ashore. The storm's getting worse, and I think the boat is settling."

Paul agreed.

When the storm eased slightly and the wind was down for a moment, they dashed to the marina. Paul carried Jeff. Brian hefted the younger boy's wheelchair. The Fenwicks followed.

Inside, people stood in clumps. Ferns, wood, and heads of dead animals filled every inch of wall space. Near the front door a particularly annoying tune emerged from the mouth of a stunningly unattractive sculpture of a singing deer. They could hear the lodge's electric generator humming despite the continuing maelstrom outside.

After they shook off the rain and took off damp outer clothing, Ian asked, "Who were those people? Do you get a lot of attacks on fishermen on the lake?"

"No," Kevin said.

Ben said, "This couldn't have something to do with those kids from last night?"

"What happened last night?" Jeff asked.

While the Fenwicks went to see about food, Paul gave a brief version of the break-in and events in the parking lot. When he described the twenty-somethings, Brian said, "I think I've seen some of those guys."

"Was it a big blond guy?" Kevin asked.

"Yeah."

"Him and four buddies? Hot car? Ugly girlfriend, kind of big and hefty?"

"She must be a prize to someone," Ian said.

Turner said, "That's how many there were."

"That's Scarth Krohn," Kevin said.

"Who is Scarth Krohn?" Jeff asked.

Kevin said, "The town bully." He sipped from a can of soda pop.

"Do you know this guy?" Paul asked Brian.

"Not much. Only what I've heard around town."

The Fenwicks returned with snacks and soda. Paul gave the Fenwicks the news that Kevin had been able to name the people in the red Mustang.

"Scarth Krohn?" Fenwick said. "Sounds like a particularly unpleasant refugee from a *Star Wars* movie."

"What's the deal with this guy?" Jeff asked.

Kevin sighed. "He and his buddies are the resident assholes. He was four years ahead of me in school. When they were teenagers they were the pranksters in town. At least they referred to themselves as pranksters. Other people thought they were mean-spirited jerks."

Ben said, "We saw them going after some of the First Nations people."

Paul said, "The police seemed ready to take the side of the white kids even though we told them exactly what happened."

Kevin said, "There's been hassles for years between the First Nations peoples and a few racists. You know how it is with teenagers. They get bored. Gang warfare isn't unique. Neither is prejudice."

"It's warfare?" Ben asked.

"That's probably too strong a word," Kevin said. "It can get serious. A few years ago a kid in Kenora was killed. The police who handled the investigation screwed it up, got officially reprimanded. But the killers got away with it because of the screwup. Scarth and his buddies have done a ton of stuff over the years. Although I don't think they've killed anybody, yet."

"How would they think they would get away with what they did last night?" Ben asked. "I thought the prejudice in Canada wasn't as bad as it is in the United States."

Kevin sighed. "Scarth is the nearest to fame this town has ever gotten. He was going to be bigger than Cathura's most famous hockey great, Cranston Broulee, a guy who was on the Canadian junior hockey team. Hockey is an obsession up here. Scarth thought of himself as greater that Gretzky. He was going to eclipse all the Great One's records."

"What happened?" Ben asked.

"He got injured. His last game in school. They'd won the local championship. He was thumping everyone, hugging everyone, shoving everyone, jumping on everyone. There was one of those big pileups of celebrating high school kids. His leg got caught. He twisted the wrong way to stand up. A clot of his clueless teammates tottered and toppled over on him. He tore up tendons and cartilage and who knows what-all in his knee."

"Hell of a thing," Ben said.

"The year before," Kevin said, "he'd played in the world junior championship. He had the most goals of anybody ever in the tournament. I'm told he had blinding speed on the rink. I never saw him play. Supposedly scouts for all the hockey teams came through town drooling over him."

Ian said, "I've always wanted to be drooled over by a whole town."

Turner said, "Is that an appropriate crack in front of kids?"

Ian said, "Depends who's doing the drooling."

64

Kevin said, "After the incident the whole town was in mourning. You'd think the Queen had died. It went on for weeks. Of course, there isn't a whole lot going on in this town anyway."

"But he gets away with bullying the whole town?" Ben asked.

"Yep. Besides the athlete crap, his dad is rich. He owned the paper mill. He sold it just before it closed. A lot of good jobs just disappeared. This town hasn't recovered from that yet. It was five years ago. Four hundred jobs gone in less than three months. Rumor was his dad sold it and made a fortune. Then the new owners just shut the place down."

"How do you make a profit doing that?" Ben asked.

Kevin said, "The forest industry has been in trouble for years. They're always talking about getting the provincial legislators to do stuff about it. Nobody ever does."

"People hate his dad?" Ben asked.

Kevin said, "Yeah. He didn't actually close the mill. Evil eastern people did, but they still hate him." Kevin paused. "Now that I think about it, Scarth's dad owns the same kind of boat that was after us, same color, too. I never got a good enough look to tell who was in the other boat. Things were going too fast. I can't even tell you if it was the exact same boat. Sorry."

Turner noted that the thunder and lightning had eased. The wind had died and rain now poured straight down.

Kevin said, "The worst was when I was in seventh grade. Scarth and his buddies terrorized everyone."

"Why?" Ian asked.

Kevin shrugged. "I could never figure it out. One day it might be because you wore the wrong color T-shirt, or it had a slogan they didn't like, or it pictured a rock band they looked down on. It was stupid, stupid stuff. Maybe somebody got a haircut they thought was weird. Finally, one of the kids had had enough. He used to wear his hair spiked, and he'd dye it different colors."

"Teenagers can be intolerant of someone different in the best of times," Turner said.

"It was the worst time for that kid. He brought a gun to school. It shocked the town. I knew the kid who was being terrorized. A fat, homely, unathletic guy. Poor kid got hell every day. Funny thing was, when he took the gun to threaten people, he didn't go after Scarth and his buddies."

"Why not?" Ian asked.

"Maybe he was too afraid of them. He threatened a bunch of his fellow seventh graders in the boys' locker room. I was one of them. Kid's name was Oliver McBride. He got off two shots. He wounded another nerdy, hopeless kid and a showerhead. Our coach was great. He got McBride to give him the gun."

Turner said, "When there's a shooting, often there are specific kids who have been making another kid's life hell, but when the shooting starts, it's other defenseless kids who die. I don't understand that."

Ian said, "And sometimes it's the tormentor who dies." He proceeded to give them chapter and verse of several incidents in the States. Turner figured he hadn't heard of this one in Canada because no one had been killed.

"Who was the woman with them?" Fenwick asked.

"That's Scarth's sometime girlfriend, Evon Gasple. According to the teenage rumor mill, she gives head but only to the toughest boys or to the ones Scarth wants her to. Nobody

I know is really sure or cares that much. I do know she clings to him, sometimes for weeks on end, and then sometimes you don't see them together for the longest time."

As they finished their snacks, they talked about filing an official complaint. Turner took a few minutes to check himself in the bathroom mirror. Ben was with him. "You okay?" he asked.

Paul examined himself. "I'm more concerned about the kids. We can't stay if they're in danger." Ben agreed.

The rain stopped at about two. Clouds and wind remained.

Without incident, they motored back to the dock from which they had rented the boats. Once Zoll had the houseboat winched up, they saw what the problem was immediately. On the bottom of most houseboats there is a corkscrew. Water often accumulates between the bottom and the deck. Usually it's not a big deal and when a boat is cleaned part of the maintenance is emptying this water. The cork is simply unscrewed.

"Yours came undone," Zoll said.

"I've never heard of that happening," Turner said.

"Happens."

Kevin said, "I agree with Mr. Turner. I've never heard of it happening."

"Could it have been sabotage?" Ben asked.

"Of course it was," Ian said. "Homophobic creeps exist everywhere. They robbed us last night."

Zoll asked, "You don't know if the people from last night are the same ones that were out on the lake today. How would they know you were homosexuals?"

Ian said, "They don't have to put much thought into it."

Ben said, "We don't make a thing of it."

"You don't have to," Ian said. "You don't make a secret of it and hide in shame. People know. Look at what those kids said and did last night."

Zoll said, "We don't have that kind of thing in Canada."

"What an odd notion," Madge Fenwick said. "You may have statistically less violence than comparable communities within the United States, but what you're saying doesn't seem immediately provable. And it doesn't make a lot of sense to me."

"You don't know us," Zoll said.

Turner said, "I've seen evidence of violence. It's in the local papers."

"Seldom directed against tourists. Unless they bring it upon themselves."

"Are you out of your mind?" Ian asked. "I've never heard 'blame the victim' so blatantly articulated."

Zoll said, "I'm sure it wasn't sabotage. I'm sorry you've taken offense."

Kevin said, "I've seen things go wrong over the years, but not like this. I think it had to be sabotage."

Zoll snapped, "You're seventeen, and Mr. Turner is here one week a year."

Kevin subsided. While he was technically an independent contractor as a guide, still he relied on owners of marinas for contacts and supplies.

Turner said, "Antigay feeling doesn't take much to get fueled."

"We're not like that," Zoll said. "Not here in the North. We believe in live and let live."

Turner didn't think there was much point in debating the universality of prejudice urban or rural.

"How would someone get under the boat?" Ben asked.

Kevin said, "You just hold your breath and swim under. Doesn't take long."

"How come the boat didn't sink?" Ben asked.

"It would take a while," Zoll said. "If you went very fast, it would tend to happen faster. You guys did the right thing by using the bilge pump."

Paul felt frustrated, but there didn't seem to be much they could do. It was nearly six o'clock. The clouds had cleared, and it was delightfully cool. They would need heavy sweatshirts tonight.

On the dock, Jeff was already burbling to everyone in sight about their adventures. Turner, Ben, Ian, Fenwick, and Madge met on the Fenwicks' houseboat. Madge and Buck's boat had been checked for sabotage. Nothing was amiss.

Fenwick said, "We have enemies."

Ian said, "We've been specifically attacked. It seems because you know us, you're among the victims."

"I agree," Madge said. "Somebody doesn't like us."

Paul said, "My family and my friends are in danger. We need to do something about this." They called the cops.

Vincent Schreppel, the cop from the night before, showed up. Turner told the story.

Schreppel didn't take any notes. Turner found that annoying. Schreppel said, "It could be accidents."

Fenwick said, "You get a lot of corks coming unscrewed from the bottoms of houseboats?"

"Happens." Same thing Zoll had said.

"People get rammed on your lake often?" Madge asked.

"That happens more than anybody could believe. It was foggy this morning."

"Not just before the storm."

"From what you said, you were aiming for them."

"You're saying we were at fault?" Ben asked.

"I've got your side of the story."

Madge said, "Are you saying we're making this up?"

"I'm listening," Schreppel said.

Paul said, "We had some problems outside the Naked Moose with the local kids last night." He began to explain.

Schreppel interrupted. "Yeah, I heard. Some of the Indian kids were causing trouble."

Fenwick said, "They weren't the ones causing trouble. They weren't the ones who came back to taunt and attack us."

Ian added, "Or who broke into our boat."

"I thought you said you didn't get a good look at them."

"Not good enough to testify in court, no, but it's logical."

"Logic and the law don't mix."

"Not so far," Ian snapped.

Schreppel chose to ignore him. He said, "We'll want to talk to the kids in the boat before we do any kind of pressing charges. Can you identify them or the boat?"

They admitted they couldn't. Kevin mentioned that it was a charcoal gray cigarette boat and that J. T. Krohn owned the same kind.

"Are you saying it was his?" Schreppel asked.

Kevin said, "I can't say for sure."

Schreppel asked, "If we do file against the kids, are you going to come back up here to testify?"

Madge said, "Tourists up here can be attacked indiscriminately because they can't come back to testify? That's absurd. I thought you people wanted tourist dollars. Keeping tourists on edge is a way to draw people here?"

"We deal with everyone equally."

The Americans looked at the Canadian official. Each of the Americans hesitated to speak the obvious truth. Fenwick's hesitation was briefest. He said, "So far we've seen that in fact that is not true. We saw First Nations kids last night getting harassed. So were we. We saw the cops not do much."

"You called about the kids getting into it, but did you call in your problem?"

"No."

"Why not?"

Paul said, "We didn't want the hassle."

"Nothing I can do if you don't call."

Back at the dock the adults debated.

"Do we go home?" Turner asked. "This is turning into a vacation from a teenage slasher movie."

Madge said, "We've got to think of the safety of the kids first."

They talked of possibilities for an hour then decided to leave a final decision for the morning. The adults were leaning toward leaving. One stumbling block was getting in touch with Mrs. Talucci. She was scheduled to be incommunicado until her return Saturday. They decided to try to figure something out in the morning.

10

It was nearly midnight. Ian was reading and occasionally grousing in his room. Jeff was on the prow fishing/practicing casting. Ben was cleaning in the kitchen. Paul was thinking of going to bed and was looking for a good book. Bachelor loons in a clutch called in the night. A blue heron screeched with its prehistoric sound that Turner thought was one of the ugliest noises of the North.

Jeff had been cranky since they'd docked. Encased in his wheelchair, he'd been sitting waiting for adults most of the afternoon and evening. He'd said he'd come to fish and he was going to fish even if it was from the government pier with the houseboat docked against it. Paul admired his tenacity. He doubted he'd catch many fish, but if the kid was content to give it a try, he wasn't going to discourage him. Jeff had a leech on the end of his line and was fishing for walleye. It was long past Jeff's normal bedtime, but it had been a miserable day, they might be leaving tomorrow, and Paul figured the boy would probably fall asleep in five minutes after he got into bed.

Brian paced up and down the deck. He'd been allowed to go into Kenora to see a movie with Kevin and several friends, but told to get back early. He clutched a blanket around his shoulders in the cool night air. Under it he still wore his going-out clothes: jeans that clung to his narrow hips, a metal belt that did not go into any of the loops, and a shimmering short-sleeve shirt. The boy had been muttering and grumbling under his breath. It had been soft enough so that Paul could safely pretend not to hear it.

Paul heard a cry that rose above the other night noises. "Dad!"

It was Jeff. The tone and timbre of his voice contained the parental summons different from all other calls. It said there was trouble and help was needed. Paul hadn't heard that kind of noise coming out of the kid since he was three. Brian, on the deck already, was instantly next to his brother. Jeff was pointing into the water and yelping. Without pause Brian jumped into the lake. Paul rushed to the edge.

"What is it?"

He heard Brian thrashing around. He knew the boy didn't have one of the life jackets on while they were at the dock. Turner also knew that most lethal accidents happened within ten yards of a landing.

"It was a face," Jeff said. "A face was looking up at me from the water."

In the running lights from the boat, Paul saw a mass of white that was far too large to be a fish.

Brian was treading water. "Dad," he called, "it's someone."

The boy was holding the head out of the water. "I don't think he's breathing."

Paul threw a life preserver to his older son. "Grab that," he shouted. Paul stripped to his boxers, donned a life preserver, and dove in next to his son. Brian had the life jacket in one hand. "Put that on," Paul said. Brian complied. The waters were cool and calm. Paul saw Ben and Ian on the deck next to Jeff. "Get a flashlight," he called up to them. He heard activity on the Fenwicks' houseboat.

"Is everything all right?" Madge called.

"We need more light," Paul said.

In moments, lights were shining onto the water. Brian and Paul hefted the body to the railing. Fenwick and Madge rushed to the end of the pier their boat was docked to, down the gangway, up the pier to the Turners' boat, then onto it. The two in the water and the four in the boat pulled, pushed, and shoved the body on board. Once it was on deck, Madge used her cell phone to call the police. The body was in board shorts, a tattered white T-shirt, white athletic socks, and shoes. The shredded and tattered clothes revealed horribly mangled flesh underneath. No blood. The lake water would have cleansed it. The corpse wasn't wearing a life jacket or a personal flotation device.

The face was clear and white. Turner realized it was the blond from the red Mustang from the night before.

Attempting CPR on the lifeless corpse was pointless. Turner hurried to Jeff and Brian. "Are you okay?" he asked.

"He's dead," Jeff said.

"Yes." Turner didn't believe in lying to his boys. The reality was the person was dead.

Brian said, "I've never touched a dead guy."

Paul put a hand on his shoulder. The boy was trembling. "You're going to be all right," he said. "You want a blanket?"

"I don't think so. What's going to happen?"

The local professionals arrived and got to work. Turner saw an Ontario Provincial Police marine unit emergency response team and underwater search and recovery unit, the Ontario Provincial Police helicopter, the Cathura police, the regular Ontario Provincial Police, and some volunteers as well in case they were needed to search for others. For a short while the OPP helicopter hovered overhead with its powerful searchlight illuminating the scene.

The Fenwicks retired to their boat to discuss the situation with their daughters.

Jeff and Brian were at the Formica-topped kitchen table. Ben stood in the background. The Cathura chief of police, Vincent Schreppel, and the commander of the local Ontario Provincial Police detachment, Mavis Bednars, entered the room.

Brian clutched a large yellow beach towel around his shoulders. Turner could see that his son still wore the shirt and pants he'd had on when he leapt into the water. He suggested his son change. When Brian returned in baggy jeans and bulky sweatshirt, the boy asked, "Could we have saved him?"

Turner said, "I think he's been dead for a while."

Schreppel said, "The dead person is Scarth Krohn, a local boy. We need a statement."

Each of them explained what they'd been doing when Jeff had raised the alarm.

Turner said, "I thought he was one of the ones in the parking lot last night when we called the police when it looked like the rival groups were going to get into it. It was some First Nations and some white kids." Turner also mentioned the sabotage of the boat, the parking lot incident, and the break-in.

Bednars said, "You didn't recognize anybody on the boat that attacked you?"

"No," Turner admitted.

"So, it might have been those kids, or might not."

Turner said, "I can't be sure. Things happened too fast."

"You didn't report the altercation in the parking lot?"

Turner said, "We reported the one between rival groups, but not when they harassed us. It seemed kind of pointless. What was to be done?"

Schreppel said, "You're a cop. You know it can make a difference."

Turner said, "It didn't seem to make a lot of difference when we called it in the first time."

"Kids," Schreppel said.

Mavis Bednars said, "We've had reports of altercations between Scarth Krohn and a number of people."

Schreppel said, "He was a good kid. His dad is going to be out of his mind with grief."

Bednars said, "What parent wouldn't be?"

Turner said, "He was not being a model citizen in the restaurant parking lot."

Schreppel said, "He was used to high living."

Turner said, "Looked to me it was more like he was used to bullying the world around him and no one put a stop to it."

"Did you know the kid?" Schreppel asked.

Turner said, "I'm only speaking based on my limited experiences with him."

Schreppel said, "He was an important member of this community, and he will be missed."

Bednars said, "Let me get my schematic of where everybody was when the alarm first came about."

Turner welcomed her change of subject. Turner's notion at this point was that the relationship between the two local cops wasn't first-rate.

After the cops were clear on the basics, Schreppel said, "Seems like a simple drowning. We'll have to let you know. There will be an autopsy."

"Why was the body torn up?" Brian asked.

Bednars said, "Most likely it got mangled by the propeller of a boat. That happens often in these cases."

Ian asked, "Have you had a chance to look into the attacks on us and on the sabotage? Maybe this guy had something to do with them."

Schreppel said, "Murder comes before domestic squabbles. I don't need some graft-taking Chicago cops trying to tell me my business or running around asking questions."

Ian said, "Graft-taking Canadian cops are okay?"

Schreppel glared.

Turner controlled his anger. He shook his head at Ian. In the middle of the night in the beginning of an investigation was not the time to ask such questions or start fights with the local cops with their prejudices about Chicago. And it wasn't the first time he'd heard this kind of crack about his city and his profession.

Hours later only Bednars and a few uniformed officers remained. The body had been removed.

Turner asked Bednars, "What killed him?"

"Most likely he drowned. He could have drifted a ways.

It's a big lake. It may not look like there are currents, but there are."

Turner said, "Schreppel must know the Krohns."

Bednars said, "Yep." She left it at that and Turner didn't pursue it.

Ian, reporter instincts on high alert, said he was going to the police station to see if he could find anything out.

Turner checked on his family. Jeff was asleep on the couch. Brian was curled in a chair looking out at the darkness. Ben was at the kitchen table. He and Brian stood up when Paul walked in.

Brian asked, "Is everything going to be okay?"

Paul said, "I'm worried about you and Jeff. Are you all right?"

"I think so. It seems pretty unreal. The biggest thing I remember is how cold the water was."

"You've been in it before."

"Yeah, but usually during the day, and mostly if I'm on the Jet Ski, I'm wearing a wet suit so if I fall in it's not so bad."

Paul said, "It's something I wish you hadn't had to go through. Now that it's happened, we'll do everything we can to make things better. Do you want to go home after this? We may not be able to leave for a day or two."

Brian thought for a minute. "I don't think so. Will Jeff be okay?"

Paul said, "We'll see how everybody feels in the morning. We'll check with the Fenwicks as well."

Paul carried Jeff from the couch to his bed and tucked him in. The boy did not waken. Paul was glad for that.

It was near four when everyone was settled down, and Paul was in bed with Ben.

Paul said, "I'm worried about the boys."

"Me, too," Ben replied.

Paul wasn't in the mood for romance, but he was in need of closeness. He snuggled up to Ben.

Much later he awakened. He thought he heard the call of sunrise birds. He heard no other indications of human movement. For a while Paul stared up at the ceiling. He listened to the shifting of the boat in the slight waves. He felt puffs of wind the screened-in window let in. He was uneasy. Death at work was one thing, but death this close to his family was disturbing. He fell asleep as the first rays of sunlight leaked through the window screen.

.11.

Paul Turner and Buck Fenwick were hunched over the Formica kitchen table on Turner's houseboat. Between them were several boxes of Timbits from the local Tim Hortons. In the Chicago area these would be doughnut holes from a Dunkin' Donuts type of place. Turner had once suggested that Fenwick call ahead to the nearest franchise in Cathura so they would be certain to have a supply on hand large enough to keep Fenwick satisfied. Fenwick had thought this was a logical precaution. They were sipping tepid coffee.

Fenwick was saying, "Why don't you gain weight from eating these? You eat as many as I do."

"No one could eat as many as you do."

"Nearly as many."

"Maybe so," Turner replied, "but perhaps my consumption of everything else is less than yours. I like these so I eat less of other stuff. I'm told that is the new diet craze, eating less."

Paul had checked with the boys after everyone was awake.

Jeff was determined to stick to the fishing trip. Paul could already imagine the eleven-year-old's voice, six months from now, bragging to his buddies about finding a body on their trip. For the moment it was still too raw an experience for all of them. Brian said he'd prefer to stay. Ian was temporarily absent, and he didn't know how to get in touch with Mrs. Talucci. Paul and the Fenwicks had consulted. The girls hadn't seen any grisly body remains, and at the moment there seemed to be more excitement than fear. For now they would all stay. And Turner was determined not to run in the face of homophobia. But if his children really needed to leave, he would consider it. Their safety and their fears trumped a fight for gay dignity.

The kids had all gone into Kenora with Madge and Ben to purchase supplies. Normally they'd have been up at five to go fishing. Today they had barely gotten to bed by then. Turner had slept until eleven. He didn't feel quite awake. Before the crowd left for town, he'd again checked with his sons. Both seemed to be fine. Jeff, the finder of the body, seemed reasonably calm although quieter than usual. During their late breakfast, his tendency to burble incessantly had mercifully been absent. Paul wasn't sure finding a corpse a day was quite the regimen he wanted his kid to start even if it would cause a halt to his seemingly endless chatter. Paul was proud his kid was bright, but there were times when he wished the kid would ask fewer questions.

At breakfast Paul had caught Brian staring into the distance. Being the first on the scene to help his brother had shaken him considerably. He hadn't been his usual self, eager to go rushing to meet his peers and make noise as only teenagers know how to do. His appetite had been blunted. Normally you couldn't fill Brian up or shut Jeff up.

Rain had started in midmorning and it had continued to sprinkle intermittently. Madge and Ben had been willing to take all the kids into town. In a situation rare for him, Brian had not objected to tagging along with the younger kids.

Paul Turner heard the thud of feet on the deck of the houseboat. Ian's face appeared at the window screen. "You won't believe this," he announced. "I've been awake all night."

"Well, throw you a fish," Fenwick said.

Turner said, "I was running around until early this morning. Could you make this short?"

Ian banged open the screen door and flourished the local paper under Turner's nose. It was the *Cathura Post* with the headline splashed across the front page LOCAL HERO DIES with a subheading about a Chicago cop's kid finding the corpse.

Turner put a hand on Ian's arm to stop the flourishing. "Yes, I know," Turner said. "Remember? My kid fished up the dead body."

"But there's been lots of them."

"My kid's been fishing up lots of dead bodies? He's been keeping them from me?"

"You hate that in an eleven-year-old," Fenwick said. "For a teenager it's still a headache, but you know how teenagers are, secretive."

Ian attempted to ignore them. "Six bodies in the past four years, seven now. All college guys."

"It's a crime wave," Fenwick said. "My life is packed with dead bodies in Chicago. I knew I felt something was missing up here."

"Well, they've got a passel of them," Ian said. "From all the communities around here."

"Maybe it's like an interlake competition, a contest,"

Fenwick said. "Maybe each of these little towns is keeping score. Where were they from?"

"Two each from Kenora, Sioux Narrows, and Cathura."

"Tied," Fenwick said. "The cable networks should be able to beat that to death. They've beaten to death less." Turner knew that Fenwick agreed with someone's analysis when cable news started—that there wasn't enough news to fill twenty-four hours. Fenwick's frequently expressed opinion was that this continued to be true. Turner agreed with him.

Ian said, "This one breaks the tie."

Fenwick said, "Cathura wins."

"How did our guy die?" Turner asked.

"He drowned," Fenwick said. "Lots of water around here. That can't be unusual. Doesn't sound like murder."

"The provincial coroner is going to do an autopsy."

"Did they autopsy the others?" Turner asked.

"No. Everybody assumed they all drowned."

Fenwick said, "Big damn lake. People drown. Sun rises in east. Stop the presses."

"But there are some locals who think it's been murder all along. They're worried they've got a serial killer on the loose."

"And they think so why?" Fenwick asked.

Turner said, "Something fishy is going on."

Ian and Fenwick glared at him. Fenwick said, "I do the ghastly puns in this relationship."

Ian said, "Listening to the two of you spouting any kind of ghastly crap is painful."

Fenwick said, "I'm also in charge of ghastly crap in this relationship."

Ian said, "Will you guys be serious?"

"I was being serious," Fenwick said.

"Is there a connection between these seven?" Turner asked. "Did they know each other? Were they friends? Drug runners?"

"Not that I know of, so far," Ian said.

Turner said, "Okay, why would it be murder? Is there a problem locally? They don't like the chief of police? The wind shifted? They had a dream? They did a tarot reading? They got a special message from their local goddess? They have forensic evidence bubbling up from the bottom of the lake?"

Fenwick said, "I prefer neon arrows above the killer's head that say 'he did it.' They have any of those?"

Ian poured himself some coffee and joined them at the table. "The people with suspicions called the Ontario Provincial Police. Those cops wouldn't intervene. They said it was up to the chief of police. Then I ran into some local guy, Howard Coates. He says it's too many coincidences. It's in the article. He thinks it's murder. Normally there's about eight or nine drownings in the lakes around here per year. In the past couple years they've had all these extras."

"Six," Fenwick said. "Stop the presses. Rewrite the statistics books."

"Seven now," Ian said.

Turner said, "Run into? You don't just 'run into' a guy making accusations of murder."

Ian said, "Fine. I talked to the reporter who wrote the articles on the other six. He told me to talk to Coates."

"They're friends? Enemies?" Fenwick asked.

"The owner of the paper edits out a lot of the speculation in the articles."

"Speculation is news?" Turner asked.

Fenwick said, "It is on the FOXNews network." Fenwick

was referring to the channel that spent most of its time shilling for various right-wing causes.

Ian said, "This Howard guy doesn't sound like a raving idiot to me. He seems sensible."

"Good for Ed," Fenwick said. "Why are you telling us this?"

"I figured you'd be interested professionally."

Fenwick said, "I'm not planning to get drunk and drown. In fact I haven't been drunk since my brother's wedding when I was eighteen. He's been divorced four times. Leaving my loony brother aside, I have no jurisdiction here. We have no standing."

Ian looked at Turner. "Your kid found the body. Doesn't that make you interested?"

"Technically it found us," Turner said.

"Yeah, it thumped into your boat. You get a lot of bodies thumping into your boat?"

"Not on this lake," Turner said, "but there was that time—"

Fenwick interrupted, "There I was, motoring through the Amazon. Three of our guides and two of the other people in the party, including an Albanian dwarf, had mysteriously disappeared. They all did a thumping-on-the-boat dance both before and after they'd been sacrificed to a variety of mysterious causes. I'd just—"

Turner said, "No, no, no. It wasn't the Amazon. We've never been to the Amazon."

"We haven't? It worked for the story."

Ian said, "I've been trying to ignore your pathetic humor. You guys are not funny."

Fenwick said, "That's been long since established in all the finer marinas on every lake within a hundred miles."

"A thousand miles," added Turner.

Ian said, "There are no fine marinas. The ones I've seen are managed by people who look more run-down than their shoddy, crumbling cabins, camps, and piers."

Fenwick said, "What were you expecting? The Wilderness Ritz? Didn't you or your family ever go camping or fishing?"

"Fishing, like golf, is not in the gay gene."

"I go fishing," Paul said.

"We've been worried about you," Ian replied.

"I'm not," Paul said.

Ian said, "You're not interested in investigating? How can you not be? One of your kids was fishing and snagged the body. What if one of you had been swimming, or"—he pointed at Fenwick—"one of your girls had pulled it out of the water?"

Fenwick said, "Maybe they'd have been tied to a buzz saw and needed to be rescued just in time."

"Or the railroad tracks," Turner added.

"That makes no sense," Ian said.

Turner said, "We try not to use the *s* word around Fenwick. Him and sense don't often get along."

" 'We' who?" Fenwick demanded.

"Anyone who's ever met you," Ian said.

Fenwick said, "Ian, you've obviously bought the whole conspiracy theory—"

"Don't," Ian said.

Fenwick continued unabashed, "—hook, line, and—"

Ian groaned.

Fenwick finished, "—homicide."

Ian said, "If I have any luck on this fishing trip, I'll be the next victim."

Turner said, "Of course I'm concerned for my kids. They may be used to my job. They might have seen a lot of death and destruction on television and video games, but the real thing is different. I don't know the young man who drowned. I'm not sure I care or why I should. He was a homophobic asshole the other night. I don't know the local law enforcement people. I don't want to be involved with them if I don't have to. The police last night seemed methodical and efficient if a little brusque and off-putting. The chief of police seemed a little too eager to believe the wrong side in a dispute. That's stupid, but not provably criminal. It's his jurisdiction, not mine."

Ian said, "We're against murdering homophobic assholes?"

"Now who's not being serious?" Turner asked. "Sure, one less homophobic asshole is in theory a good thing." Turner remembered one of his favorite sayings from *The Lord of the Rings,* when the wizard Gandalf is speaking to Frodo, who has just wished death upon the villain Gollum. Gandalf says to him, as Turner now quoted to Ian, " 'I daresay many that live deserve death. And some that die deserve life. Can you give it to them? Then be not too eager to deal out death in the name of justice.' Maybe I've seen too many dead bodies in my career. This one has nothing to do with us. Take our Chicago police detective stars and add two bucks and you can get a cup of coffee at Starbucks."

"But this Coates guy can't get a hearing from the local cops. They ignore him."

"Then he's lucky," Fenwick said. "If he's that interested or that much of a pain in the neck, he should be their number one suspect."

88

"Just because somebody's interested doesn't make him a suspect."

"Too interested, makes a suspect, does," Fenwick said.

"You swallow a Yoda pill recently?" Ian asked.

Turner said, "So Howard thinks what?"

"That somebody pushed them. They were all drunk. They had all been drinking at the same local establishment on the waterfront."

Fenwick said, "You said they were found at various points around the lake."

Ian said, "But all were seen drinking in Cathura the night they died."

Turner pointed out, "There aren't that many local establishments that stay open on the waterfront after ten at night. It's a small town."

"Guys get drunk, fall in the water, die," Fenwick said.

"These were all young, athletic college kids," Ian said.

Fenwick said, "College kids drink a lot."

"So do cops."

"You got a set of them turning up dead in the lake?" Fenwick asked.

"Not yet," Ian said. He swirled his coffee around in his cup. "Several people from the earlier drownings have filed lawsuits against the bar for serving them drinks."

"Dead people have been filing lawsuits?" Turner asked.

"Their relatives," Ian said. "And they're suing the town for not putting up barriers along the waterfront."

"But it's a parkway along the shore," Fenwick said. "Hundreds of people stroll along there every night. We've strolled along the shore. Big deal."

Ian gulped more coffee. He said, "No, you guys have got

to listen. There is intrigue in this town. It is a veritable hotbed of dastardly doings."

Fenwick yawned. "I hope you don't use that many clichés when you write."

"Everybody's a critic. Come on, you guys. You're cops. You've got to at least be a little bit interested in this, maybe at least as an intellectual exercise."

"Let me give it due thought," Fenwick said. He paused for three seconds. "I have given the subject all the consideration it deserves, and the answer is, I don't care. I'm on vacation. I'm fishing. We have nothing to do with this. They have police here. Let them earn their doughnuts."

"But there's all kinds of cloak-and-dagger crap. What about the big lodges who are fighting the conservationists?"

Turner said, "What does that have to do with dead college-age kids?"

"Scarth Krohn worked for some of the lodges. As far as I can find out, he took a few college classes. Supposedly still did. Maybe he met some of the dead kids."

Turner said, "Half the kids up here work for one, some, or all of the lodges. They do freelance guide duty. They tote barges and lift bales. They do a million things for the tourist trade."

Fenwick stood up and said, "It is nap time on the Fenwick vacation time schedule."

"Nap," Ian said. "You can nap when there's murder afoot?"

"I can nap when there's murder underfoot, above foot, horizontal and vertical foot. Naps are the staff of life. I'm good at them. Like I always say, when you're good at something, stick with it. Always go with your strength, and one of my great strengths is napping." He washed his coffee cup out, stuck it in the dish drainer, strolled onto the deck, and lumbered over to his family's boat.

Turner knew Fenwick would be asleep in seconds. Fenwick always declared that naps were second only to chocolate as the loves of his life. Turner had noted that he never uttered this sentiment within hearing distance of his wife or kids. Turner knew that Fenwick was totally devoted to them although Fenwick would rather rip out his tongue than admit that to very many people.

Ian said, "Come on, Paul, even if you're not interested, let me tell you, there is some nasty stuff in this town. Look what's happened to us since we've been here."

Ian was a friend. They'd been lovers many years ago. Paul kept his sigh to himself. He said, "Don't go getting involved in this. There is no benign amateur sleuth immunity. Not in the real world. If they are halfway competent cops, and you seem like you're too interested, they will go after you."

"When have you not known me to be discreet?"

"I have a list that has grown extensively over the years. Big charts, dates, times, who was present."

"Fenwick has had an evil effect on you. How about this: Did you know the owner of the houseboat company that rents you these things is a homophobic pig?"

"And how did you find that out?"

"I have four sources."

"How did you get them to talk?"

"Everybody wants to talk about the murders. You get them talking, they tell everything. It is the topic of discussion up and down Main Street. People are talking—tourists, year-rounders, everybody."

"And murder and homophobia came up in the same conversation how?"

"Well, funny you should ask. There I was."

"Yeah, right, once upon a time. Get on with it."

"The guy who rents you these houseboats owns the dock, the marina, that little restaurant, and the bar. The bar where supposedly all these people had been drinking before they bought it in the briny deep."

"This is freshwater. I don't think it's briny."

"He owns the damn bar. It's a popular spot in town. There's only three really big establishments. During fishing season it's packed. Well, Howard Coates, the guy the reporter told me about, also owns a restaurant/bar."

"They're rivals?"

"I guess."

"So he's definitely objective."

"Just listen. You've seen the place. It's down the highway just the other side of downtown. It's called the Dangling Fisherman. I like the logo."

Turner remembered that the front of the bar had four gigantic picture windows so that as many diners as possible could have views of the dilapidated buildings across the street as they ate. In the top half of the last window going north there was a three-by-six-foot picture of a fisherman caught on a giant hook. He was dangling above the mouth of a gigantic fish, which was about to devour him.

Turner sipped coffee while he listened. The lake water quietly lapped against the hull and the shore. He heard birds and insects. A distant motorboat thrummed for a moment.

Ian said, "Howard was holding court in his restaurant this morning. Seems there's been political fights in the town as well and squabbling fishermen up and down the lake. You know how the conservationists and the resort owners are always fighting? And the loggers are pissed off at everybody since the plant closed?"

"I'm sort of peripherally aware of it. The one week I'm here I don't usually attend political meetings in town. That may be what you go on vacation for, but it's not my thing."

"Well, this is serious. This kid who is dead is the son of the richest guy in town. You've heard of him, J. T. Krohn. That's why this is such a big deal."

"I don't care if the corpses are rich or not."

"But the community does. And I found out all kinds of inside dirt on the kid." Ian clamped his fedora further down on his head. "What Kevin said yesterday was true. The kid was the town bully."

"I didn't doubt Kevin's word."

"No one ever dared lift a hand against Scarth. He was a big kid, six feet four, the star of every team at the local school for years. He was *it* for Mr. Stud Athlete. Remember yesterday Kevin said he had an injury?"

"Yeah."

"My sources told me he was also a lazy-ass jerk who preferred to stay around here and sponge off his dad, screw as many of the local girls as he could, commit petty thefts, and live off ill-gotten gains."

"Mr. Coates didn't like him."

"Mr. Coates knows everything about everybody."

"And he confided all of this in you because?"

"We became good friends very quickly."

"Do I hear wedding bells in an international relationship?"

"Right now we're just friends."

"I've got to meet this guy."

"You will. He's willing to talk to you. He wants to talk to you. Even if it does piss off the local police. I don't care if it gets me in trouble. They may be pissed off already, but how would they know who I talked to? Or care?"

"It's a small town. Everybody knows everything and the cops can get more pissed off. Why don't you solve it? You know all this. You've got the contacts."

Ian looked abashed. "I want to. I can't. I tried going to the police station. They threw me out after demanding to know my name, address, country of origin."

"They were suspicious and should have been."

"They won't be suspicious of you."

"Probably they would be. Even more likely they would be irritated by what they would see as unnecessary interference from someone who has no standing."

"You're a cop."

"Which is not a universal set of permissions to torture suspects in various countries or to conduct investigations even without torture. I have no access to files, to the usual suspects. These guys all drowned, Ian. There is no mystery here."

"The whole community hated this guy."

"You took a poll?"

"You should have heard how the people talked. Every single one said he was the classic bully."

"A coward and an asshole. So what?"

"He tore up people's property. He hurt people. He abused every girlfriend he ever had. On the hockey rink, he smashed into guys after the final buzzer. He was known as an enforcer. He took cheap shots. He ended a lot of kids' careers or at least their interest in the game."

"Don't people cheer at hockey games the more violence there is?"

"People in this town hated him," Ian reiterated.

"You talked to all of them?"

"Well, a few of them."

"He probably did do all those terrible things, but that gets you nowhere close to a murder or a suspect. Unless someone confessed to killing him, you don't have much of a case. Yes, many guys abuse wives and girlfriends, and sometimes it's the other way around. But you still need witnesses and facts. You have anybody who saw him fall in? Hold him down? No. If you did you'd have told me. If he's a big kid and athletic as you said, how'd they manage to hold him under? He must have fought back. Maybe it was a group? You have anybody, individuals or groups, confessing? No. You'd have probably told me that. Better yet, do you have anybody who saw him pushed? No. Do you have the slightest scintilla of concrete evidence?"

"Lack of concrete evidence doesn't stop people from getting convicted."

"In my police work I have yet to begin working on the theory that if somebody looks like a killer, they're guilty. Juries in California can do that. I'm an intelligent cop or at least I try to act like one. Ian, he drowned. He got drunk. He slipped. He fell. He's dead. He drowned. Period. The town bully is dead. You should be happy. Were all six of the others town bullies?"

"Not that anybody said."

"Do you know anything about the other six?"

"No."

"Do you have background on any of them? Some connection between all of them?"

"They all died by drowning."

"A connection while they were living? Backgrounds, data, inside information?"

"They all went to St. Croix College, the local place."

"Did they know each other? Have classes together? Come from the same town?"

"I don't know."

Turner sighed, then said, "We don't have the resources here to find out. Why don't you relax, get into the vacation? There's nothing you can do."

Ian's jaw set, and he gave Turner a steely glance. "Perhaps I'll nose around."

Turner said, "You're not interested in this because Coates and you got acquainted?"

Ian said, "Does it make a difference?"

"Might."

Ian said, "When it does, ask me again." The reporter wasn't ready to relent just yet. "What if the murder has something to do with you or your family?" he asked.

"I don't see how," Turner said.

"Those other things did Sunday. The kids in the car. The break-in."

"Murder is different."

"You hope so."

"Ian." Turner's voice was stern. "I don't need you stirring up the kids."

"I wasn't going to."

Turner gave it up. When his friend was in reporter mode, there wasn't much to be done. He hoped he didn't get himself into trouble.

ˎ 12 ˏ

That afternoon the fishing was quiet. No bodies. No storms. No sabotage. He and Ben took out their powerboat. The two of them always spent some time together alone on the trips. It wasn't as much as they liked, but when you've got kids, supervision happens.

As the sun was setting, the cigarette boat with Mrs. Talucci sitting in magisterial splendor arrived at the dock. Her visiting between arrival and departure was unprecedented.

Paul caught the line from the elegantly slender young man who drove. Paul helped make the boat secure. He offered Mrs. Talucci his hand. She moved more slowly these days.

After she stepped onto the dock, she touched the side of his face. "Are you all right? The boys and Ben?"

"We're okay. You heard about the body?"

"Of course. I had to come. Is there anything I can do?"

Paul said, "It's been a strain. Ian thinks it was murder."

Mrs. Talucci smiled. "Doesn't he always?" She bustled to their houseboat. In minutes Mrs. Talucci and Madge Fenwick were creating a dessert for the whole crew. Both families gathered on the Turners' boat. There were even a few tentative smiles as they devoured cake, chocolate sauce, and vanilla ice cream. Paul noted that Mrs. Talucci made sure to pat each of his boys on the shoulder and ask if they were all right. They had each nodded and smiled. At some point when each boy had a modicum of privacy, she had leaned down close to their ear and whispered something. Each boy had whispered back. It was a brief exchange. Turner guessed Mrs. Talucci was telling each boy that she loved them. Turner smiled to himself.

An hour later Mrs. Talucci and Paul were on the dock again. Mrs. Talucci pulled a sweater close over her shoulders. She said, "If I can be of any help, contact me." She gave him a card. All it had on it was a phone number.

Paul said, "Are you going to be safe at night on the water?"

"Yes, even I have learned to navigate by the GPS, and I'm not driving the boat."

Paul accompanied Mrs. Talucci as she walked back down the pier to her boat. She had taken his arm. At the end of the dock she said, "I love you and your family." She kissed his cheek and stepped with surprising dexterity onto the deck of the boat. They motored away.

Paul was still restless as the others settled down for the night. He said to Ben, "You want to try a little late-night fishing?"

Ben got a gleam in his eye. The Fenwicks agreed to keep

an eye on the boys. Fenwick nudged Madge and winked. She patted his arm. "Not tonight, dear," she said.

The night was cool and they huddled in sweatshirts as they fished. They took out downriggers and trolled the depths trying to keep the bait close to the bottom. After half an hour, they went ashore, cleared some brush, slathered on more bug spray, spread a blanket under them and a blanket over them, and under the stars and with the pine trees as witnesses, they talked about fear and the kids and what could be done. They held each other, which led to more. Under the stars and the moon and the trees and with the wind and the bugs around them, they made love.

.13.

The Cathura police chief, Schreppel, was at the marina when they returned. A police cruiser was docked at the pier. The cop was talking to several of the locals. When Turner was ashore, Schreppel approached him and said, "Can I speak with you, Mr. Turner?"

"Sure," Paul said. He turned to Ben. "I'll be back in a minute."

The cop began to walk away. Turner followed.

"Something's come up," the cop said. Turner said nothing. He'd learned to use silence as an interrogation tool a long time ago. As they neared the path into the woods, the cop turned and faced the shore. Finally, he resumed. "We have at least two witnesses who saw Scarth in town away from the shore after he was done drinking."

"What was he doing?"

"Cruising in his Austin Healy Sprite."

"No Mustang?"

"He has several cars. His dad has plenty more."

"Isn't that kind of an expensive car for a kid in Cathura?"

"For the kid, maybe; for his dad, no. His dad drives a Porsche. Either of your kids off the boat that night?"

Turner swallowed cracks he wanted to make about his kid in the wheelchair. This guy was a fellow cop trying to do his job. Sarcasm wasn't appropriate. He evaded the question. "So, somebody had to get him, with or without his car, back to the water. He was big. It wouldn't be easy. How drunk was he?"

"Very."

"Was there anything suspicious about any of the other six deaths?"

"No."

"Have you looked back into them?"

"Looking back into other deaths would make it less likely that your kids had anything to do with it."

"They didn't—"

"You'd protect your own. So would I. In this town J. T. Krohn has a lot to say. He's the richest man around. He has influence."

"With you?"

"Yes. He knows his boy was seen around town. He's pressing hard for an investigation. Very hard. He wants to know what happened. He wants to know why his son died."

"I heard Scarth was the town bully. You ever do anything about that? Any schoolteacher, school principal?"

"He came within my radar a few times. Nothing serious. Kid stuff."

"What kind of kid stuff?"

"I can't help you with that," the cop said. "The reason I stopped by was that your kid was seen in town that night."

"What significance does that have? So were all the several thousand people who live in town."

"You know this reporter, Ian Hume?"

"Yes."

"Come on, I'm a cop. I'd think you'd be willing to help. Short, snappy answers aren't going to help."

"Earlier I was an annoying interferer from the evil big city. Now I'm supposed to be cooperative and friendly. Which way do you want it? You're not going to get it both ways."

"Your boy old enough to be in a drinking establishment?"

"Was he somewhere he didn't belong? If he was, why don't you just say so? Where was he? What was he doing?"

"I'm just asking questions."

"No, that isn't all that you're doing. You're using innuendo to suggest something. Are you accusing him of murder?"

"No."

Turner was annoyed. One, at himself for getting annoyed and cutting off a conversation. Two, at the cop. What did the guy know? He wanted to try and get a few answers himself. He held his emotions in check and said, "Is there any indication of what time he went into the lake?"

"Not yet. I'm not answering your questions. You have no inherent protection here just because you're cops. This isn't Chicago."

"And this isn't Baghdad," Turner retorted.

"You and your group sticking around all week?"

"That's the current plan."

"Good." The implication was clear: don't leave town. Turner was determined to find the killer if only to spite this asshole.

The cop left.

Turner strode over to the Fenwicks' houseboat. Fenwick was in baggy jeans shorts and a navy blue sweatshirt.

"What's up?" Fenwick asked.

Turner told him about the cop conversation. Fenwick said, "We need to talk to Ian and his buddy."

Turner said, "He asked about Ian and Brian. Something is up. We've got to find Ian. He's probably in bed with any number of hot local men."

"Pissing off the local police is not a good idea," Fenwick said.

"We're going to be doing that if we start investigating."

"Yeah, but we're saints," said Fenwick.

"Cop saints?" Turner asked.

"There's got to be cop saints."

"We'll probably find Ian before we find any cop saints."

Ian was nowhere to be found. Turner and Fenwick vowed to hunt for the local reporter, one of Ian's sources, after the next morning's fishing.

Before he retired for the night, Paul knocked on Brian's door and stepped into his bedroom.

"Are you okay?" Paul asked.

"Pretty much. I think so." He glanced up at his dad.

Brian sat on his bed. Paul leaned against the wall. Brian said, "What I remember most was how cold the water was, and how cold the body was. When I think about it, I get weird goose bumps."

Paul said, "It's okay to think about it. Talking about it is okay, too. With any of us. Burying the experience won't make it go away."

"Yeah, I know. I talked with Mrs. Fenwick today. She was really helpful. It's like this really adult thing happened."

"You handled yourself mostly right. Next time please try to remember a life jacket. Even this close to shore there can be problems."

"I know. I won't forget. I'll never forget any instant of it."

"It'll fade. You did right. Your brother was frightened. You make good decisions. You have for a long time now."

"Thanks," Brian said.

"The police chief Schreppel was just here. He said you were in town last night. You didn't go to the movies in Kenora?"

"Nah, Kevin and his friends wanted to stay in town. We just hung around."

Or was he out necking with Kevin for a second night in a row?

"Did you see Scarth Krohn at any time?" Paul asked.

"If he was around, I didn't notice him."

Turner let it go. He wasn't going to bring up the scene in the forest from the first night.

Paul said, "Fenwick and I may need to do some investigating. Unless you want to spend a father/son day tomorrow."

"Nah. I want you to catch the son of a bitch who did this. I'd feel better. I'm not sure why, though. This Krohn guy was a shit."

"That he seems to have been," Paul said. "Language?"

"Sorry."

Strong language was discouraged in the home especially around Jeff, who'd gone through a stage two years ago of testing the house's language limits.

Paul checked on Jeff. He was asleep. He crawled into bed next to Ben, who rolled close. Ben said, "The boys seemed pretty okay today. At dinner Jeff talked a blue streak about anything but the body."

"He's asleep. I'll check with him tomorrow morning." They cuddled and then slept.

14

Fishing at five the next morning was difficult for Paul. He'd have suggested canceling if he hadn't wanted to keep things as close to normal as possible and to check on how Jeff was. The younger boy did burble continuously as they motored out to the nearest fishing ground.

Paul took him out in the rowboat. Jeff continued to burble until Paul said, "What's wrong?"

Jeff stopped. Water lapped against the boat. Paul knelt next to his specially arranged chair in the middle of the boat. They were on the same eye level.

Jeff got teary eyed. "It was weird and sick, and I got scared last night. I had a nightmare."

"You could have called me."

"I know. I didn't. I heard Brian snoring. I felt better. I fell back to sleep pretty quick."

Paul said, "Two nights ago you called for help. That's

what you're supposed to do. There was nothing else you could have done."

"I wish I could have jumped in. I'm never going to be able to do that. Never."

Paul was sure this was the heart of the upset. Jeff was very used to his spina bifida, but there were times when he desperately wished to be like all the other kids. He seldom said anything to Paul, but the feelings did surface on occasion. Paul and his son looked at each other. Jeff said, "I know what I am and my limitations. Sometimes it's a pain in the ass."

Paul said, "Everybody has limitations. Everybody has gifts. You know yours better than most eleven-year-olds. That's a tremendous accomplishment."

"I know. It was just so weird. So, so weird."

"Are you scared something might happen again?"

"More like, I want to be able to make it stop."

"You know none of us can stop bad things from happening. I can't make the criminals of Chicago do that, and I'm a very good detective."

"Are you going to find out who did it?"

"If I can."

"Good. I'll feel better."

Jeff's burbling eased for the next hour. They fished quietly. Talked father-and-son things. They motored around dock and shoreline. Jeff caught three perch.

After they returned to the dock, Turner collected Fenwick and Ian.

Turner said to Ian, "You were out late last night."

"All night," Ian said. "I was making friends." Which could have been Ian's euphemism for saying he was having sex or could mean he'd been investigating. Turner knew he could have been doing either one all night. Turner well knew how strong Ian's libido was. Rookie cops at the same time, they'd also been lovers years before, and it had been exhausting. More fun than Turner had had in his life up to then, but exhausting.

"We're investigating," Turner said.

"Excellent. What brought this on?"

"I had a visit from Schreppel last night. He pissed me off."

"Good."

"I'd like to start with your reporter source."

Ian accompanied Turner and Fenwick as they walked to downtown.

Steve Fournier was the reporter with whom Ian had spoken. He worked at the *Cathura Post*. The newspaper office was in a storefront on Main Street.

The receptionist told them they could find the reporter having breakfast at the Old Forest Café, three doors down.

In the restaurant Ian spotted his erstwhile friend, waved, strode over, and introduced Turner and Fenwick.

Fournier was in his late twenties. He was lanky, and, even sitting, his torso stretched quite far above the table. Turner saw black-framed glasses, thick black hair, knotted fists, and ropes of veins on his hirsute arms. Turner knew this was Ian's favorite-looking kind of guy. Fournier also wore a large gold wedding band. Turner knew this would cause Ian to be discreet, but would not stop his interest. Ian, as did Turner for that matter, preferred more masculine men.

They sat. The waitress brought coffee. Fournier wore a short-sleeved white shirt, a dark blue tie, and faded blue jeans.

Ian said, "We're off the record?"

"Absolutely." Fournier's voice was well into the baritone register.

"These guys got a visit from Chief of Police Schreppel last night."

Fournier said, "Schreppel is a moron."

"How so?" Turner asked.

"What I say goes no further?" Fournier asked.

Ian said, "Reciprocal silence."

"But I get any story?" Fournier asked.

"Absolutely," Ian said.

The two detectives nodded.

"Schreppel has been in charge for ten years. He's been on the force for about twenty-five. On his way up he was an ass kisser and licker. How come he was after you guys?"

Turner said, "My son was in town the night of Scarth Krohn's murder."

"So were a lot of people," Fournier said.

"What's the deal with the family?" Turner asked.

"Scarth's father, Joseph Thomas Krohn, was the town bully in his day. His son is the same. The man who started this, Great-Grandpa Krohn, supposedly killed several people, including a Mountie, in the Northwest Territories in 1904. He was never convicted. Scarth's granddad, Blake Krohn, made a fortune in timber back when fortunes could be made in timber. Not like today. It's been a long time since the family's well-being was tied to timber. They diversified during World War II. Blake Krohn was also a stud. He fathered seven kids. Many of them and his grandkids are still around. Scarth had a passel of uncles, aunts, and cousins. A lot of the town is connected in some way to the Krohns, either working for them or related to them. Blake put other timber barons out of business. He was supposedly quite ruthless. Scarth's dad, J.T., is equally so. This town does what he says. We don't put anything in the paper that would reflect badly on them. Nobody stands up to that family."

Turner described the incident in the parking lot with the twenty-somethings.

Fournier said, "Problems with the First Nations people occur a lot. Scarth would feed on that kind of thing."

"Did you know him as a kid?"

"I was ahead of him in school by about eight years. He had a reputation as an athlete and as a troublemaker. The athlete stuff triumphed over everything else. There wasn't much the rest of the people in the town could do about his wild behavior."

"What did he do?"

"By this time it's hard to separate fact from legend. Among certain parts of the population every minor crime at this end of the province was eventually set down to Scarth Krohn. We're talking property damage, broken windows, drug sales, fights. There were more than a few who felt it was just retribution when he got injured in a celebratory frenzy."

"We heard about that."

"I was at the game. Scarth was jumping up and down out of control. He slapped people, punched, shoved. He spent time taunting the other team. They just lost a championship game, and he had to rub it in. He could never do anything halfway. He could never just be happy in and of itself. Somebody else had to be miserable. He's the kind who would taunt an opponent after he beat him. He's an asshole, but so is his dad. I don't feel a lot of sympathy for the kid, but coming from that family couldn't have been easy."

"Who would want to kill him?"

"It was murder?" Fournier asked.

"No one is sure," Turner said.

Ian said, "Steve thinks the other drownings were."

Fournier said, "More 'might have been.' The key is, none of them were investigated. Most of them were out-of-town kids who were going to the local college, St. Croix. Nobody asked questions. The parents who came were too grief-stricken to go beyond the obvious. I wasn't going to pester them with my suspicions."

"What were you suspicious of?"

"All of them, except Scarth's, happened on Saturday nights. It was always the first Saturday of the month. The people with each of them all said that the friends who died left the bar on their own. Someone could have been watching for who was leaving alone and waiting for them. You watch for who is drunk enough, a push, a shove, especially if the water is a little rough, and they drown."

"Nobody got pushed, shoved, and survived?" Turner asked.

"No. Or at least no one who came forward. Nowadays there are some of us, lots of us, who when we go drinking in the local pubs make sure we don't walk out alone."

"Could Scarth have been committing those murders?" Fenwick asked.

"As with all these things, it's possible, just not provable. It's the kind of thing Scarth and his buddies would do just for a kick. Just to be mean."

"And they would get away with it?"

"If it was murder, so far whoever did it has gotten away with it."

"But Scarth's murder would imply Scarth's buddies had turned on him," Turner said.

"I've got no proof for any of this," Fournier said. "We're just discussing oddities and possibilities."

Fenwick said, "Evon Gasple was with them the other night."

"Good old Evon," Fournier said. "There are almost as many rumors about her as about Scarth. Evon has a wild reputation. One rumor I got was that she was the actual drug connection in town and the guys she hung around with were distributors."

Ian said, "That would account for her popularity."

Fournier said, "I've never confirmed any of it. She may be the town slut, but she's never offered me her services. Supposedly she and Scarth would have these big fights and then get back together. I've never been able to find out the truth."

15

Fenwick, Turner, and Ian's next stop was Howard Coates's bar and restaurant. They found Coates in conference with a woman in her sixties with iron gray hair, and a man in his early twenties with short, spiked blond hair and a gold nose ring.

Ian introduced them. The woman was Christine Jenkins. The man was Bill Foster.

Coates said, "We were discussing the serial killings in town."

Coates was a man in his early forties. He had salt-and-pepper hair and a wiry frame. He wore a leather vest over a bare chest. Turner noted the torso was hairy and the abdominal muscles rippled. His jeans hung low on his hips. Turner knew Ian would be attracted to this type as well. After introductions, Coates asked, "Is there anything you can do? We're sure there is a serial killer on the loose."

"How are you sure?" Turner asked.

"There can't be this many accidents."

"How many people drown on this lake every year?" Fenwick asked.

"These have been the only ones reported with no witnesses."

"But there's been no sign of violence on any of them," Turner said.

Christie Jenkins said, "It's a cover-up. The chief of police here is an incompetent moron. He thinks that he's the only one with the expertise to do anything. He never listens to anyone, especially us. We're the liberal lefties in town. Actually, nobody listens to us. This is rural right-wing Canada. We hold meetings and three people besides ourselves show up. What do people think is going to happen when they don't care? If they even do think. And if they don't pay attention, they get idiots for police chief."

Her I-told-you-so rant lasted five minutes. Turner wasn't interested in their political fights unless it led to a murderer.

When she stopped, Coates said, "Schreppel is a god-damn know-it-all. He thinks every decision he makes is best for everyone. He doesn't have a clue how people really work. He's tried to get this town under his thumb."

Bill Foster said, "And he's pretty much succeeded. People are afraid of him." When he spoke, Foster tended to touch his nose ring with his right hand. When others were speaking his hands were in motion, gripping his forearms, rubbing his legs, clutching his sides.

"Was Scarth Krohn afraid of him?" Turner asked.

Jenkins said, "Scarth Krohn was the local bully. Everybody hated him and his dad. The police ignored everything he did because J. T. Krohn, father of the bully, owns this town."

Fenwick said, "He committed crimes and got away with it?"

116

"I think so," Jenkins said.

Turner asked, "Why not call on the Provincial Police? Or if they're under contract with the city, why not elect a new slate of representatives who were willing to stop with the contract? If those things didn't happen, somebody must like him."

"A lot of people in this town owe J. T. Krohn," Coates said. "That's not the same as liking him."

Jenkins added, "Or are related to him. They won't go against him. They won't go against Schreppel either. This town is so indifferent. You can't get them to take any kind of stand. Remember the vigil we tried to set up last March to protest the war in Iraq? Six people showed up. One of whom was not you, Howard."

"Let's not get into that now," Coates said. "The point is you can get away with anything in this town as long as your name is Krohn."

Jenkins added, "And the antipoverty petition. Seventeen signatures after working on it for six months. You'd think people would be against poverty."

Coates sighed. "Christine, these gentlemen are working with us on the murder. Let's focus." She glared at him a moment and then nodded. Coates said, "The cops are backed up by J. T. Krohn's money."

"He bribes them?" Turner asked.

"Probably," Jenkins said.

Coates said, "It might not be as blatant as that, but he is rich. He gets away with anything."

"But it's J. T. Krohn's son who is dead this time," Fenwick said.

Jenkins said, "That's what makes everybody so unsure. We feel unsafe. Schreppel has been like a crazed man. First, he

117

does nothing for six drownings. Now he scrambles like mad. He's the one who insisted all the first killings were not the work of a serial killer. He's the one who said they were all accidents."

"Yeah," Coates added. "Now he's stuck with his initial analysis. Either he was wrong about all of them or he's wrong about this one."

Fenwick asked, "What if he was right about them and this one was the only murder?"

Foster said, "It's hard to imagine Schreppel being right about anything. It's like watching somebody get things wrong time after time. It's as if there was a brick wall in front of him, and he just kept running at it full tilt, leading with his head."

Turner said, "Okay, Schreppel wins prizes for stupidity and did a lousy job on the first six, or he's a saint for how he handled the first six and for doing too good a job for the person everybody hated."

"Saint cop," Fenwick said.

"Huh?" Coates said.

"Skip it," Turner said. "What did people know about the first six who died?"

"College kids, young people from out of town," Coates said. "It was an easy group to dismiss. Only one of them had relatives who lived in the area. That was the first one."

"Who was that?" Turner asked.

"Scott Cromelin," Coates said. "He was a quiet kid. Tended to get drunk like a lot of kids. There's not much to do here in town. Kids get bored. After they graduate, lots of them leave. He died three years ago this month. He'd been drinking at Michael Zoll's bar. No one saw him leave. He turned up dead."

"He have any enemies?" Turner asked.

"Not that anyone knew. Like most of the kids he had jobs helping out the tourists. He was a part-time guide. He did fishing and hunting trips."

Jenkins said, "We're suspicious now because of all the others. There is no reason for these people to be dead."

From his detective work Turner knew there were more times than anyone cared to admit that there was no reason for someone to be dead. And sometimes there were reasons and sometimes those reasons made sense and sometimes they didn't.

Fenwick said, "But this latest one, Scarth, you're saying there are reasons for him to be dead?"

Foster said, "You bet. Anyone my age or younger hated him and his crowd. They were the town bullies. They were the ones who could make your life hell."

Fenwick said, "Why didn't anyone speak up?"

"You can't tell on your peers."

Fenwick said, "That rule was made up by the bullies of the world. Who does silence serve? Only them. Silence does not serve the victim. It's bullshit."

"We didn't tell, okay? We just didn't. You don't know what bullying can be like in a small town."

"I've found that bullying is pretty much the same all over," Fenwick said.

"What exactly did he do?" Turner asked.

Foster said, "Sometimes he did things just to be mean. People were desperate not to be noticed. Scarth was the star of the local teams. He'd lead the pep rallies. If he spotted you not cheering, they'd visit you sometime when you were alone."

"How would he know you weren't cheering?" Fenwick asked.

Foster said, "Maybe he caught your eye in the crowd. He watched everyone. He was very possessive. If he thought you were talking to a girl he was interested in, he'd arrange another meeting." Not only was he touching his nose ring now, but actually twirling it in its socket.

"Did he have a steady girlfriend?" Turner asked.

Jenkins said, "He had a continuing set of conquests and then an off-and-on steady."

"Kind of a big woman," Fenwick said. "Pink glasses?"

"Evon Gasple," Jenkins said. "He put her in the hospital once. Beat her up. Since sixth grade she's been the town slut."

"Beat her up?" Turner asked. "Nobody pressed charges?"

"Scarth can get away with anything," Foster said.

"Sixth grade?" Fenwick asked.

Foster said, "I was in the same grade as Scarth and Evon. She's worn skirts too short, jeans slung down to her pubic hair, clothes too tight, and too much eye makeup since she was twelve."

"When was the beating?" Fenwick asked.

Jenkins said, "Just after they got out of high school. Nobody pressed charges. I assumed money passed hands. They were back together the next week."

Fenwick said, "You mentioned meetings. What would happen at them?"

"Depended on his mood," Foster said. "On a really bad day, you'd get the crap beat out of you. It didn't start when he was an athletic star. When he was eight or nine, he'd take your lunch money. If you had something prettier or shinier, it had to be his."

Turner said, "And parents wouldn't notice this?"

"Nobody ever did. Or kids didn't tell. Or he'd wreck your car. Or the paddles on your boat would be missing or all the contents of your locker would be gone. They'd be dumped in the lake. Or you'd slip on the ice, and he'd be behind you, and somehow no one ever saw him do it. No one except his buddies. Or in the hallway of the school, you'd be smashed into. Or shoved or pushed. Or dumped upside down in a trash can. Or given a swirly in the boys' locker room when the coach wasn't watching. Or maybe the coach was and told you to be a man about it. That was Mr. Sterling. He loved Scarth and excused everything he or his buddies did. Or maybe you'd get the hell beat out of you in back of the gym after school." His right fist clenched the left sleeve of his shirt, his left fist the right. The material was twisted tightly. The memories were grim.

"Teachers didn't try to put a stop to this?" Turner asked.

Foster said, "When they saw it, sure. Usually. All the athletic coaches at the school loved Scarth. There was pressure on them to let him succeed for the sake of the local hockey team. It was disgusting."

"Why would he do all this?" Fenwick asked. "He's rich. He's athletic. He's Mr. Success."

Jenkins said, "Why does any bully do it? And ultimately what difference does it make why they do it? They do bully you, and it goes on and on, and you think it will never end, and you wonder why you go on. And sometimes you don't. And you think of killing the bully or yourself."

Turner said, "Are you claiming that the six who died were suicides because of bullying?"

"No, no, no," Coates said. "We're creating a picture for you."

Turner said, "Anybody specific in town who made actual threats against Scarth?"

Coates said, "I hate to admit it, but we've got to mention everybody. That's why this has gone on too long, all kinds of silence and secrecy."

Foster said, "Silence, secrecy, and death. This is no goddamn Eden up here. This is hell on Earth. I'm moving as soon as I make enough money to get myself the hell out of here."

Turner asked, "Who are you talking about?"

Coates said, "Our local Boo Radley."

Jenkins said, "Ralph Bowers is not that bad. He's a good boy."

Foster said, "A good man. He's twenty-one, the same age as Scarth Krohn and me. We were in school together as long as Ralph Bowers attended school."

Jenkins told the story. Ralph Bowers was the son of two local truck drivers, a male and female couple. They took him and his brother on the road with them starting only a month after he was born. When he finally started school, in the first grade, after no preschool, he was far behind his peers. Then early on the teachers found out he was not right. The other kids made fun of him mercilessly. Scarth Krohn led the charge. He was cruel and drove Ralph to tears numerous times. The truck driver couple confronted Krohn Senior. The town expected violence. Didn't happen. Like usual, everyone assumed money changed hands. Ralph got a job at the local hardware store starting when he was thirteen. He was too loud and too friendly. At that time, he didn't know how to tone himself down. A few of the people of the town understood and were kind. He'd startle the tourists and some of them were rude. He got the job because the manager, Jerry

Scarianno, lived next to the Bowers, and he felt sorry for him. Jerry was kind and stuck up for Ralph. As Ralph got older, his parents would go out on their cross-Canada trucking expeditions and would leave him alone. This was when he was eleven and twelve. The kid would exist on cereal for days. He'd get himself ready for school. The parents gave him minimal sustenance, minimal affection. It was a crime.

At the end of the backstory, Foster added, "Ralph could be violent. He had a temper. When they picked on him, he would fight back with the kids at school. Or try to. There's something wrong with his coordination. He'd throw a ball, but it wouldn't go in the direction he wanted it to. He'd try to hit his tormentors, and he'd miss, and he'd get more angry."

"No adult," Turner said, "no teacher stood up for him?"

"He had one champion," Jenkins said. "Beverly Fleming, his third-grade teacher. But there was only so much she could do. Beverly is a good person."

Foster said, "It got worse over the years. There was one time when he was chasing Scarth Krohn down Main Street at the height of the tourist season. Ralph was swinging a hockey stick. If he'd connected, he'd have killed Scarth right there."

"How old were they when this happened?" Turner asked.

"Thirteen or fourteen."

Turner asked, "Where were the police, the authorities, school personnel, social workers?"

Coates said, "Schreppel did nothing except protect the Krohn family. Nothing but protect. Vincent Schreppel is little better than a Nazi goon."

"I've met him," Turner said. "He wasn't pleasant."

Jenkins said, "As Ralph got older, if there were petty,

unsolved crimes, Schreppel would lock Ralph up in a cell overnight and try to get him to confess. Ralph would scream all night. It was as if Schreppel enjoyed having him scream."

"Does the man have a conscience?" Turner asked. "He feels no guilt?"

"That's Schreppel," Jenkins said, "the Nazi of the North, and I use that word deliberately." Her eyes glittered with tears. "I'm sorry," she said. "What he does makes me so angry. I get so upset. Cruelty is one thing. Needless cruelty to a harmless creature is unconscionable."

Turner asked, "Are you saying that Ralph would be able to plan seven murders?"

Foster said, "He'd be angry enough to kill Scarth Krohn. As Ralph got older the townspeople turned even more against him. He was 'not right.' He was violent. He'd become enraged."

Turner said, "Enraged violence is not an acceptable response in anyone, but it is very understandable coming from a frustrated child."

Coates said, "I agree, but Ralph scared people. Parents told their kids to stay away from him. The crueler ones used Ralph to scare their kids. You know, like, 'Do you want Ralphie to get you?' That kind of crap."

Jenkins said, "Such cruelty from children or adults is inexcusable. Adults should know better."

Foster said, "He takes walks at night along the waterfront. He has for years."

Turner said, "At the least he could have seen something Monday night."

"Schreppel claimed to have talked to him," Jenkins said.

"He confided in you?" Fenwick asked.

"His secretary is my sister. She said Schreppel kept Ralph for six hours last night, but he let him go this morning. Even in this town you need some kind of evidence, and they didn't have any."

"Ralph has been real quiet since the murder," Foster said.

Coates said, "Before he was picked up, when I was in the hardware store, he wouldn't meet anyone's eyes."

"He knows something," Foster said.

"Why wouldn't he tell?" Jenkins asked.

"It's obvious," Foster said. "He did it."

"Or he's protecting who did," Turner said.

"Does he have the wherewithal to do that?" Coates asked.

Jenkins said, "I've always wondered how smart he really is."

"These are young people," Fenwick said. "Were Krohn and his buddies into drugs?"

"Not in an organized way," Foster said. "They weren't a particular source that I know of, but I'm not into drugs that much. Sometimes they had them, like most of us."

"Anybody into hard drugs?" Fenwick asked.

"Nah, it was mostly dope and booze. Normal kid stuff."

A woman in her early twenties entered the bar. She had flowing golden hair, a patch of freckles on her nose, and eyes so dark blue Turner thought they must have been enhanced by contact lenses. She walked up to Foster and said, "I heard you were meeting here." She eyed the two Chicago cops and Ian. "Who are they?" Her voice grated like Jean Hagen's character, Lina Lamont, in *Singin' in the Rain*.

Foster introduced her as Marilyn Gwinn. Foster explained,

"They're going to help. They're going to find out who killed all seven of those people who drowned."

Gwinn said, "Why find out who killed Scarth Krohn? He was a menace to all decent people everywhere. I hated him. When I heard he was dead, I wanted to do a dance of joy. I'm sure every woman who's ever dated him felt the same way. He was a pig."

"Why did women date him?" Fenwick asked. "This is a small town. Didn't his reputation precede him?"

"Yeah, sure," Gwinn said. "Rich, good-looking guy asks you on a date. Everybody says he's impossible. But you figure with you, he'll be different. You want to catch him, or change him, or tame him, or some other empty-headed notion. He's a sports star. He looks hot no matter what he's dressed in. All the popular, athletic boys are his friends. You want to be popular, too. So you date him. Then you find out he's total slime. Total. From the first minute, his hands are all over you. Then you go to your friends to complain and they all say, 'I told you so.'"

"And no one said no?" Turner asked.

"How would we stop him?" Foster asked. "Do you know of a teenager who would dare stand up to a popular, big, strong, athlete? Nobody does that. Nobody. Not in Canada. Not in the States. Athletes have their own rules."

"So he got lots of dates," Fenwick said.

"Yep," Gwinn said. "Turns out he was a lousy lover. His breath was always foul, whether from booze, cigarettes, or lack of breath mints. He didn't take showers often enough. He would have his orgasms within minutes, sometimes seconds, and you were supposed to be happy about it. I figured it out early on. I preferred to turn him on so he came in his

126

pants. Better his underwear getting soaked than for me to touch his flesh. He'd brag to all his buddies about what a stud he was. Ha! We girls might not have been able to stop him, but we knew enough to talk to each other. A hand job early in the evening would generally keep Scarth quiet for most of the night as long as the date was over before he got too drunk."

"He get drunk often?" Turner asked.

"Night after night in establishment after establishment or out in the woods, or driving around in his car. The bars loved having him around because then his buddies would be around and there would be singing and laughing and people would buy lots of beer."

Turner said to Gwinn, "They were telling us about him and Ralph Bowers."

"Ralph is the town loon. We were warned against him when we were kids. He was the one your parents told you not to get near. Ha! He was probably the safest one to be around. And Mr. Screwed-Up Popular Scarth Krohn? We should have run from him. Ralph was odd, sure. I wouldn't want to be alone with him for too long, but he was always gentle, always."

Foster said, "Except when Scarth made him mad."

Gwinn said, "You think Ralph killed him? All those other six guys died. Why is this one murder? I didn't know any of them. They weren't locals. Ralph wouldn't have killed them. He might have killed Scarth, but the list of people who would have happily murdered Scarth is miles long. You'd have to interview everybody in this province and then start on the major cities on both sides of the border. He was internationally slimy."

"Won't Schreppel have talked to key people?" Turner asked. "Won't he be angry that we're interfering?"

"Do you care?" Ian asked. He'd been silent, listening while standing more than companionably close to Coates. The leather-clad barkeeper had not moved away.

Turner said, "He may not be extending professional courtesy to us, but I'm going to extend it to him. If he was in our jurisdiction, I'd be polite and helpful at the least. He's a cop."

Coates said, "He's an asshole. A first-class asshole. He's one of the bullies in this town. He was the Scarth Krohn of his day."

Fenwick asked, "If things are so awful, then why do people stay here? Why do people put up with this? I thought this was the rugged North where men were men and women were women and everybody had too many shotguns to put up with any crap."

Jenkins said, "So many of the women who weren't his victims said that it wasn't their problem. They didn't want to get involved. They didn't want to believe there was a problem if they weren't having the problem."

Foster said, "Lots of people think that if a problem doesn't directly affect them then everything must be fine."

Coates sighed. "It's an atmosphere made for the tough and rugged, but there are basically some pretty nice people. They've got a decent living. They are not boat rockers."

"So to speak," Fenwick said.

"I want to start with background," Turner said. "Let's talk with that teacher who helped Ralph."

Jenkins said, "I'll call Beverly Fleming. She did wonders with him. Scarth and Ralph were in the same grade until Ralph quit. I think that was when he was fifteen." She took out her cell phone and pressed the numbers. She spoke briefly then looked up and said, "She'll talk to you."

128

16

Ian made as if to come along. Turner said, “No. Fenwick and I are going to do this. You are not official.”

“Neither are you. You planning to tie me down? That hasn’t happened in a few years.”

“Not often enough,” Turner said.

Fenwick stuck up for the reporter. “Let him come. We probably won’t get anywhere anyway.”

Ian said, “Why be pessimistic?”

Fenwick said, “Obviously you weren’t a cop long enough.”

Turner was adamant, however. Two strangers asking questions would be a lot; three, too many. Leaving Ian behind, they picked up Turner’s SUV from the houseboat rental’s parking lot. Beverly Fleming lived in a log house at the edge of a small stream that fed directly into Lake of the Woods. The trees surrounded the cabin and extended right down to the lake. When they got out of the SUV, Turner could not hear sounds from the town about a mile away. He heard birds chirping and leaves rustling.

Beverly Fleming met them on her screened-in porch. She was a diminutive woman Turner judged to be in her seventies. She had on a flower-print blouse, deep-indigo blue jeans, and flat sneakers. She wore a chain around her neck that held her glasses. Everyone except Fenwick sat on wicker rockers. As he put it, his bulk and wicker weren't likely to get along well. Turner never did understand why people purchased wicker. It was uncomfortable and wasn't particularly pretty. Fleming had placed comfy, green-leaf-patterned cushions on the wicker. She offered them tea. They accepted.

She returned moments later with a polished-silver tea service. She had dainty plates with bits of cookies and cakes and scones on them. Turner wondered how she could have put together a tea service so quickly. Did she have high tea ready for casual visitors? Instead of questioning his host, he accepted his cup and saucer and bit into a homemade scone. It was delicious. Fenwick contented himself with a small finger cookie. In the center of the tea service was a small pedestal topped with a two-inch-long wooden carving of a muskie. The detail was magnificent and the coloring exquisite.

Turner summarized what they'd been told about Ralph. When he was done, Fleming took another sip of her tea, sighed, smiled, and said, "Howard Coates is a fool."

"How so?" Turner asked.

"He convinces people to go along with his silly theories. He's determined to prove that there has been murder going on, and now poor Ralph Bowers is caught up in his madness.

Is he telling you that all of these are murders and that Ralph committed all of them?"

"No," Turner said. "You don't think Ralph did it?"

"If I was picking murderers for the first six, I'd have picked Scarth and his cronies."

"Why would they do it?"

"Why not? Just to be mean? Because they could? Because they're ignorant bullies? Ralph is a gentle soul. I don't care what those crazed semisuburban moms want to believe."

"What was that?" Turner asked.

"They would try and scare their kids and themselves with comments such as, 'If you don't behave Ralph Bowers will come and do any number of bad things to you.' Children were told not to play with Ralph. When he was in first grade, he had no friends. Bullies seemed to accumulate around Ralph. This community can be pretty unforgiving. So can children. A few teachers tried to help. His fifth-grade teacher tried to get Scarth expelled."

"Why?" Turner asked.

"The only reason you expel someone that age is if they are a danger to others. Scarth was."

"What happened?"

"For some reason with Scarth Krohn, the paperwork that year went slower than ever. Meetings were postponed or never happened. Eventually nothing happened. The torture went on and on."

"What did he do to Ralph?" Turner asked.

"Even in third grade, when he was in my class, I couldn't shelter Ralph completely. He begged to stay in for recess

131

every day. He always offered to help me in my classroom. If it saved him from even a few minutes of playground hell, I was glad to have him. Then over the years he'd stop in to talk, to get away from the yammering. Many a time he would come in sobbing from lunch or recess."

"Is there actually something physically wrong with him?" Fenwick asked.

"He was always a skinny kid and terribly uncoordinated. He had a slight limp from a childhood birth defect. His IQ was at the very low end of the normal range."

Turner said, "We were told he could become violent."

Fleming said, "What do you think a sane response to years of abuse would be?"

"I'd be pissed," Fenwick said.

"Exactly," Fleming said. "He'd flee from recess in tears. He'd walk home in tears. I'd see him. I did my best. Of course, his tears only encouraged the bullies. It was so sad. I could control them in my classroom, but outside, oh my. And some of the teachers were part of the problem."

"Beg pardon?" Fenwick said.

"They'd let the other children's cruel comments go on in class. I found out it was happening one year. I marched the teacher down to the principal's office. He quit at the end of that year. Ignorant fool. I didn't blame Ralph for being angry. He'd sob so hard. He just didn't understand. He was always so mild and so polite. He'd say, 'Mrs. Fleming, I didn't do anything. Why do they hate me?' Sometimes when he left, I would weep for him and for all of Scarth's silent victims who didn't have at least a teacher to go to for a few minutes of respite. It is so, so sad."

"At least you did something," Turner said.

She nodded. "I did what I could. Ralph was happiest working on his own. Doing things very carefully so he wouldn't make a mistake. Sometimes it took him so long, but the key was to give him the time. He'd be so proud when he did something himself and got it right." She pointed to the carving of the muskie in the center of the tea service. "Ralph did that when he was twelve. It took him the better part of a year. I cried when he gave it to me. He still does them." Turner saw her eyes glisten. She sighed. "Then he'd get outside the classroom door and the torture would begin."

Turner said, "When did he start fighting back?"

"I remember that day well. It was one of the greatest moments of my career. It was after school. They were twelve-years-old. Ralph still often came to talk to me, but he hadn't been in that day. His teacher that year was fired later. He did nothing to help that boy. Although that wasn't why he was fired."

"Why did he get fired?" Ian asked.

"He was another incompetent fool," Fleming snapped. She took a sip of tea and then continued more mildly. "He was a pro-Scarth jock fan. At twelve Scarth was playing with the fifteen-year-olds. Ralph didn't get big until after he was fifteen. Then he blossomed and bloomed. But before all that, it was difficult for Ralph, very hard. That day I heard a noise after school on the playground. It was a group of kids in a circle jeering. That's a sure sign something is wrong. I hurried out. Kids saw me and began to disperse. I saw Ralph, skinny, helpless little Ralph, sitting on top of Scarth, who was at least a head taller mind you. Ralph was hitting, kicking, gouging, biting, scratching, and Scarth was bleeding, crying, and hollering. Scarth was fighting back as hard as he could, and he was losing. As soon as I saw what was happening, I stopped hurrying. I walked as slowly as I could. By the time I got there, Scarth was curled in a small ball. He was whimpering. I called softly to Ralph to stop. He looked up at me. Stopped immediately. He began to sob. Scarth shoved him over hard into the dirt. Scarth got up, all scratched and bleeding, and began to taunt Ralph for being a crybaby. I did something quite unprofessional. I grabbed the little son of a bitch by the ear, gave it a sharp twist, held on, and marched him to the office."

Turner eyed her slight frame. She smiled at his look. "I'm still a teacher at that school. You'd be amazed how easy it is to cow the largest, most hulking football lineman, much less some twelve-year-old."

Turner said, "I don't think I would be amazed." She had a presence and command that didn't need heft.

"Didn't Ralph's parents complain?" Turner asked.

"Getting in touch with Mr. or Mrs. Bowers could be difficult. He was never around much. Mrs. Bowers was a small slip of a woman who never said much of anything. She was ineffectual and sad. Mrs. Bowers would ask for advice about what to do. I'd give her a list of what to say and precisely what to do, and specific details on how to help. She'd smile and go away and nothing would change. More parents than I care to admit are like that."

"Toxic parents," Turner said.

"It happens," Fleming said. "Oh my yes, it happens. In any event, Scarth got the beating he deserved. That boy was a danger to the world."

"After the incident, did Mr. Krohn try to make trouble?" Fenwick asked.

134

She chuckled. "He came in all fuming. I reminded him about one day when he was in third grade, and I was his teacher. He pissed his pants in front of the class. J. T. Krohn has no terror for me."

"Does he for others?" Turner asked.

"Money," she said. "It's all about money."

"So, did Scarth's behavior stop?"

She frowned. "He became less bold around school. That was about the age he became sneakier. He might not be the direct cause, but it always seemed like a friend of his was in trouble. Perhaps Scarth would urge the friend to give the teacher a hard time or urge his friend to steal something or deface something. For whatever reason, they listened to Scarth and did his bidding. And remember, after grade school, he went to the high school, where his athletic prowess had far more influence. I thought the favoritism Elijah Sterling showed to him was disgusting."

"What was that?" Fenwick asked.

"Sterling would beg teachers to let him pass their classes, or forgo assignments, or turn the other way. The sports people were among the worst. The usual enshrinement of athleticism over morals or decency." She sighed. "The fight with Ralph did have one other effect."

"What was that?" Turner asked.

"If Ralph saw Scarth picking on somebody, Ralph would step in. He was quite the little protector. He may still be in his own quiet way. I think he has as little to do with the town as he can."

"Where's Mrs. Krohn?" Turner asked.

Fleming sighed. "You'd see Mrs. Krohn in a local restaurant trying to discipline her ten-year-old son. The kid would choose not to behave. She'd be dragging him out by the arm and wrestling with him."

Fenwick asked, "How is that different from you grabbing his ear and dragging him to the office?"

"Mine worked. He behaved for me. I scared the hell out of him. Still do. Last week we were in the grocery store at the same time. He and his cronies hung their heads and said, 'Hello, Mrs. Fleming.' I said hello back. A most satisfactory exchange. Mrs. Krohn would try talking to him, and he'd laugh at her. Mrs. Krohn would claim her little dear was bored because he was so intelligent. Bored my ass. So being bored translates into being the town bully? I'm bored so I get to hit, pick on, call names, hurt anyone or anything I can get my hands on? Oh no, Scarth Krohn was a shit." The word from those calm, precise lips seemed to echo in the wilderness. She paused a moment, then resumed. "But it was his parents who were incompetent morons. They tried excuses: 'He was bored.' 'Evil television and movies corrupted him.' 'Violent video games made him do it.' Bull hooey."

"We heard the girls were especially afraid of him," Turner said.

"If you were Evon Gasple, you weren't. They were boyfriend and girlfriend off and on for years. I think it was sick. They were the male and female sluts of their year in school. She got the pejorative label. He was named a stud. They were made for each other. Most of the other girls, unless they were very stupid, stayed away from Scarth Krohn and Evon. Evon could be as mean and cruel as her erstwhile boyfriend."

"Does Scarth have brothers and sisters?" Turner asked.

"A brother, Trent. Three years younger. Quietest, most

mild-mannered child. Smart. Did extremely well at college this year. He's back this summer. He works for one of the tourists' lodges. I've heard said that he's mostly cut himself off from his family. He lives by himself on a little spit of land on the lake. He's got a small tent. Does some fishing. I hear he gets lots of tip money from the tourists. That's one way you can tell a successful guide in these parts. He goes out of his way to be kind and helpful. I never saw the two brothers together unless it was some occasion where they were both dressed up. Scarth would always be sitting on his father's left and Trent would be sitting on his mother's right, as far away as they could get from each other. I never heard about actual physical fights between them. I imagine there must have been although Scarth was three years older. That little incident with Ralph, now there was a beginning. Ralph stood up to Scarth from that day on. Nobody in this town will forget the day Ralph was chasing Scarth down Main Street. Ralph had picked up a hockey stick and was twirling it round and round his head. If he'd have caught Scarth then, he'd have killed him."

"Would he have killed him now in the same kind of rage?" Turner asked.

"No. No. No. Ralph has it under control. Whatever puberty did, it made him bigger than Scarth and made Ralph a quiet and reflective boy. Getting bigger was the key. Ralph went from being a head smaller to being a head taller than Scarth. Scarth wasn't the brightest bulb in the socket, but he wasn't totally stupid. When confronted successfully, he would stop, at least to your face."

"Where is Ralph nowadays?" Turner asked.

"He works at Scarianno's Bait and Hardware Store on the

end of Main Street that's nearest the lake. The owner felt sorry for him."

Turner and Fenwick drove back to town. Turner said, "I wish we had a million more teachers like her."

Fenwick said, "I think we do. They don't get their names in headlines, but my guess is most of them are closer to Beverly Fleming than not."

"I hope so. I feel sorry for Ralph."

"Where the hell were his parents?" Fenwick demanded.

But they both knew the truth of the matter from their detective work. Parents abused each other, their kids, drugs, alcohol. No matter what a horror they were as a human being, society had decided because they could procreate, they were worthy of having and keeping kids. So, with rare exceptions, they perpetrated the agony of the world all by themselves in their own little corner.

.17.

Turner and Fenwick found Ralph at Scarianno's Bait and Hardware store. It was a ramshackle affair of storefronts and corrugated tin stretching for half a block in from the lake. A large table saw whirred near the entrance. Ralph was working in a side yard. He wore a rubber suit that covered him up to his nipples. He was standing in a vat of smelly bait. He saw them and said, "Arthur is up front."

Turner said, "We wanted to talk to you. We talked to Mrs. Fleming."

"She called me a few minutes ago. She said you were okay." He eyed them carefully. He slowly got out of the vat and walked to a toolshed, which had open double doors. He had a slight limp and a squint in his left eye. Turner saw that the walls of the shed had rows and rows of tools with their outlines painted behind them. Ralph placed each piece of equipment he was working with back in its correct spot.

When he was done, he led them into the store. He said, "Scarth was bad, and I'm glad he's dead."

Turner said, "We heard you protected people from him."

Ralph sat on a high stool. He swung one foot in a precise arc that did not vary. He looked slightly to the left of Turner's ear.

"Scarth was bad."

"Who did you protect?" Turner asked.

"Whoever needed it. Whenever I saw it."

"You helped people at school," Turner said.

"The teachers were afraid of him. Scarth was bad. Except Miss Fleming. She was good. She was tough. Scarth was bad."

"Did you see him the other night when he was drunk?"

"I don't go out at night."

"We were told you usually take a walk at night along the waterfront. That you've done it for years."

For the first time his eyes met Turner's. They did not waver. "I'm not lying. I work. I go home. That's my waterfront. I live down by the water. I walk a little ways beyond my house. I don't bother anybody. I don't talk to anybody. Nobody wants to talk to me. Most of the kids run from me." He looked away again.

Turner said, "Did you see anything the night Scarth died?"

"No."

"Has Scarth bothered you lately."

"No."

"What about his buddies?"

"All kinds of people come in here to buy fishing gear and tools and stuff. Or to talk. I stay in the back. I work hard." He began rubbing his fingers together.

Fenwick said, "People in town have said some bad things about you."

"They always do. Anybody who is different. I'm always different. I can't be like them. I'm just me."

Turner said, "I don't think you did it either, Ralph, but I'd like to ask you a few things."

"Sure."

"Do you know Evon Gasple?"

"Yeah. She offered to let me have sex with her one time. I know she was making fun of me. I could hear her crowd laughing while she asked."

"When was this?" Turner asked.

"Ninth grade."

"Did she bother you?"

"No. I'm not going to have sex until I find someone I'm going to marry. I haven't had a lot of dates."

Turner found himself wishing he was in a *Lifetime* television movie so he could find someone Ralph could love and who would love him back. He didn't hold out much hope for the reality.

"Do you know anyone who would want to hurt Scarth?" Turner asked.

"Yeah, me."

"Anybody else?"

"I don't worry about anybody else. I worry about me."

A burly man in a red beard came through the door into the store. "Hey, Ralph, we got work here. You can't be gabbing with people."

"I gotta work," Ralph said.

He went back to his shed and began taking down the same tools.

Turner introduced himself to the new man, who turned out to be Jerry Scarianno, the owner.

Scarianno said, "Word's already round town you guys are asking questions. You can't count much on the chief of police or the OPP on this. J. T. Krohn's got too much clout. I figured somebody would try to blame Ralph. He gets blamed for every unexplained crime perpetrated in this town. These people don't have a clue. He's worked for me since he was thirteen. Has to be taught, but what kid doesn't? He's always on time. He's always respectful of me and all the customers. He's a treasure as an employee. I wish I had more like him. A few very good teachers and dedicated social workers got him to the point he's at now. He was a hellion in the lower grades. Couldn't be controlled. He learned. He works hard. Once he learns, he's very good at what he does. Always does precisely the same thing. Can't think on his own much. Makes him nervous. He's a good man. Lives by himself. Takes care of himself. He didn't kill anybody. Scarth Krohn deserved to die. Wasn't worth the pine needed to build him a coffin. Don't care if he's dead. I couldn't think of a good thing to say about him and his friends when he was alive. Can't think of a good thing now."

"You know Evon Gasple?"

"Evon is sad. She only knows how to make friends by giving away sexual favors. What an awful way to live. How rotten she must feel about herself."

Turner wondered if they'd run into the philosopher of the local bait and hardware clique.

Scarianno was still talking. "Kids in this town, they got nothing, and they're going nowhere. I tell them to get out while they can. This town will deaden the best of them."

"You're still here," Fenwick pointed out.

"Yeah, but I'm a tough old son of a bitch. I keep my mouth shut. Work my business. I'd defend Ralph anytime."

"Where are his mom and dad?"

"Ralph's parents couldn't stand the strain of raising a kid who was different. He was a tough kid to handle, and they were ill-equipped to handle a normal kid. He has a brother ten years older. He left town ages ago. He's in the merchant marine. Just after Ralph graduated from school, mom and dad moved to Windsor, Ontario. He didn't kill anybody. Get that out of your head."

Turner and Fenwick thanked him.

In the street Turner said, "My money is not on Ralph as a killer."

Fenwick said, "We're gathering more and more evidence of what a total shit Scarth was. A live, breathing hunk of shit is a notion that I don't find appealing. A dead one doesn't have that much more charm either."

Turner said, "Somebody must have liked him."

"Presumably his mom and dad, but we don't have an 'in' to talk to them."

Turner said, "We should try to talk to those First Nations guys. Coates or someone in his crowd must know where to find them." He used his cell phone to call the restaurant. After he hung up, Turner said, "I described the kids to him. He knew the tall, skinny one right off. Billy Morningsky. He works at the local diner in the summers."

Turner and Fenwick took the SUV to the North Woods Dairie Delight Diner on the road to Kenora. In the middle of the day it wasn't crowded. They found Morningsky cleaning in the back.

18

Billy Morningsky was washing out trash cans with a hose. His loose-fitting jeans hung low enough on his lanky frame to reveal three inches of maroon boxer shorts. His gray T-shirt had moons of sweat around the armpits. Turner asked if they could talk.

The kid gave him a neutral nod. They moved farther toward the woods and stood next to green, industrial Dumpsters that were on their sides, dripping water.

Morningsky rested a foot on one of the wheels of the overgrown trash cans and leaned toward them. "What's up?" he asked.

"We're trying to find out more about Scarth Krohn," Turner said.

"You saw him in action the other night."

Fenwick said, "They were assholes."

Morningsky said, "You stuck up for us."

"Yeah."

"Some people wouldn't. Is it because you're gay?"

"Is that a problem?" Turner asked.

Morningsky shrugged. "I always look for a motive when somebody's nice to me, especially a white guy."

"I did what I did. You can assign whatever motive you like. I can't stop you."

Morningsky caught Turner's eye and held it. Then lowered his head for a few seconds, nodded. "What can I do for you?"

"What can you tell us about Scarth?"

"He led the prejudice against us among the kids our age. It wasn't just me and my people. If he thought you were different, he'd pick at you. If he was in a bad mood that day, you could be a target. I was tall and skinny. That was enough to draw his attention. Added to that, I'm from the First Nations. He was a racist pig. When we were younger, in the lower grades, it wasn't so bad. Back then you never really knew which Scarth Krohn was walking into the classroom. Sometimes he'd be completely indifferent to you. I used to pray for indifference. I guess it was around when we were thirteen, he turned completely into an asshole all the time. That's also when people began talking about him as being the next great Canadian hockey god. Some of us weren't willing to worship at Scarth Krohn's altar. Eventually, I got pissed and I got some pride. There's only so much dignity you can lose. Not to the Scarth Krohns of the world. He never accosted me without a group."

"Why was that?"

"Ralph Bowers wasn't the only one to beat the shit out of Scarth."

"What happened?" Turner asked.

146

"Five years ago, the day before he won that stupid championship game, and then screwed up his leg for the rest of his life. I cheered when I heard about that. I thought, at last the son of a bitch is getting what is coming to him."

"How'd you wind up fighting?" Turner asked.

"I was in the woods checking some traplines. We have the right to hunt on our land. My traps had been messed with. I'd gotten there earlier than usual to try and catch who was doing it. I saw fresh tracks. I followed quickly and very quietly. It was bitter cold that afternoon but the wind was dead calm. I found him at the last trap as the last rays of the sun were touching the tips of the pines. A small rabbit was caught in the trap. The animal wasn't dead. Scarth twisted its neck and killed it. I'll never be sure if he was being cruel or merciful. Then he used a tire iron to start bashing my trap. He'd brought the tire iron with him. You don't bring a tire iron with you to walk through the woods. It was deliberate. I waited until he was at the top of a swing. Then I jumped him. Scared the piss out of him. Literally. He stank. He tried to hit me with the tire iron, but I got it away from him. I tossed it yards away in the snow. Then I started hitting him. I bashed him in the head, throat. He was choking. It's hard to get good hits in when you're both in parkas and layers of clothing, but I got in a few solid blows. I busted his nose, I think. He'd had it busted in hockey a few times. At the end I rubbed and pushed his face so hard into the snow that it created a hollow through the drift down to bare ground. By the time I was done, his nose was scraping on bare earth. I told him if he ever got near me or mine again, I'd kill him."

"Nobody noticed his injuries?"

"I don't know if he ever told anyone what happened. I guess they were the kind of thing that would be easy to pass off as wounds from hockey."

"Who'd you tell?" Turner asked.

"My friends. They know. They'd never say anything."

"Did you know the other kids who drowned?"

"Nope. I didn't go to college. I don't go to the downtown drinking establishments much. I prefer places closer to home. Do the cops really think it was murder?"

Turner said, "It's hard to tell in this town. Some people want to connect all seven deaths. That seems a stretch."

"I'll be a suspect."

"Why?"

"Prejudice. The cops don't know we fought, but everybody knows we were enemies. We were leaders of our groups. It's like rounding up the usual suspects, but in a very *West Side Story* kind of way."

"You guys ever do out-and-out gang war?" Fenwick asked.

"It's too cold most of the year for that," Morningsky replied. "It was more simmering prejudice that got let out at opportune moments or maybe when one side or the other got bored."

"What can you tell us about his buddies?" Turner asked.

"Followers. Kind of useless mini-Scarths. I sometimes wonder if without Scarth, they might have been okay guys."

"What about his girlfriend, Evon Gasple?" Turner asked.

"That girl has a mouth on her. She would egg them on. She would shout the loudest at us. She'd use words nobody used in polite company. She's hard and tough. If she's the town slut, she must have a cast-iron pussy. I can't see anybody finding warmth and affection there."

Turner decided he kind of liked the kid. He also didn't think he was a murderer.

"Do you know Ralph Bowers?"

"Yeah, he's weird. I used to be scared of him when I was little."

"You ever pick on him?" Fenwick asked.

"I guess, sometimes I did. Not like Scarth. As I got older, I realized Ralph was doing the best he could. I stopped. So did my friends. A lot of kids who should have known better never stopped. Still today even adults who should know better use him to scare their kids. He doesn't have a lot of friends. Scarth hated him, but Scarth steered clear. Ralph has a very short temper. I wouldn't cross him. He leaves us First Nations kids alone."

"Anybody else who you think might have wanted Scarth dead?"

"A lot of people probably, but most of them keep their mouths shut. There are only a few of us who spoke up and we became targets. Krohn might not have accosted us openly, but like my traps, sometimes things got broken or disappeared."

"Were Scarth and his friends into drugs?" Fenwick asked.

"No more than any kid in the North Woods."

"He wasn't a dealer, distributor?" Fenwick asked.

"Not that I know of."

The detectives could think of no other questions. They thanked him.

Morningsky said, "You stood up for us. I wish I could help. Do they really think it might have been murder?"

"Hard to tell," Turner said.

Morningsky said, "If I get arrested, I'll need help."

"We'll do what we can," Turner said.

They left.

"Hell of a thing," Fenwick said, "cops working on prejudice instead of facts."

"Billy Morningsky certainly thinks so. Can the police up here be that unprofessional?"

"Are there police that unprofessional in Chicago?" Fenwick asked.

"Yeah," Turner admitted.

"There's your answer. Who's next?" Fenwick asked.

"His buddies? His hockey coach?"

"Are the buddies going to talk to us?" Fenwick asked. "We were not their friends the other night."

"We can give it a shot, I suppose."

They grabbed burgers at the Dairie Delight and then drove back into town.

▪ 19 ▪

It wasn't hard to find Scarth's buddies. A few questions
downtown and Turner and Fenwick were on their way. The
dead boy's cronies were encamped at the Frosty-Freeze ice
cream drive-in. Compared to the Dairie Delight, the Frosty-
Freeze was a remnant of fifties décor: outfits on the carhops,
parts of dead flies encrusted on screens, dirt strewn on the
floors and caked in the corners. Not much changed in de-
cades. Music blasted from several cars and boom boxes as
Turner and Fenwick pulled up. Three of Scarth's buddies
clustered near the driver's-side door of the red Ford Mustang. They leered at and ogled passing carhops, slouched
and swaggered, smoked cigarettes, made loud, caustic comments to the people nearby. The fourth member of the group
sat in the backseat of the car. He was eating a burger.

"You guys are the cops from Chicago," said a solidly built
kid. Turner had given descriptions of the crowd from the
other night and had gotten names from Coates and thought

he could identify which one was which. This one was the shortest and blockiest. He had to be Frank Doran. He stood with an elbow on the driver's-side mirror.

Turner listened to the sound of traffic, the murmuring of people on the waterfront walk, and the bugs zapping themselves to death on the traps outside the drive-in.

"Where's the tough lady?" Doran asked. He cracked his knuckles in a way Turner guessed must have driven his teachers nuts in school.

Fenwick said, "Waiting with a baseball bat behind the drive-in."

"You serious?" Doran asked.

"Do I need to be?" Fenwick asked.

Turner said, "We've got some questions about Scarth."

Doran said, "Why should we answer you? Why are you even talking to us? We were going to beat the shit out of you the other night. You weren't scared."

"Should we have been?" Fenwick asked.

"You guys are really cops?" asked one whose face was dominated by a nose that had been broken more than once, Turner guessed. Coates had said the nose kid's name was Abel Verinder.

"Detectives," Fenwick said.

"Like on television?" Verinder asked.

"Fuck you guys," said the third. The acne-encrusted skin led Turner to guess that this was Gordon Nagel.

Turner said, "If it was murder, wouldn't you want to help us find who killed him?"

"Was it murder?" Doran asked.

Verinder said, "I know who did it then."

"Who's saying it's murder?" Nagel asked. He scratched

a yellow zit and drew pus and blood. He wiped the residue on his jeans.

"It's a rumor we're getting," Turner said. "My son found the body. I'm interested. The police weren't real helpful."

"Cops," Nagel said. "Screw 'em. They're nice to you one minute, then they hassle you. It's always, 'Move along. Get a job.'"

Turner understood the cops' impulse.

"I was kind of curious," Fenwick said. "Whose idea was it to attack us?"

General shrugs. "We do whatever we want, whenever we want," Doran said.

"Does anybody really do that?" Fenwick asked. "You must need money for food and clothing and essentials. It just falls from heaven like manna?"

Nagel laughed. "Dude, we do what we want. Anytime we want, anyplace we want."

Turner said, "You couldn't prevent Scarth's death."

They glanced sideways at one another. Nagel said, "Our buddy is dead. There's nothing you can do about it."

"We could help find his killer."

Verinder pointed at Fenwick. "How come you're friends with a gay guy?"

Fenwick said, "How come you're friends with these guys?"

The kid actually seemed to think for a minute. "I just am."

"Friends are friends," Fenwick said. "Doesn't change, no matter what country you're in or what sexual orientation you are."

Nagel asked, "Why didn't you call the cops on us after we came back?"

"Would you have liked us to?" Fenwick asked.

"That's a dumb question," Doran said.

"You want to argue about it?" Fenwick asked. "I suppose I could call now if you want."

Doran looked at Fenwick's bulk, back at his buddies, and at the crowds of people lounging inside and outside the restaurant. "I guess not right now," he muttered.

Turner said, "We didn't call them because we weren't sure it would do any good. We're going back to our own homes in a few days. If you attack tourists that can't come back to testify, maybe you're getting away with more than you should. We knew we could defend ourselves."

Turner wasn't sure what the reply would be to his blunt answer.

Nagel said, "Yeah, tourists are easy marks sometimes."

Verinder said, "Was it really maybe murder?"

Turner said, "We figured you'd care if you thought Scarth had been murdered. You don't have to like us to want to help track down a killer."

"Didn't he drown?" Frank Doran asked. "That's what the cops are saying."

"Maybe they're wrong," Fenwick said.

"Schreppel's wrong about almost everything," Verinder said.

"You guys give him trouble?" Fenwick asked.

"We've never spent the night in jail," Verinder said. He sounded like he was bragging. "We just have fun sometimes."

Nagel added, "Nobody's ever caught us and nobody would mess with us. They know better."

Doran said, "Nobody would put Scarth in jail. He's the town sports hero, and his dad's rich."

154

"Yeah," Nagel said. "He was a great guy."

The fourth, who had been sitting in the car listening, got out and stood behind the other three. He was the heavyset one with the hurt arm from the other night. Turner knew his name was Cory Dunsmith.

Turner said, "We wanted to ask a couple questions about Monday night."

Doran said, "Schreppel said we didn't have to talk to anybody."

"Warned us not to," Nagel said.

"Why?" asked Fenwick.

"You gonna beat it out of us like Chicago cops?" Nagel asked.

"Only if you want me to," Fenwick replied.

Turner said, "We were wondering why you weren't with your friend all night. I got the impression you always hung around together."

Gordon Nagel said, "Scarth did what he wanted. We hung around with him a lot. He hung around with us a lot."

"What happened that night?"

"We all got high." Snickers and nudges with elbows.

"Just booze?" Fenwick asked.

"Anything we wanted."

"You guys into a lot of drugs?" Fenwick asked.

Verinder said, "Less than some, more than others."

"Was Scarth into selling? Any of you guys?"

Smirks all around.

Verinder gave them the lie Turner expected. "Nah, he wasn't our source."

"When was the last time you saw Scarth?"

"He left the bar about ten."

"By himself?"

"Yeah."

"Where was he going?"

Shrugs.

"Did he go off by himself a lot?"

"Sort of."

"What does that mean?"

"Scarth was his own guy."

"Who would want to hurt him?" Turner asked.

"Ralph Bowers," Nagel said.

Doran said, "Ralph is a whack job." The others nodded.

Abel Verinder said, "Ralph is violent. Nobody gets in Ralph's way. Him and Scarth used to have fights when we were kids."

Fenwick said, "The way we heard it was that you guys picked on him unmercifully."

"Ralph didn't mind our teasing," Nagel said.

"He say that?" Fenwick asked.

Doran said, "He never said anything."

Turner said, "We were told that you guys reduced him to tears nearly every day."

"No way," Doran said. "We're not like that."

But Turner knew they were. As sure as he was that he was on the planet Earth, he had pegged these guys as heartlessly cruel and very much unable to have the insight to know they were. Certainly they showed no evidence that they would have been capable of such insight in grade school.

Turner asked, "We heard Scarth was pretty rough with the girls."

"Bullshit," Nagel said. "All the girls wanted to date him."

"What's the story with Evon Gasple?" Turner asked.

"She's great," Doran said. "She and Scarth were mostly friends. She's hung around with us since we were ten. She always had ideas on stuff to do."

"The rest of you ever date?" Fenwick asked.

"Sure, we've all had girlfriends," Verinder said. "We're not—" He halted then tried again. "We're all—" He took refuge in silence.

Turner asked, "Anybody know where she is at the moment? We'd like to talk to her."

They all shrugged.

"She and Scarth were close," Turner suggested.

Doran said, "Sometimes. Other times not. She just hung around with all of us."

Fenwick said, "She friendly with everybody?"

"What does that mean?" Doran asked.

Nagel said, "He means did she have sex with all of us. What do you think?"

Fenwick said, "That would have been convenient as long as Scarth didn't beat the crap out of you."

Nagel leered. "Evon enjoyed every bit of attention we showed her."

"Did he date any of the other girls for very long?" Turner asked.

"Nah," Verinder said. "Scarth was a love 'em and leave 'em kind of guy."

"There weren't hurt feelings about that?" Fenwick asked.

"Why would there be?" Verinder asked.

Fenwick said, "Maybe some girls would be interested in a relationship."

Verinder said, "So? Scarth got what he wanted. He could get any girl he wanted. Girls want to be friends with us."

"Was he out looking for sex that night?" Fenwick asked.

Verinder said, "Isn't everybody all the time?"

"Was he drunk?" Turner asked.

"We all like to drink," Doran said. "We like to stop for a few beers. It's no big deal. Nobody is going to stop us."

"Was Scarth driving that night?"

"I guess he had his dad's car."

"Who else might have wanted to hurt him?" Fenwick asked.

"His brother, Trent, is weird," Verinder said.

"Weird how?" Turner asked.

"He's always off by himself. He's probably a—" He caught himself again. "He acts like he's gay."

"How's that?" Turner asked.

"He's always reading books. He never dates girls."

"Does he date boys?" Turner asked.

They all shrugged. If shrugging, slouching, swaggering, leering, and ogling ever became virtues, these guys would be candidates for sainthood.

Verinder said, "Talk to Ralph. People should be afraid of Ralph. He's nuts."

Turner said, "We heard Scarth and Evon had big fights sometimes."

"Nah," Doran said. "Don't believe that shit. Sure, they'd yell and scream sometimes, but that was normal. Hell, you're with some woman, and they give you a hard time, sometimes you gotta take action. It was never serious." The others nodded.

"You guys give the First Nations kids a hard time," Fenwick observed.

Doran said, "Don't start with that bullshit. They give us a

158

hard time. First Nations bullshit, man. That is so bogus. They get preferred treatment for everything."

Verinder said, "Billy Morningsky was always in everybody's face about his heritage, and how we were shits."

Turner didn't see a reason to disagree with Morningsky's analysis. Turner found their misogyny and ignorance appalling.

"The fights go back a long way," Fenwick suggested.

Verinder said, "Since we were kids."

Nagel said, "Talk to those goddamn First Nations kids. They were always causing trouble. They'd wait until your back was turned and then attack."

Doran said, "Scarth always was standing up to them. They tried to push us guys around and, dude, they had to be put in their place. They were always messing with us."

Fenwick said, "It seemed kind of mutual."

Nagel launched into a rant that was mostly barely disguised racism. The others chimed in with anecdotal episodes of alleged mistreatment.

Fenwick asked, "Anybody ever try sitting down and talking about your differences?"

Collective and random snorts greeted this suggestion. Doran said, "Man, the bleeding hearts around here were always trying to get us to sit down and talk. What's to talk about? We know our place, and they should know theirs."

Fenwick asked, "And what is your place?"

The four of them looked a little confused.

Fenwick said, "What is it then that is your place that is not their place?"

Verinder said, "They should just keep the hell away."

Doran added, "Morningsky was always looking for trouble.

He was an instigator. They did most of the petty crimes in this town that we were accused of."

Fenwick said, "Did you bring your proof to the police?"

"Screw proof," Verinder said. "The people in this town just believed them."

Turner asked, "You guys know anything about the other six kids who drowned in the lake the last few years?"

Nagel said, "What's the deal with them? Were they murdered? Nobody said they were murdered."

Doran added, "They started dying years ago. We were teenagers."

Fenwick said, "Probably big enough to push someone in the lake and hold them down."

Doran said, "We don't know nothing about that shit."

Turner and Fenwick left them. They strode a block down to where they'd left the SUV. Dunsmith, the one who had been silent, emerged from the woods on the far side of the SUV. He glanced furtively left and right then raced to the passenger side of the SUV out of sight from the clustering teenagers. An attack? Turner wondered. An escape? Dunsmith stood in the shadows of the SUV. "I gotta talk to you guys." Turner unlocked the SUV. Dunsmith scuttled into the backseat and scrunched down far enough so that he couldn't be seen from outside. Turner slowly drove to the edge of the city park and let the vehicle idle.

"What's going on?" Turner asked.

"I hate those guys. I hated Scarth. He was a shit to me. He busted my nose. Twice."

"Why hassle us?" Turner asked.

Dunsmith said, "The rest were doing it. I didn't dare not

do it. It was kind of fun to watch people get scared. I'm a coward and as big a shit as them. I didn't have the guts to get away."

"Why'd you hang around with him?"

"Not hanging around with him could be even more dangerous, but Evon was worse. She was a total shit to me. She cheated on Scarth when they were dating."

"They both knew what they were doing with other people?" Fenwick asked.

Dunsmith said, "She'd cheat with animals, vegetables, minerals, dildos, women, and men. She's great at what she does. I hate the bitch. She gave everybody head. All of us."

Fenwick said, "She do something specific to you? Did she break your nose?"

Dunsmith said, "She let everybody know I had a small prick and that I came real fast and then couldn't get it up again. The whole goddamn North Woods knows I'm a lousy lover. I wanted to pound the crap out of her, but Scarth would protect her. Well, he's not around now. I can speak my mind. Some Saturday nights she'd do all of us one by one in the backseat of Scarth's car."

Fenwick said, "Everybody would watch?"

Dunsmith said, "I think everybody else did at one time or another. Everybody knew her reputation. Supposedly she and Scarth were each other's 'first' back in fifth grade."

"They were sexually active even then?" Fenwick asked.

"Tell me you aren't really astonished," Turner said. "You know kids have sex. The studs like Scarth start early. He was handsome and an athlete from an early age."

"Got that right," Dunsmith said.

"I'm not surprised," Fenwick said, "just in awe."

"I think they were sort of sex outlets," Dunsmith said. "Convenient without any commitment on either side."

"This was mutually agreeable?" Turner asked.

Dunsmith shrugged. "I guess."

"Any arguments about who was doing what to her when?" Fenwick asked.

"Nope," Dunsmith said.

"Scarth didn't get pissed?" Turner asked.

"He and his hard-on were in line like the rest of us," Dunsmith said.

"But weren't they boyfriend and girlfriend?" Fenwick asked.

"Sometimes," Dunsmith said, "but that mostly meant if there was, like, somebody getting married, it was them two that went together. They were like convenient dates for each other. Nobody got pissed. No, dude, the point is Scarth is dead. I'm free of him. I'm dumping those other three assholes and clearing out of this screwed-up end of nowhere."

"How did you know I was gay?" Turner asked.

"You've been up here a few years. You go around town with another guy. People notice."

"Whose idea was it to attack us the other night?"

"Scarth's," Dunsmith said. "Everything we did was Scarth's idea. If we sat around being bored, that was Scarth's idea, too."

"Why did you stay friends with him?"

"Better to be a friend than to piss him off."

He knew nothing specific about Scarth's movements late Monday or Evon's current whereabouts. After several furtive glances outside the SUV, he left.

162

As the detectives drove down Main Street past the cafés and tourist shops, Turner said, "Seem like a normal bunch of aimless thugs who don't know how to deal with their emotions except to turn them into violence."

Fenwick said, "Evon doesn't shine as an example of feminist liberation."

Turner said, "Desperate to be popular and liked? A psycho bitch?"

"All of the above?" Fenwick said.

Turner said, "These guys kill their buddy?"

"Nah," Fenwick said. "They're followers. If Scarth killed somebody, they'd go along. Except maybe Dunsmith. He's a traitor and he's pissed, but he's our pissed-off, angry traitor. For now, he's on the Definitely Maybe list. Who's next?"

Turner said, "We could try Scarth's hockey coach."

⟍ 20 ⟍

They found the coach, Elijah Sterling, sitting in front of his double-wide trailer in a clearing in the woods. Weeds and scruffy, uncut grass swept from tree line to mobile home. Tires and rusted toys and half-chopped logs dotted the clearing. Sterling's bulk oozed from every opening in a cheap plastic lawn chair. The mound of beer cans and fast-food containers around him attested to the source of his bulk. Even Fenwick paled in comparison to the heft of this man.

Sterling glared at them in the glint of the sunlight. As they walked up the driveway, the corpulent coach said, "I hear you don't like my boy, Scarth."

"Lots of people didn't like him," Turner said.

"Jealous of his daddy's money. Jealous of Scarth's athletic ability. The losers and whiners and complainers in town didn't like him. They were jealous of his looks, of his success, of his humor, of his joy at being alive."

"Didn't he make a lot of people miserable?" Fenwick asked.

"A lot of people prefer to enjoy their misery. I'll show you the kind of boy he was." He beckoned them into the trailer. The kitchen had dirty dishes heaped in the sink. The living room had three pieces of furniture: a thirty-six-inch television, a recliner, and a trophy case that stretched along one whole wall. Sterling drew them close to it.

He said, "See them. All of them. They were for teams of mine that won championships. Scarth could hit a hockey puck through the eye of an opponent at fifty paces. The boy was the best athlete I ever coached. He was the one who took the other kids on the team to another level. He knew how to play and how to inspire his teammates. He had a work ethic that I've never seen matched. He'd get to school early every day to work out with weights. He had specific exercises to do for specific muscle groups on specific days. He kept charts of his progress. Hell, he inspired me. It always made me proud to be a coach when I watched him play. He'd listen to suggestions. He wanted to be better." He wiped incipient tears from his eyes. He abruptly walked out of the trailer back to his seat on the patio. He grabbed a handful of chips, stuffed them in his mouth, chewed a moment, took a long drink of beer, belched, farted, and scratched his balls. The escaping gas was loud enough to silence the local birds for several seconds. He took another gulp of beer, then used the back of his hand to wipe away tears.

"Hockey's a violent sport," Turner said. "Was he a violent kid?"

"No more than your average player."

Fenwick said, "He had the strength to make his emotions felt in physical ways that other kids couldn't stop."

"He knew his strength. He knew when to stop."

"He drank a lot," Turner said. He noted the empty beer cans and liquor bottles.

"So do I. So does everybody in this godforsaken corner of the planet. You ever try and find something to do night after night in the middle of a cold, cold winter? You do what you can to warm up." He took a long pull from his beer can. "Don't you put this on Scarth. Don't you dare. Scarth was a fine boy."

Fenwick said, "He drowned while he was drunk."

"Somebody tried to kill him. The current isn't that strong. There was no storm Monday night. Someone had to get him while he was drunk."

"Who did?" Turner asked. "If he was such a great guy, who would have reason to kill him?"

"Everybody has enemies. Even the best people."

Fenwick asked, "Did he get drunk every night?"

"He liked his beer. There's no crime in that."

Fenwick asked, "He get along with his younger brother?"

"Kid wasn't much of an athlete."

"Is that the only criteria you have?" Fenwick asked.

"It's as good a way as any to judge somebody. The younger one was a wuss. He was worthless. He kept out of my way. Always had an excuse not to be in gym class. That's fine. I don't want that kind in my gym class."

Fenwick said, "You're not much of an advertisement for an athletic life."

"Neither are you."

"Yeah, but I'm not a gym teacher and don't pretend to be

someone who works with or for the physical well-being of those with whom I come in contact."

Sterling gave him an odd look. "You talk like that much?"

If they were alone, Turner would tease Fenwick about his verbiage.

"Did he have fights with anybody?" Turner asked.

"Some kids might have been jealous of his ability. I never noticed. I was too busy to care about silly complaints."

"No enemies at all? You didn't hear about him picking on other kids?"

"Exaggerations. He was a good kid, a good man. I was proud to call him my friend."

"Did you know his girlfriend, Evon Gasple?" Turner asked.

"A sweet girl. She always made time for Scarth. She'd bring cookies for him and the team. He took her to the prom. I thought they might get married."

Fenwick said, "We heard she had the reputation around this town for being a slut."

Sterling stood up. "Look, I'm putting up with a lot from you two. You hear rumors about famous people all the time. Even about not famous people. Like the rumor you two are fags."

"I am," Turner said, "but he's not."

"Does that make it okay?" Fenwick asked Sterling.

"That's enough questions. This town needs to mourn that boy. He—" And he actually began to cry. They were the first tears they'd seen for the dead youngster. He paced back and forth on his minuscule patio, stopped for a moment, lifted one foot, then the other. For a few seconds he shuffled like a dancing bear.

168

Turner wasn't through yet. "Some people are saying that this death is connected to the other six college-age kids who died."

Sterling paused in his pacing. "Those six? I coach at the college most winter evenings. Gives me something to do. They were all on one team or another of mine."

Fenwick said, "It didn't seem funny to you that it just so happened that kids who were on your teams were dying?"

"A couple of them were only on the team for a week or two the year before they died. I didn't know any of them others real well. They weren't great athletes. I don't really remember them that well."

"It wasn't sad that they died?" Fenwick asked.

"Well, yeah, sure, but I'm not going to pretend that I was all broken up. They weren't friends of mine or anything."

"Would Scarth have known them?" Turner asked.

"Maybe the last two. He was too young to play in the earlier one's division. Don't pull this shit that you think Scarth had something to do with those murders. That's bullshit absurd."

"Did his buddies know the other guys who died?"

"Scarth's friends were loyal to Scarth. They wouldn't harm anyone."

"They were harassing some First Nations kids the other night."

"Billy Morningsky, right? That kid has a mouth on him. He was the rudest teenager I've ever had in any of my classes in all my years of teaching. He needed to have somebody beat the crap out of him."

Fenwick said, "Sounds like Scarth could have used some crap pounding."

Sterling crunched his beer can. His breath rasped out of his throat. "Billy Morningsky could have been a great athlete. He wasn't willing to put out the effort. He wasn't willing to work. Billy Morningsky thought the world was going to be given to him."

"Seemed like a nice kid to me," Fenwick said.

Sterling glared. "Get off my property."

Turner and Fenwick retreated.

In the SUV Turner said, "We finally have a connection between all these dead guys."

"I don't think Elijah Sterling did it. Hell, he'd never catch them, no matter how drunk they were. All they'd have to do is walk slowly away from him."

Turner said, "He'd be big enough to hold them down."

"He'd have to catch them."

"They were drunk," Turner said.

"This is a connection," Fenwick said, "just not a very murderous one, as far as I can see."

"Me neither."

"That makes it unanimous."

Turner said, "Who's next?"

"The kid who brought the gun to school to kill Scarth sounds like a good possibility."

﹀ 21 ﹀

Oliver McBride no longer sported spiked hair. Its red color didn't look like a dye job. He may have been a portly child, but as an adult he was a rail-thin six feet three. He was a part-time mechanic and salesman at a used-car dealership out on Route 17. A sign over the door said MCBRIDE AND SON AUTO DEALERS, NEW AND USED CARS SOLD. CARS FIXED WHILE YOU WAIT.

The man they wanted to question was leaning over the engine of a Lamborghini. A chubby man in a rumpled business suit hovered near him. This man said, "You're sure you can fix it?"

"Part'll be here tomorrow," McBride said. He tapped the engine and stood straight. "You're lucky you broke down near here. There's not another shop that can fix it in a hundred miles."

Turner excused himself and said, "We'd like to talk to you about Scarth Krohn."

McBride turned very blue eyes on them. "You're not the Provincial Police."

"No," Turner said. "We're interested in what happened. We're hoping you can help us get some insight into him."

McBride called back into the shop. "Dad, I'll be on the lot for a while." He left the customer wringing his hands.

McBride led them outdoors. They stood between a 1955 Chevrolet and a 1964 Rambler. McBride said, "You know about the shooting or you wouldn't be here."

They nodded.

"I wish I'd have killed him then and a thousand other times. I wish I'd been the one to kill him this time."

"You think it was murder?" Turner asked.

"I hope it was. I hope someone was getting even for all the rest of us. I hope someone made him suffer for the ass-hole, son of a bitch he was. His life was an intrusion on the rest of us. He was the puke in the middle of the cheese dip at anyone's party. He deserved to die. They say he drowned. I hope he knew he was dying. I hope he suffered. He deserved to."

Turner asked, "Why didn't you try to shoot him the day you brought the gun?"

"I was crazed. I didn't know if I was too scared of him, or his whole gang, or the whole world."

"Yeah, but you hit an innocent kid."

"It was an accident. He was trying to pull the gun away from me. I'm not sure I wasn't trying to commit suicide. Life, when you were a target of Scarth Krohn's, was hell. He'd whisper to me when nobody was around, 'Your ass is mine,' or 'I know you like being corn holed.' Even when I dated girls he would hound me. I screamed it at him once, told all his buddies about the threats he had made to me. They all laughed. Nobody believed their straight hero was even slightly a fag."

"He never actually touched you?" Turner asked.

"I was a master at hiding. When I finally got taller and lost weight, I could outrun almost anybody in school. He never caught me. I don't know what he would have really done. His straight credentials topped my straight credentials. I'm married and I've got a little kid. More than Scarth ever had or will."

"Where were you Monday night?" Fenwick asked.

"At home with the kid. My wife was out at a library town meeting. Why are you asking these questions? I thought he drowned?"

Turner said, "Some people in town think Scarth's death and that of the other six young men might be connected."

"You mean a serial killer? In this burg? Get real."

Turner asked, "Did you know his girlfriend, Evon Gasple?"

"Evon the slut or Evon's mother?"

Turner and Fenwick looked puzzled.

McBride explained, "It's Evon Junior and Evon Senior."

"They were both dating him?" Fenwick asked.

"Sort of. I heard Scarth had screwed both of them."

"Both?" Fenwick asked.

"I heard Scarth brag that he made it with both of them."

"Did mother and daughter know about the other?" Turner asked.

McBride shrugged. "Evon's a sad case. She's got a juvie record longer than anybody in town."

"What'd she do?" Fenwick asked.

"Petty stuff. Mostly trying to show off for Scarth, I suppose, or the other boys. When she was younger, she was thirteen going on slut. Rumor was she put out for any boy. Sometimes she and Scarth were exclusively dating. Sometimes not. I never did get that. Scarth could have almost any girl he wanted."

"If he was such a creep, why would anyone date him?" Fenwick asked.

"He was pretty and his daddy was rich. He was a hot guy. He always had the hottest car or when we were kids he was the first one with an Xbox or whatever the chosen toy of the moment was. His stuff was also the best and newest. The girls liked that. Sure, I was jealous, but I knew my place."

"It must have been difficult," Turner said.

"The worst was when I got in some trouble a couple years ago. I was on the sidelines of smashing some windows in the school. I never picked up a rock. Scarth lied. He blamed me. My daddy isn't rich. I got sent to a juvenile facility for six months. I survived. Barely." He shut his eyes and shuddered. Finally he resumed. "I wish I had killed Scarth. I might even be out now for doing that."

"Tough taking the blame for someone else."

"Tough being the object of ridicule. Why they didn't turn on Scarth for being a rat, I never could figure out. No one would listen to me when I tried to tell them. Krohn money and Scarth's looks beat anything in this town."

"You know any of the other kids who drowned?"

"What do they have to do with Scarth?"

"Nothing that we know of," Turner said. "A few people in town think there's some kind of connection."

"It's a lake. People drown. I don't go down to the waterfront. Unless you work there, there isn't much point. It's jammed with tourists."

Fenwick asked, "Did Scarth make love to tourists?"

"Locals. Tourists. If it was female, and it was breathing, Scarth was trying to get into its pants. He was the town stud. I don't think anybody could ever sort out the rumors about his conquests. Scarth never did anything to quash them. Supposedly he even did some porn videos."

"They make porn around here?" Fenwick asked.

"Anybody can make porn," McBride said. "All you need is a little camera equipment, a sophisticated computer, and a little knowledge of lighting and setting. Doesn't take much."

Fenwick asked, "You mean he made this in his bedroom or there's a place around here that makes porn?"

"Bedroom stuff is anybody's choice, but supposedly the guy who owns the photo shop, Nick Broder, makes porn on the side."

"You have proof of this?" Fenwick asked.

"Scarth and his buddies hung around the one photo shop in town way more often than made sense."

"So what?" Fenwick said.

"None of them owns a camera."

He gave them the name.

In the SUV Turner said, "Making porn? This isn't the San Fernando Valley."

"Porn as a reason for murder? It can happen. We've seen murder for less."

"Half the town wanted him dead," Turner said.

"Hell," Fenwick said, "the Trans-Canada Highway is only a few miles away. Anybody could have come in off the high-way and done some dirty."

"Killing Scarth?"

"And the drunk college kids. Serial killers have murdered far more people for less motivation. We've seen killers who were acting on the voice of God."

"I thought that was the Pope," Turner said.

"Hey, you're the one who takes his kids to Catholic Church every Sunday."

"Believing equals accepting every bit of bullshit that's in the manure pile?"

Fenwick said, "It all smells the same."

Turner said, "These are the strangest theological comments I ever hope to hear, and I made one of them."

Fenwick said, "So, we are not buying the passing trucker who likes to off college kids?"

"Do we ever discount possibilities?"

"All the time," Fenwick said.

"Good. Then lets dump that one until we hear the voice of God or the Pope."

"Hell of a trick," Fenwick said. "What else do we have?"

"They all hated him."

Fenwick said, "Except those that didn't."

"A small number. We need to talk to the parents of all these kids."

"Can you believe that about Scarth doing the mother and daughter?" Fenwick asked.

"Right now, I'd believe that Scarth was the anti-Christ."

Fenwick said, "It's been a long day, and we're not on overtime. We should check in with our families."

"And you haven't been fed in a while."

"Got that right."

22

Brian and Kevin sat at the end of the dock. The long twilight of the North Woods had begun. Each boys' shoulders were slumped, and they kicked their legs sporadically and aimlessly over the side of the pier. Turner could hear Madge's raucous laughter and Fenwick's grumbling from the kitchen of their boat. Ben was rowing Jeff around the cove. Ian was reading Proust in his cabin.

Turner sat down next to his son. He asked, "How you guys doing?"

"Is this how you feel after working with a dead body?" Brian asked.

"Sometimes it gets me down," Turner said, "but I've learned to keep working through it. I don't expect that of you."

"Kevin's hung around all day. We didn't do much fishing."

Turner noted that the boys sat together with their shoulders, elbows, and legs touching. He said nothing. It was not his business what his son may have been doing, except it was his business, but he was not going to ask about it. He assumed his son had lied to him before this. He knew there were lots of things it was better for parents not to know. Certainly there were things he'd done that he hadn't told his parents about, nor would he ever. This was not his secret to tell, if there was a secret here and it was worth knowing. And he wasn't going to slyly hint about it, hoping for a mistake or for his kid to figure out that he knew.

Turner said, "I've been talking to people around town about Scarth Krohn."

Brian said, "I've run into him a few times. He always stayed out of my way. He never gave kids a hard time around me."

"You're bigger and stronger than he is," Kevin said.

"But I'm five years younger than he is."

Kevin said, "But you don't put up with crap from anybody."

"I don't make a big deal out if it," Brian responded.

"Nobody ever messes with you," Kevin said.

Brian shrugged it off.

Turner said, "Almost everybody in town agrees he was a bully. We talked to Beverly Fleming."

"Mrs. Fleming is great," Kevin said. "She's the best lady in the world. She was a good teacher. I wish all the teachers were like her."

"Did you guys see him Monday night in town?" Turner asked.

They had said that's where they were going. He waited for a lie.

Brian said, "Kevin and I just hung around for a while. We

didn't do much of anything. We took a walk, watched the stars."

Turner didn't pursue specifics. He said, "We're supposed to talk to Trent Krohn."

"I've met him," Brian said. "He seems nice. Never says much."

"Scarth's brother is real quiet," Kevin said. "He was a grade above me. He's a nice guy."

"Do you know where he is?" Turner asked.

"The place where he camps now isn't far." He gave Turner a set of directions. "You can get there and back in less than half an hour. It's a tiny, rocky little peninsula so the hunters never go there. Not a lot of fishermen either. He just has a little tent there. He doesn't bother anybody. You should go by yourself. Mr. Fenwick might intimidate him. He's shy and suspicious."

Turner decided to give it a try.

23

Turner took the motorboat and followed the directions. The full moon was rising behind him as the sunlight turned to golden orange above the trees. He heard loons calling to loons. Occasionally he heard the plop of a fish or voices from the shore. It was fishing time. He saw boats out. Most had their lights on already.

Turner pulled close to an island he thought was the correct one. There were actually two of them, with a ten-foot passage in between. He circled the first one but found it completely deserted. Halfway around the second, he saw a light and motored closer.

When he shut down the engine, a voice called from shore. "Who's there?"

"Paul Turner," the detective said. "I'm Brian Turner's father. He says he knows you a little. Kevin Yost is his friend. Kevin is our fishing guide every year." About ten feet inland a teenager stood with a shotgun pointed at Turner's head.

Turner said, "I'm not here to hurt you, son."

"Scarth is dead."

The boy's quiet voice barely reached the boat. When the engine had died completely, the sounds of the northern night surrounded him. Full darkness was coming on fast. He'd be motoring back in the night.

The boy was skinny. He wore a black T-shirt that was too small and rode up on his torso revealing his tight jeans with black knit briefs peeking above them. He wore high-top tennis shoes. He held the shotgun on Turner as the detective climbed out of the boat. Turner felt his heart hammering in his chest. His gun was tucked into the belt on the back of his pants. He didn't want to make any sudden moves to startle the boy. He didn't want to end up at the wrong end of a shotgun blast.

Turner said, "I'd like to sit down and talk with you."

"About what?"

"Scarth."

"I didn't kill him."

"Could you put the gun down, please? And the bugs are getting pretty fierce. I could use some bug spray."

The flies had risen. They could drive him away if the shotgun didn't. Turner said, "I'll leave or if you could get me some spray, we can talk."

"You're Brian's father?"

"Yes."

The boy nodded. The shotgun came down from his shoulder. "I have Bug-Be-Gone in the camp." He walked backward toward his camp. The shotgun hung loosely, but close by his side. Turner didn't try to grab for it. The boy sat on one side of the small fire and nodded toward a stump on the other.

When Turner was seated, Trent reached into a side pocket of his small tent and pulled out a can. He tossed the Bug-Be-Gone to Turner, who slathered it on every exposed surface of his skin. He didn't care about the antiseptic smell. After thirty-six hours, no matter how many showers you took on these trips, almost everyone smelled of a mix of smoke, bug spray, and lack of deodorant.

"What about Scarth?" the boy asked. His voice was soft. His eyes seldom left the fire. The shotgun was leaning against one leg. In his other hand he fiddled with another can of bug spray. He hung his head so the firelight hid his eyes.

"Some people think he was murdered."

"Wouldn't surprise me."

"Would you kill him?"

"I stayed out of Scarth's orbit."

"Hard to stay completely out of his way when you share the same house."

"Hard not to be outdoors in the summer helping fishermen and hunters. Hard not to be outdoors in the winter helping skiers. You make a lot of money. Scarth helped when my dad had big rich clients. I never let on how good I was at this to them. They thought I was this nerdy thin kid who couldn't do much. Anybody would kill him. Anybody with enough balls. Even his idiot friends. I thought he just drowned."

"Do you know his friends?"

"Those guys and Evon Gasple? Yeah, I know them. Sort of. I didn't hang around with them."

"How did they think they would get away with everything they did?"

"Do people in Chicago get away with crimes?"

"Sure. Sometimes."

"It's the same here. It's quiet and bucolic and filled with flawed humans. Teenagers do stupid teenage stuff here just like in the States. And daddies cover it up."

"Has your dad covered up for Scarth?"

"Yep. Scarth could never do anything wrong. And he turned out to be a sports jock from an early age. I won every chess championship in Ontario when I was ten. He was thirteen and playing hockey. He was a saint. I was an afterthought. Am I bitter about my brother? I've had a lot of time to try to not think about him. That's another thing I do. I have thoughts. I'm sure Scarth never had one, other than how to satisfy his dick. His world revolved around his prick."

"Your mother wasn't on your side?"

"My mother does what my dad says."

"You don't live out here year-round?" Turner asked.

"I spend eight months of the year here. I know how to keep warm. I know how to take care of myself. My dad owns this spit of land. Nobody else gets near it. The other four months I'm down in Montreal working odd jobs and trying to sell my paintings."

"Where were you Monday night?"

"Here. With no witnesses. I hated my brother, but I didn't kill him."

"Do you know Ralph Bowers?"

"Everybody in town knows Ralph. I felt sorry for him. At the dinner table, Scarth used to talk about the things he did to Ralph. My dad would laugh. I think I started hating my dad from then on. I couldn't understand how anyone could be that mean. I still can't."

"Would Ralph kill your brother?"

"I have no idea. I doubt it. Ralph, despite his reputation, is a gentle guy."

"What can you tell me about Evon?"

"The slut. Everybody knows her. They should have gotten married when they graduated from high school. I heard she took the morning-after pill so often they were thinking of giving her a year's supply, except it was too expensive. I would have given them a lifetime supply as a wedding present. It might have been a way to keep them from reproducing."

"She ever get an actual abortion?" Turner asked.

"Their last year in high school. I wasn't sure if it was on Scarth's insistence or my dad's. I was a kid, and I didn't always scan on what they were talking about. It was a nasty time. My father was furious. He screamed about condoms for hours."

"How often did Scarth bully you?"

"Not as much as you'd think. We had a big house. He was always out doing sports, and I kept out of his way. I hid. My parents glowed at him across the dinner table every night. I knew my place. Sure, I'm pissed about it. I should get therapy for years. I haven't had the time. But I was never angry enough to kill him. He got that done to himself on his own."

Turner couldn't think of any more questions. He said, "I appreciate your help."

"Kevin's a good guy. We hang out sometimes. I've met your son. He seems like a decent kid."

Turner got up to go. Full dark had gathered in the forest's glens.

Trent said, "I'll lead you back. You won't find your way."

"I kind of know it," Turner said.

"Would you like to be kind of out in the middle of the lake for several days?"

"How will you get back?" Turner asked.

"There's a land path back to this piece of land. It's a peninsula, not an island."

"You can find your way in the dark?"

"Yep. I found the way in when I was seven. I may be the only one who knows it. No one else ever goes that way. You have to get a little wet and the path is not clear."

Turner accepted the help. The boy stayed in the stern of the motorboat. He pointed the light several times and in a short while the houseboats began to come back into view.

As Turner cut the engine and began to dock the boat, the boy said, "I'm not gay."

"Oh?" Turner hadn't noticed any gay "characteristics" that night. The boy didn't try to discuss color and fabric or sing Broadway show tunes. Turner didn't care if he was or wasn't.

"Everybody thinks I am. I guess I am kind of femmy. I'm not. If anybody thinks you're gay in this town, you're a target. Always gotta be acting macho. That was the only benefit of being Scarth's brother. They let me alone."

At the dock Turner said, "I'd like to be able to talk to your mom or dad about Scarth."

"They don't have a clue as to what he was really like. They adored him."

"Still, it might help. Can you contact them and maybe get me in?"

"I can try with my mom. She notices I exist."

"Thanks," Turner said.

186

24

They went out fishing for only an hour or two the next morning. Jeff burbled less. Brian was quiet. Ben and Madge and the Fenwick girls caught fish.

After returning, Turner wanted to get into town and begin questioning people, but it was still barely seven in the morning. He also wanted to find out if Ian had discovered anything in his questioning the day before. He invited Ian for a stroll in the woods. Ian had on a long-sleeved white shirt, heavy jeans, a scarf, and his slouch fedora. The few visible bits of skin glistened with the residue of bug spray and suntan oil. Turner was in jeans, a short-sleeved sweatshirt, and bug spray.

Ten yards into the woods, Turner asked Ian what he'd found out.

Ian said, "Screw this case." He swatted at several bugs hovering near his right arm. "I'm walking in the goddamn woods. If I see another green leaf, I'm going to puke on the nearest person with a fishing pole."

Turner said, "There's millions of leaves. You'd have to be a puke master to heave that much."

"I'm a master—"

"Don't go there," Paul said.

"What if we get lost in these woods? What if we come upon a bear?"

"What did I tell you to do?"

"Don't run. Look big. Make noise? Don't make noise? I don't remember which. Be carrying a bazooka? What good is a bazooka going to do if we get lost?"

"It's your bazooka," Paul said. "This is a nice path. It's maintained by the province. Some of the woods are parkland. It's quiet, peaceful. There are little markers here and there giving details about the various trees and flowers."

"Who makes a living doing that kind of thing?"

"Somebody must want to do it," Turner said.

"Maybe it's Canadian torture," Ian said.

"Maybe your imagination is running away with you."

"What did you guys find out yesterday?"

Turner filled him in.

"I get no sense of who did it," Ian said. "Sure are a lot of people who didn't like him. Motive never solves murder," he ended with the oft-repeated cop axiom.

Turner knew that was true. They were taught from day one it was clear physical evidence that won convictions. Here half the town would be locked up in jail forever if motive was the answer.

"What did you find out?" Turner asked.

"I tried to talk to his friends. That went nowhere. You had better luck than I did with them. I visited the parents of the friends. The parents of Cory Dunsmith, the one who blabbed, and Oliver McBride's mom and dad had a few things to say."

"They didn't try to minimize their kid's involvement with murder?"

"They all did that, but I got an earful from Dunsmith's and McBride's folks. The McBrides hate the Krohns. Passionately. Either mother or father would cheerfully take a gun to the entire Krohn family. They would start with Scarth. They claimed that son of a bitch tortured and teased their kid for years."

"Hard not to be angry about that, but didn't they try to do something about it then?"

"Their kid kept quiet. He suffered in silence until the gun incident. It just kind of boiled over. They didn't have a clue."

"How could they not have?"

"They claim they didn't. Dunsmith's mother was apologetic in the extreme. His dad thought his kid was a lazy bum who was in with the wrong kind. He thought his kid should have gotten a job. He blamed 'that crowd that he runs with' for all of his problems."

"It's everybody's fault but mine," Turner said.

"Got that right. He didn't seem to be as angry at J. T. Krohn as some others. That could be because, as I found out later, Mr. Dunsmith has one of the few jobs left at the mill since it closed. He's some kind of security guard. However, Dunsmith's father is pretty pissed at Scarth. He's not part of the Scarth-is-a-saint chorus."

"Something I never want to hear," Turner said.

Ian said, "I talked to people at the local college. The officials were reluctant to talk about the deaths."

"Understandable."

"I finally got the story." He drew a breath. "Which was

absolutely boring. Nobody knew of any connection between all of them. No one knew all six of them. I tried to piece together connections from the bits different people said. Not a clue in sight."

"We've got what the coach said about them being on those teams, but that has neither an obvious nor obscure connection to murder that I can see."

Ian said, "I dug into the Krohns' family background. Mrs. Krohn is a whack job, certifiably on her way around the bend."

"What's the problem?"

"She's married to a hard-driving, heartless gazillionaire whose money does not meet her emotional needs. According to this town, she was the sweetest kid as she was growing up. She and J.T. met in grade school. They are the only one each other ever dated. Then they got married. Supposedly, she's been faithful. Supposedly he's a philandering, lying sack of shit who would be happy to screw any woman in town."

"And did he?"

"What?"

"Screw them."

"According to my source, if he didn't, it wasn't for lack of trying. The dad matches the son in having multiple partners. I've seen pictures. He's as good-looking as his kid in an I'm-a-pirate-and-I-may-make-you-walk-the-plank-any-minute kind of way."

Turner said, "He's rich. He's pretty. I got that."

"He's a son of a bitch. He led the chorus in the-kids-drowned scenario for the first six of them. He's invested in every big development in town. More tourists, more money.

He's an Amityville throwback. Don't alarm the tourists that there's a shark devouring half the town. That type. But now that it's his own kid, the sky is falling."

"Do the mother and father have alibis for the time of the murder?"

"Nobody in this town would believe that he would kill his own kid."

"Yeah, well, I'm not from this town. I only come up here to not go fishing."

Ian paused in the middle of the path. He stared forward and back and then forward again.

"What?" Turner followed his friend's gaze.

"Hush," Ian whispered. "I thought I heard something."

Turner listened to the birds, the wind, the trees. Then he thought he heard a faint noise, which quickly grew in intensity.

Soon they could make out panting, crying, brush being disturbed. Then a crescendo of screeches rose for several seconds then fell in a gurgling wail. Moments later a woman appeared on the path. She wore a red jogging suit. Turner had never seen her before.

She ran up to them, stopped, and bent over. Between great gasps for breath she said, "Help! Help!"

"Are you hurt?" Turner asked.

"In the forest," she gasped. "Oh help!"

"We'll follow you," Turner said.

"I can't. I can't."

"What is it?"

"Someone."

"Are they hurt?"

"Yes. I think so. Yes." She knelt on the ground and began

to vomit. When the heaving and sobbing stopped, and her breathing was under control, Turner said, "Please, could you help show us the way?"

"I don't know if I can go back."

"Was the person on the path? We could find them."

"Her, I think. On the path or off the path."

"Pardon?" Turner said.

She took a deep gulp of air. "I was running along the shore path. I saw something. I went to look. It was awful. I panicked. I ran. The wrong way. There were woods all around. I heard all kinds of sounds. I ran and ran. I stumbled onto this path. Something horrible has happened."

Turner said, "Can you go back with us as far as you can? We can go on from there. Was it someone you know?"

"I'm not sure."

"How far back is this?" Turner asked.

"Maybe two miles. I've run along the shore path for years. It's quiet. That's why I like it. Hunters use it in the fall. That's why it's pretty smooth and even." She looked down at her feet. "It's like this one. Pretty regular."

She led them back the way she had come. "I came out here. I sort of recognized this path. I mean I know there's the shore path and then this one farther inland." She pointed. "There's a clearing through there about a mile. I was on the halfway point of my run. There's a quiet little secluded beach. I like to sit there and meditate. Today, it was awful." Tears started. She pointed. "It's that way."

Turner said, "Why don't you go for help? We'll check it out."

She nodded and hurried off down the path. Turner and Ian plunged into the woods. At times they had to clear brush in front of themselves. Ian said, "It can't be another dead body in the North Woods?"

"The last one was in the lake."

"That's no comfort."

Turner said, "Just a guess, but whatever it is, it's not going to be pretty."

"Are we still going in the right direction?" Ian asked. "It would be easy to get lost in here."

Turner said, "I checked the sun's position when she pointed." He looked at the sky. "If we don't find something in the next few minutes, we can turn back. We should mark our path." He began breaking tree branches about every ten feet. When they'd gone another fifty yards, Ian pointed. "I can't make that out."

Turner followed his friend's finger. He was looking between two larch trees. A bit of pink tinted with red reflected in the sunlight. The wind briefly touched the leaves, and the apparition was covered in shadow.

Ian began to walk toward it.

"Stop," Turner said.

"Maybe it's just somebody in trouble."

Turner nodded. "Be careful." As young cops together when they were first lovers, they'd been taught to take every precaution with a crime scene.

The two stepped forward, barely rustling the weeds, leaves, and dead branches that lay on the forest floor. Closer they could see it was a person. By the time they were twenty feet away they knew they were at a crime scene.

The body was that of a young woman who wore clothes two sizes two small for her. She had on a bright orange and yellow sweater that hung in shreds from her enormous chest. Turner remembered the garment as the one worn by Evon Gasple when they were accosted by the crowd of six in the parking lot. He spotted a pair of glasses with bright pink frames on top of a bush. One lens was cracked.

Turner could see dark bruises on exposed portions of her skin. She'd been brutally beaten fairly soon before her death. He could also see tooth and claw marks.

"Was she attacked and killed by a wild animal?" Ian asked.

Turner said, "More likely they've been snacking after she died."

Turner tried to take in the whole scene at once. He saw that the lakeshore was only about forty feet away. The body was in a small clearing about thirty feet in from a stony beach that stretched the rest of the way to the shore. They moved off to the side to avoid disturbing the crime scene and to wait for help that they hoped the woman they'd met was sending.

Eventually, Chief of Police Schreppel and Mavis Bednars, the commander of the Ontario Provincial Police detachment, showed up. Ian and Tuner gave their statement and were told to wait.

Half an hour later the Canadian medical examiner was talking to Schreppel and Bednars. Turner and Ian were brought in.

"You found the body?" Schreppel asked.

"Yeah."

"Finding lots of bodies."

"It's a curse," Turner said.

"It's not time to be cute."

"Is this a good time to be cop clumsy and officious?"

194

Turner replied. He turned to the medical examiner. "How did she die?"

"Somebody beat the hell out of her. She scratched, hit, and bit back."

Turner said, "Scarth's body was pretty mangled."

The ME said, "He probably got himself caught in the propeller of a boat. It might be hard to distinguish which wound was inflicted by what. Could have been Scarth who attacked her, but I'm not sure you're going to be able to prove it by the markings on his corpse."

"Could she have killed Scarth and then died from her wounds?"

"Anything is possible."

Bednars said, "Maybe she wandered around wounded in the woods."

"No, she was beaten and died there. The ground was trampled. The footprints of human and animals were too blurred for them to yield any record of what had happened."

"Were they Scarth's shoes?"

"I'll need to check. The beach is stony, but they could have walked here or come in a boat. On the grassy surface there are a lot of different tracks. You've also got critters who have been through here and obliterated a lot. At least one bear has been by having several meals and any number of smaller animals have had their fill."

Ian said, "At least she didn't suffer."

"Actually, she probably did. She didn't die right away. Critters nibbled at her. She couldn't move. Her neck was broken. Whoever bashed her was incredibly strong. She wasn't a small woman. Animals would have been attracted by the scent of blood. Her throat was crushed. She couldn't have called out. She was bleeding before the critters got to her. She's got bug bites on most of the exposed surfaces of her body. Those bites are disturbed by various things snacking on her. She was watching herself be devoured."

Everybody was very silent.

"Would she have lived if someone had found her sooner?" Turner asked.

"No," the ME said. "If she'd had the same injuries in the middle of the most up-to-date hospital in Montreal, she'd have died. They'd have been able to save her a lot of pain, but that's about it."

"She was the local slut," Schreppel said. "She'd been shared by more guys than a whore in Amsterdam."

"That's harsh," the ME said.

"That's reality," Schreppel replied.

Bednars said, "She was Scarth's sometime girlfriend."

"They were together the other night," Turner said. He explained the parking lot encounter.

"This is definitely murder," Ian said.

"Yes," the medical examiner confirmed. "She's got bits of flesh under her fingernails. Defense wounds on her arms. She fought her attacker."

"Could she have killed Scarth prior to her injuries?" Ian asked.

The ME said, "Sure, but if she did, who injured her? Trust me, she didn't kill anybody after she was injured."

Turner said, "We don't know if they attempted to kill each other or if there was a third person here who attacked them both." Head nods.

Schreppel said, "We shouldn't be talking in front of civilians."

The ME and Bednars gazed at him evenly. They also remained silent.

Schreppel said, "We'd like Mr. Hume to come back to town with us."

"What?" the reporter demanded.

"You've been around town asking questions for two days. We need to know what you know."

Turner said, "I was around asking questions yesterday."

Schreppel said, "Right now we're interested in Mr. Hume."

Ian said, "Bullshit. What is this crap? You have some evidence connecting me to this crime?"

"You've expressed an inordinate amount of interest in this case."

"Which case? This one was just discovered. Unless you've known all about it and haven't reported it. I have better things to do than indulge you in whatever criminal fantasies you are choosing to have at this moment."

Turner normally didn't believe in antagonizing the local police, but he sympathized with Ian. Nor did he understand the cop's bullheadedness.

Turner said, "We're not planning on leaving town. Is Ian under arrest?"

"No," Schreppel said.

Bednars spoke up. "We have a lot of paperwork to do and people to talk to. We know where to find him if we need him."

"Got that right," Schreppel said.

Not seeing an arrest as imminent, Turner led Ian away. Ian groused for the entire walk back to the dock. Madge and Buck Fenwick accosted them on the shoreline.

"What the hell happened?" Fenwick asked. "A million

emergency vehicles drove up and people trooped into the woods."

"Murder," Ian said.

"Without me?" Fenwick asked.

"Who died?" Madge asked.

"Evon Gasple," Turner said, "the woman who was in the red car the other night in the parking lot. Scarth's girlfriend."

"Somebody killed them both?" Madge asked.

"Hard to tell," Turner said. "They must have died the same night. It's going to take the medical examiner some time to fix the time of death as precisely as possible. If Scarth killed her, then who killed Scarth, or did the third person kill them both?"

Ian said, "They wanted to arrest me."

"Why?" Madge asked.

Turner said, "They wanted to question you some more. I think the chief of police is pissed off because you've been sticking your nose into things around town."

Fenwick said, "So have we."

"But he's taken a dislike to Ian. Remember when he came out here the night of the break-in? He wasn't ready to believe much of anything. And Ian, you were your usually charming self."

Madge said, "Schreppel was rude."

"So was I," Ian said. "Sometimes I don't know when to keep my mouth shut."

"What do we do next?" Fenwick asked.

"Talk to the people who knew Evon," Ian said.

Turner said, "Right now, I don't think you should be talking to anybody."

"Somebody has to."

Fenwick said, "Leave it to us. At least we are currently working cops."

Ian said, "Start with the mother. I talked with her yesterday. She lives in a trailer park on the edge of town. She was pretty drunk and that was at one in the afternoon. She didn't seem real happy with her daughter. Called her a slut and a whore."

Fenwick said, "I love dysfunctional families in murder cases."

Madge said, "You love anything weird and kinky—" She saw the smirk on Ian's face. She rushed to add, "—connected with murder."

"We'll go see her," Turner said. "It's a place to start. If she'll talk to us."

Ian said, "I'll go with."

Turner said, "You'll stay here."

▲ 25 ◢

Evon Gasple Senior lived in a trailer park on the road to the Trans-Canada Highway. The parking lot was in the front. A hand-painted sign announced NORTHERN LIGHTS TRAILER PARK. Many modern mobile homes might be close to luxurious or at least be the equivalent of a real house. Gasple lived in a collection of trailers, sad lumps of tin, that might have been new in the thirties. Most were aluminum gray. A few had flower pots with desperate flowers trying to make a dent in the assorted gloom. Someone had cut down all the trees within a hundred yards and replaced them with concrete, which was now cracked and crumbling. Shade was at a premium. There would be nothing to break the howling winds of winter. Enquiring at the manager's office gave them the information that Mrs. Gasple lived in the last trailer on the left down the main thoroughfare of the camp.

Turner and Fenwick walked down the cement drive to

the back. A few kids clustered in the dust that inched out a foot or two from the front of most of the trailers.

Mrs. Gasple was on her patio—or at least Turner thought of it as such. The portion of concrete she sat on was on the shady side of the trailer. It was near the door and two aluminum fold-up lawn chairs sat next to her. She had her shoes off, her feet up on a lump of log that looked like it was only a few years short of petrification. She wore a waitress uniform, and she was smoking a cigarette.

Turner introduced Fenwick and himself.

She spoke in a whiskey snarl. With no preliminaries or prodding, she said, "That boy killed my girl."

"Why do you say that?" Turner asked.

"Scarth Krohn had his way with my daughter when she was not of age. He was evil, and now she's gone. She was my baby."

She wiped her tears away with the hand that held the cigarette. Turner feared she might set fire to the front of her dyed-blond bangs.

"Back then why didn't you call the police?" Turner asked.

"They were both thirteen. How was I going to have my own kid arrested? I walked in on them in there." She jerked her head at the overgrown heap of metal behind her. She took a drag on her cigarette.

Turner mused. How do you tell a mother that they'd heard her daughter was the town slut starting at eleven?

Mrs. Gasple motioned them to the other chairs. She leaned forward. "It was that boy's fault that my daughter had the reputation she did. He spread it around. He made up things."

"Why did she still date him?" Turner asked.

"He had a hold over her. Some men can do that especially to impressionable youngsters. They have ways. I told her and told her to stay away from him. I tried to break them up. I told her she'd be sorry." She lit another cigarette from the first one. She flipped the still smoldering butt of the first into the square of dirt that passed for a yard. He noted a huge cluster of yellowed butts in her ersatz ashtray. "I know what this town said about me. The usual gossip crap about an idiot controlling mother driving her daughter into the arms of the local boob. Her father never took an interest." Turner and Fenwick endured five minutes of an anti-ex-husband diatribe. She finished with, "That son of a bitch hasn't been around since she was five. He was useless. Most men are. No offense." She flicked her ash into the slight breeze.

"Do you know where your daughter was Monday night?" Fenwick asked.

"She left around six. I have no idea where she was going. Six months ago she was supposed to get her own place and leave me out here in peace. She could never hold a job. I don't know where she got her money." She glared at them. "She was not selling drugs or herself. I'm her mother. I know my own daughter."

Turner wasn't ready to bet the ranch on this mother's level of insight.

"Did your daughter have any enemies?"

"Not a one. She had tons of friends. Everybody liked her. There were always kids around. She always had places to go and people to go out with. You go talk to her best friend, Matalina. She'll tell you. I'm not making any of this up. You ask her. She's a good girl."

"Did you know Scarth's brother?"

"Kid's got to be homosexual. He's always quiet. Lives by himself. Isn't friendly with anyone. He never came around here. You'd see him around town with his nose in a book or going to the library or coming back from the library with stacks of books. I never heard of him dating girls."

"How about the mom and dad?" Turner asked.

"You must already know J. T. Krohn owns this town. He controls what gets developed and who develops it. He sold that mill at a convenient time. He owned tons of property before that. For all I know he owns the entire western end of the province."

Turner figured they could listen to her numerous ill-founded insights until the next Ice Age. He decided to forgo the pleasure. When she drew sharply on her cigarette in the middle of her third repetitive tirade about Scarth, Turner stood up. Fenwick followed immediately.

As they neared the exit, the manager accosted them. She was an older woman, maybe in her late seventies or early eighties. She used a cane. She jerked her head at them. They followed her lead into the office. She said, "You can't be coming in here in daylight. I won't have it."

"I beg your pardon?" Fenwick said.

"Those Gasples can get away with their two-person cathouse at night. I can't stay up at night. I fall asleep. Since my Harold died three years ago, there's not much I can do. Even he couldn't do that much. Those two are out of control. I won't have it during the day. You keep your filth out of here."

Fenwick said, "We're police detectives from Chicago. We were here on vacation." He pointed to Turner. "His son found the body of Scarth Krohn."

"That boy was always nice to me, always. Used to help

out sometimes. Taking the garbage out or doing some cleaning. Never asked to get paid."

"He didn't come here for service from the Gasples?" Fenwick asked.

"He tried to make that girl respectable."

"Mrs. Gasple didn't seem to like him much."

"Some people liked him. Some didn't. I did. Mrs. Gasple is more of a slut than her daughter, but that girl was catching up, fast. The mother works at the diner at the intersection with the Trans-Canada Highway. She brings all kind of strangers in here. We only have thefts after she's entertained some of her temporary friends."

"Why don't you kick her out?"

"You see this place? We get all the dregs and dirt and riffraff of this town. You don't get a lot of folks who keep up their rent on a regular basis. She does. I do know mother and daughter had a huge fight Monday before she left. They have huge fights most nights. They both used that trailer to turn tricks. I'm surprised they didn't have to give out numbers like they do at the meat counter in the grocery store."

"Would Scarth come to visit Mrs. Gasple when Evon wasn't here?"

"He was a good boy. He came sometimes to help me. He'd visit a few people as well."

In the SUV Fenwick said, "He was banging mother and daughter?"

"And anything else that moved," Turner said, "if we are to believe the local gossip."

Fenwick said, "I'm willing to be pretty progossip by this point."

"You're such a pushover," Turner said.

~ 26 ~

Turner and Fenwick visited Matalina McMahon, Evon Junior's best friend. She lived above a dry cleaner in downtown Cathura.

She greeted them with a baby in her arms. Turner thought the infant might have been three months old. McMahon wore the same waitress uniform as Mrs. Gasple. She chomped on a large wad of gum. The kid was sucking on a bottle.

Turner introduced them. She let them in. When they were seated on a plastic-cushioned couch, he said, "We're trying to find out who would want to kill Evon."

"Scarth Krohn, or her own mother."

"Did you get along with Scarth?" Turner asked.

"I hated him."

"Why's that?" Turner asked.

"He raped me." She nodded toward the baby. "This is his."

"Did he support the baby?"

"Money? I didn't want shit from him."

"How did Evon feel about all this?" Turner asked.

"We used to be best friends."

"Her mother left the impression that you still were."

"Her mother is clueless. We still talked sometimes. It's a small town, but we weren't friends anymore."

Turner said, "I thought she and Scarth were dating."

"Love-hate. All the time. Fights. Make-ups. Screaming. Carrying on." She shifted the baby's weight.

"Did they ever hit each other?" Turner asked.

"All the time. Evon was tough. She didn't put up with shit from him."

"She hit him?" Turner asked.

"It was like wrestling matches and boxing matches and then they'd do sex again the next minute."

"People saw this?" Turner asked.

McMahon said, "They'd do sex at parties, and they didn't care who they did it in front of. I'd tell Evon, 'Get some respect for yourself. He's just using you.' She wouldn't listen. Of course, he was just using her. Like he used all the girls in this town."

"Even you?" Turner asked.

"Yes." She chuckled. "Before I got pregnant. I bit Scarth's ass once. I hope I left a scar. I know I drew blood."

"How long did she and Scarth have this kind of relationship?" Turner asked.

"Since forever. I told Evon to at least be more selective. She bragged about doing Scarth and all of his buddies at once. I didn't believe her."

The baby gurgled and McMahon shifted the child in her arms.

208

"There was one strange thing," McMahon said.

"What's that?" Turner asked.

"Evon claimed she had sex with all those guys who died in the lake. You know the ones they're saying got killed by a serial killer? Them."

"Did you believe her?"

"Evon tended to brag."

"On the night they died?" Turner asked.

"I don't think so. She never claimed that. She'd say a lot of stuff. Starting in eighth grade, every few months she'd claim she was pregnant."

"Was she?"

"Not until the end of high school."

"What happened to the baby?" Turner asked.

"She had an abortion. Evon claimed Scarth's father paid to get that swept under the rug. She never looked pregnant to me. It could have been true. Hard to tell. Evon was a good liar."

"We heard the guys were into making porn tapes."

"I never heard about them making movies. They were always horny. Boys have only one thing on their minds."

"Was Scarth into drugs?" Fenwick asked.

"He made Evon become a dealer. I told Evon not to."

"Evon was the local pusher?"

"Well, you could get drugs from her, but it was Scarth's fault. Always Scarth's fault. Everything that has gone wrong in my life was Scarth's fault. Everything that has gone wrong in this town is Scarth Krohn's fault. He was an awful, terrible shit." A tear escaped down her face and the baby fussed a moment.

"You said Mrs. Gasple didn't have a clue. Did Evon have fights with her mother?"

"All the time. Evon used to come over here to get away from the shrew. That woman never let up. I hated to go over there when we were kids. I finally refused. If Evon wanted to see me, she'd have to come over here, or we'd meet someplace else."

"What did they fight about?"

"What didn't they fight about?"

"Did Scarth get along with his parents?" Turner asked.

"No. He hated them. He wanted them to get a divorce. He was desperate. If they split up, he could get his hands on all kinds of money and be a rich, worthless piece of trash."

Fenwick said, "Mrs. Gasple claimed she tried to break them up."

"She tried to screw everyone up. Hell, she screwed Scarth."

"Evon?" Fenwick asked.

"The mom."

"You have proof of this."

"Scarth loved to brag."

"Did Scarth get Mrs. Gasple pregnant?"

"If he did, she had an abortion. She never had any kids besides Evon."

Back in the SUV Fenwick asked, "Am I missing something? Did anybody in this town like this kid?"

"His buddies, his coach, the manager at the trailer court."

"Oh, yeah," Fenwick said, "easy to forget. Evon was the local drug connection?"

"Maybe she was her own little Canadian cartel," Turner said. "Abortions. Sex with mother and daughter. My view of Canadians is changing."

"From what to what?"

Turner glanced at Fenwick. "I'm not sure."

"What do we do with all this information?" Fenwick asked.

"Nothing yet," Turner said.

"Who do we try next?" Fenwick asked.

"The porn guy? We've got wild sex all around this town. Might as well dip our feet in it. I should probably go by myself. If he's doing porn, he'd be less likely to talk to two guys. Especially if he's doing gay porn. What do you think?"

"Are you saying you're an expert on gay porn?"

"Enough of one to hold up my end of a conversation. I hope."

▗ 27 ▖

Turner strolled down to the Cathura Photo Shop. The picture windows on the outside were filled with wilderness photos: grizzly bears rampant, glaciers calving, moose rutting, forest fires burning, prairie wheat blowing in the wind. He entered. A tall, slender man in his late twenties stood behind the counter. He wore a gold, short-sleeved seersucker shirt. His arms were covered in thick black hair, a matt of which sprouted beneath his shirt opened to the last button above the large belt buckle of a cast-iron beaver. His black jeans were neatly pressed and tight at the crotch. They clung to his thighs and calves. He wore silver thin-framed glasses. His hair was dark black and cut short. Turner walked up to him. He said, "I'm looking for Nick Broder."

The man said, "You found him."

Turner said, "I'm Paul Turner. I'm a detective from Chicago here on vacation. My kids fished up Scarth Krohn's body."

"That's terrible. Are they okay?"

"Yeah. I heard you knew Scarth Krohn."

"Everybody knew Scarth Krohn."

"That you were friends."

"I wasn't in that crowd."

"But they came to your photo shop."

"I'm the only photo shop in town."

"Scarth Krohn didn't own a camera."

Broder said, "I heard you were here with your partner. A guy. You're gay with two sons."

"That's right."

"That's kind of brave."

"How so?"

"This is rural Canada."

"We've never had any problems."

"Not to your face."

"And that means?"

Broder said, "Rural anywhere is not safe for gay people. We all know that. And before you ask, yes, I'm gay. No, I don't hang out with Howard Coates and his ineffectual human-rights clutch of desperate fags. They want to change things. Ha!"

"So why do the local boys come here?"

"Somebody must have told you."

"I heard rumors."

"I make straight-guy porn. It's called Wilderness Studs on the Internet. All the guys are supposedly straight, and I don't ask, and they don't tell. I make more from my Internet porn sales than I do from this store."

"And why aren't you discriminated against?"

"Because I pay these local studs lots of money. And

I probably pay more in taxes than half the businesses in town. Hell, since the mill closed, I might be in the running for biggest employer in town. You got bored guys who don't mind putting out a little."

"Is that why they perform for you?"

"I don't care why they perform for me. I act straight. I talk in a deep voice. I'm masculine. I can play their sports games better than most of them."

"How do you recruit your subjects?"

"Word of mouth."

"Isn't that dangerous? What if the wrong person found out?"

"What I'm doing isn't illegal. They're of age."

"How did Scarth Krohn get involved?"

"Daddy and Mommy weren't keeping him in the style with which he wished to become accustomed. He needed money. They all do in this no-job town. You have the fishing and hunting seasons. Every kid claims he's a guide. A few are good and make decent money. In winter you don't get enough skiers up here to pay the bills. Along about February you get really bored. Scarth was somewhere around my twentieth model."

"These guys all put out?"

"Sure. Some of the guys wouldn't appear with another guy. Some of them would permit another guy to sit next to them, and they'd beat off together. Some guys would permit themselves to give each other hand jobs. A few let themselves get blown. Two of the guys really got into each other all while watching straight porn and talking about how into women they were."

"Into each other?"

"Kissed, took it up the ass. It's my biggest seller. Two of Scarth's buddies. I'm sworn to secrecy. Why they haven't figured out all you have to do to identify them is check my Internet site, I don't know."

"How'd you convince them to do all this?"

"Money. The more they did, the more cash they got. Kissing straight guys who suck and screw could get a few thousand."

"Lot of money."

"It's a fraction of my cost. I make a lot."

"Why haven't the police shut you down?"

"It's an Internet porn site. Like a live show but with archives. I don't actually have to ship much of anything. Somebody looks at my site, likes the preview, and then subscribes with their credit card."

"And the guys around here haven't beat the shit out of you?"

"I have a studio out in the woods. They don't know where I live. Only a few of them actually come from around here. I get guys from as far away as Thunder Bay, Saskatoon, and even a couple from Minnesota. Lots of them are rural guys who just don't give a shit. Some are married. It's a little fun and a little money."

"Who recruited Scarth?"

"I place a small ad in porn magazines and on the Net. He said he saw it and was curious. I'm careful when I meet them."

"Did you grow up around here?"

"Kenora."

"Did Scarth do anything besides beat off?"

Broder said, "He made six."

"That sounds like a lot."

216

"It is. Five of them were solo jobs. He was a hot man. He's a big seller."

"But he did one with someone else."

"Yeah. Not somebody from around here. I can tell usually in the first two minutes what they're really going to be willing to do. Some gay guys and women really get off on straight guys kissing, making out, and having sex. A surprising number of women order DVDs of guys beating off. Scarth claimed he wouldn't do anything with another guy. I had to offer him a whole lot of money just to sit next to the guy. I put porn tapes on to get them in the mood. I tried a bisexual one. Scarth made me switch it. For a short while at the start, I thought he might be a little flexible. With the guy, he was out of his clothes in seconds and his dick was hard before his boxers came off. I offered him good money to interact with the other guy, but he said no. His two buddies gave in when I suggested lots more money if they'd beat off with another guy. They gave me this big show of reluctance. I get that a lot. Once they got started, it was no holds barred."

Turner asked, "What tips you off to their willingness to experiment?"

"They look at the other guy too often. A straight guy who is totally straight barely looks at the other guy. Scarth looked a little."

"Scarth doesn't know about his buddies?"

"They haven't confided in me." He hesitated. "I guess I could tell you. You're smart enough to check the Net. The two are Dunsmith and Doran. They got done with each other and made all kinds of protestations about doing what they'd done for money, only for the money. They kept repeating to me and to each other how many girls they'd had. What

I don't get is what all this has to do with Scarth getting drunk and falling into the lake and drowning."

"It gives me insight into who he was, what made him tick. Did any of the other guys who drowned appear on your Web site?"

"That would be convenient for you, wouldn't it? One of them was, only one. I didn't get started with this business until after the first two deaths."

"Tell me about the one who did."

"He was the fourth one who died. He was friendly enough. Most of them get shy and nervous at first. He was silly and goofy. He'd smile, and nod, and do everything I asked for not that much money."

"Do you have sex with these guys?"

"Sometimes."

"With Scarth?"

"Unfortunately, no."

"And do you put the ones with yourself and them on the Internet?"

"No. That's my little private bonus for living in this god-forsaken corner of the world."

"Why do you live here?"

"It's quiet. It's a world I know. I'm actually an artist. I sell my paintings in Vancouver. I make a little money doing that. I do a little guide work for the tourists in the summer. In the winter sometimes I work at a university in British Columbia."

"What do you know about Evon Gasple?"

"Town slut. I heard she got an abortion, but I have no idea if that's true. She wouldn't do porn. She was also the local drug connection."

"As in occasionally she had stuff for everybody or as in major market supplier?"

"Major market. She'd get Scarth and the boys to sell and distribute for her. I'm not sure Scarth was much into the organization although I guess he often kept stuff hidden for her. Everybody figured that since his dad had money, he'd be able to pay somebody off, or somehow pay their way out of any trouble."

"Evon was the leader?"

"Yeah. Women aren't drug kingpins in Chicago?"

"I guess they could be if they wanted." Broder knew no more.

28

It was midafternoon. Turner met Fenwick and went back to the houseboats. Brian was on the lake with the Jet Ski. Jeff was racing his wheelchair along the dock with another kid in a wheelchair. Madge and Ben joined the two detectives. Paul and Ben put together a large plate of cold cuts, bread, pickles, chips, mayonnaise, and mustard for a late lunch. Madge panfried several perch that her daughters had caught that morning. The Turner and Fenwick kids bolted their food and rushed off to their own interests.

After the kids left, Ben asked, "Any luck with the investigation?"

"No," Fenwick said. "Scarth was a shit, but his friends liked him."

"Isn't that always the case with friends?" Madge asked. "Otherwise they would come under the heading of enemies."

Ben said, "No wonder you married him. You have the same ghastly sense of humor."

All of them knew the truism that you were more likely to get useful information out of the enemies of the dead person than from the friends.

They spent the rest of their lunch speculating about numerous possibilities. As they were settling down on the comfy chairs on the top deck of the Turners' boat, a gray Honda Civic drove up. Howard Coates, the bar owner, and Ian emerged. They strode to the seated assemblage.

"What's up?" Fenwick asked.

Coates said, "I have inside information. There's no question that Evon was murdered, and now Scarth's death is definitely being considered a homicide."

Madge asked, "Could they have killed each other? Maybe they had a huge fight. You've described them as constantly battling."

Ben said, "That would work very neatly and get rid of two boils on the butt of life."

Turner said, "That can't be ruled out. Did they say what Evon died of?"

Coates said, "My source would tell me only so much. He did say there had been pressure to rule Scarth's death an accident, but he's sticking to his guns. He's a new guy. He never dealt with the other six deaths. I heard he may reopen the inquiries into those. The shit is about to hit the fan in this town."

The silver cigarette boat with the man who had picked up Mrs. Talucci entered the bay and headed for their dock. As the boat pulled in, Turner grabbed the line the man threw. After securing the boat, he walked up to Turner. This was the first time Turner had seen him up close. He was five feet eight, slender, with blond hair. He wore a blue blazer that was cut to emphasize broad shoulders and a slender waist. His deep voice was soft. He might have been in his middle-to-late twenties.

"Mr. Turner?" Polite, deferential.

Paul nodded.

"Mrs. Talucci sent me to ask if you would accompany me to see her."

Everybody exchanged looks.

Ian said to the young man, "Do you want me to go with?"

Fenwick guffawed.

Madge said, "I teach a course in subtlety. It meets once a week for the rest of your life. For the entire hour we practice keeping our mouths shut so we don't embarrass ourselves."

Ian said, "I'm going to look for a burly Mountie who will come back and arrest you all." He stomped off. Turner heard him mutter, "Can't blame a guy for trying."

Through all this the young man had remained impassive. To Turner he said, "Sir?"

Turner said, "Of course." He didn't ask what it was about. If he was supposed to tell, he guessed this young man would have told him.

Ben said, "I'll watch the kids. We could try and get in some more fishing."

"Thanks."

As Turner put his life jacket on and buckled himself into the boat next to his driver, the young man said, "Mr. Turner, my name is Phil. If I can do anything to make your journey more comfortable, please let me know. This will be a straightforward shot. We have about an hour and a half ahead of us."

Turner said, "Thank you. I think I'll be fine."

Phil turned the boat on. Fenwick threw them the rope. Everybody waved as they pulled away.

29

Conversation over the roar of the cigarette boat's twin engines would have had to occur at the shout level. The young man stood at the wheel and dodged marker buoys deftly. Turner would never have gone this fast through parts of the lake he was familiar with, much less these parts, which he didn't know. An errant rock could tear the hell out of the bottom of your boat. The sun was warm, but the lake was cool. Turner was glad he was wearing his heavy sweatshirt. By the end of an hour they were on parts of the lake Turner had never been.

Abruptly, the boat slowed. Turner looked around. They were miles from land. The engine noise was down. He looked at the driver, who said, "We're being followed."

Turner looked back. In the far distance he saw a speck of black in the middle of the water. It could have been a rock, except in a few moments it began to get larger.

"Someone who happens to be on the lake at the same time?" Turner asked.

"They've been behind us since we started out." Phil shoved the throttle down and the boat flew off. They were heading due south. In about ten minutes they closed in on a series of islands. Phil took the boat around the first three then doubled back. He drove in under a wide swath of overhanging trees. He tied the boat up and began to disembark.

"I'm coming with," Turner said.

Phil nodded. They crossed a small isthmus and were able to look back on the way they'd come. In a few minutes a charcoal gray boat approached going at high speed. Turner saw four men in the boat. They were about a half mile away so he couldn't be sure who it was.

Phil said, "Scarth's buddies."

"You're sure?"

"I recognize the boat. It's the one Scarth Krohn always used. I assume it's them."

The boat raced past their observation spot. Turner began to go back to their boat.

"Wait," Phil said.

Minutes later another, much smaller powerboat drove past. This one was much closer to the shore they stood on.

Turner said, "That's Ralph Bowers. What the hell is going on? Is he following us or them and why is anyone following us?"

Phil said, "I don't have the answers to those questions. We need to go. They'll probably figure out we're not ahead of them fairly soon."

They returned to their boat and took a different channel out into the lake. Phil pushed the throttle on full and they raced away toward the north.

Twenty-five minutes later bright red, elegantly lettered

signs began to appear warning them that they were entering private property and that there would be no trespassing. Another five minutes and Turner saw they were approaching the largest log structure he had ever seen. It was a mansion built with lodgepole pines. There were outbuildings with horses in front of them being led in circles around a paddock. A wide green lawn led up from a small dock. Another cigarette boat, which matched the first, was pulled up to the pier. A young man about Phil's age hurried from a boathouse and helped with the lines. Turner noted that this man, like Phil, carried a deftly concealed handgun.

Turner spotted Mrs. Talucci on a shaded veranda. She waved. Accompanied by Phil, he strode forward. The backdrop to the home was tall pine trees and solid oaks. His feet sank into the well-manicured lawn.

When Turner touched the door of the screened-in porch, two large dogs rose from the ground within. One was a black German shepherd, the other a Doberman pinscher. They neither barked nor wagged their tails. Phil said, "Excuse me, sir." Turner stepped back. Phil touched the door and said, "Friend." The dogs subsided. Turner entered. Phil followed.

Mrs. Talucci rose and greeted him. She introduced a man sitting in a two-seater swing, which was next to her chair. "Paul, this is my brother, Dominic Antonetti. You've heard me speak of him?"

Turner remembered Mrs. Talucci had nine brothers and sisters. He recalled that Dominic was the youngest. He looked to be in his late seventies. Turner shook his hand. Turner noted that the swing did not squeak as it moved with the man's motion. Somebody kept it well oiled.

Dominic said, "Forgive me for not rising. The doctors say I am to take it easy for three more weeks."

"Nothing serious, I hope," Paul said.

"With old people, things break down," he said. His voice was soft and raspy. He looked thin and frail. He wore a brown cardigan sweater over a blue, long-sleeved shirt, and khaki pants.

Next to Mrs. Talucci on a white wrought-iron table sat a glass of iced tea and a book of Kierkegaard's writing. Paul knew in the fall she was planning to take another philosophy course at the University of Chicago. The pine chairs on the veranda had deep, soft, flowered yellow cushions for the occupants to relax on. The veranda was cool and pleasant, the giant oaks in the yard casting vast shadows.

Phil said, "Mr. Antonetti, we had two boats following us." He gave his report.

When he finished, the young man said, "I'll order the usual precautions."

Antonetti said, "Thank you, Phillip."

Another gentleman emerged from the house. He was about the same age as Dominic. This new person was introduced as Pierre LeBec. He sat down next to Dominic on the swing. He put his hand on Dominic's shoulder and asked, "Do you need anything?"

"I'm fine for now, thanks."

Pierre put his hand around Dominic's shoulder and left it there.

Paul wasn't stupid.

Dominic said, "They came with an entourage." He explained to LeBec what Phil had told them. He finished, "We'll double the guards for a while."

A man in his late twenties appeared with a cart that he wheeled down a smooth concrete path that snaked around the property. On the cart were a variety of snacks, a silver tea service, and a small coffee urn. Turner recognized a plate of Mrs. Talucci's fudge. The combination of miniature marshmallows, pistachios, and cashews was her signature. Dominic served. Paul took a small piece of each pastry and a cup of coffee. Serving her guests food and drink was a time-honored activity for Mrs. Talucci. If you came to her house, she fed you. Obviously her brother had the same approach with visitors. Paul felt little occasion to refuse; besides, it would be rude. He took a bite of fudge. Delicious as always.

When they were each settled with their bits of confections, Mrs. Talucci said, "Are the boys all right?"

"They're coping pretty well. I've talked to them both. I'll want to keep talking to them."

"You always do," Mrs. Talucci said. "Now, you've been having adventures. Tell us what's happened."

Turner told the story.

When he finished, Pierre said, "The sabotage that happened to your boat worries me more than anything else. And you were attacked. And you were followed out here."

Dominic added, "And you had the break-in that first night."

Pierre said, "Be careful who you trust."

"I agree," Dominic said. "It's a big lake and accidents can happen awfully conveniently."

"I'd never endanger my family," Paul said.

Mrs. Talucci said, "We will do our best to make sure nothing happens."

"Thanks," Paul said. He didn't know what they could do, but Mrs. Talucci was a marvel.

Paul asked, "What can you tell me about the Krohns?"

Dominic said, "I knew Scarth Krohn's great-grandfather, Arnold, best. He hired me in his mill when I came up here when I was fifteen. I had to run away from home."

Turner could guess why, but he kept silent. Listening to people's stories was a good part of his job as a detective. He was fairly good at getting people to talk or letting them talk. He was hoping to hear a new bit of Mrs. Talucci's family history.

Dominic said, "I was a wild kid. I didn't think the world could hold me." He smiled. "I was also flat broke. I did every rotten, low-level job in the mill. I boarded in a house near downtown." He smiled at Pierre. "He was fourteen then. What a time we had running in the woods, falling in love. I worked for the mill for fifty-two years. Eventually, I became foreman. I saved my money."

Pierre said, "I became an attorney and worked for the mill. I also inherited some money."

Dominic said, "We bought an acre of land out here in 1946."

Pierre added, "We used to always come out here separately. We were always careful. We bought more and more land and eventually built this place. We did much of the work ourselves."

Dominic said, "Well, to business. I feel bad about Scarth Krohn dying. Not because he was a good person. He was terrible, awful, but it's sad when any young life is snuffed out. I always hold out hope that people can change."

Mrs. Talucci said, "You are kinder than I am."

Dominic said, "Old Arnold Krohn, the great-grandfather, was a merciless skinflint. He drove all his rivals out of business, then created rivals so he could pretend there was competition. If he cut prices one place, he made a bundle in another mill. He didn't care if he ruined the lives of hundreds of employees."

"It was all secret," Pierre said. "Arnold Krohn specialized in secrets. The more harmful to someone else the better. I was a lawyer for the mill, and I thought I knew secrets, but he was a master at creating them, keeping them, and crushing people with them."

Dominic added, "He was the most rotten of all to his son, Blake, who was even more rotten to his son, J.T."

"I'd like to talk to Scarth's dad and mom," Turner said.

Dominic said, "I will arrange it."

Turner noted that there was no mention of "trying" to do it.

"I appreciate that."

Mrs. Talucci said, "I'm worried about you and your family. What else can we do to help?"

"Tell me more about these people. I need background."

Dominic sipped from his coffee cup, put it down, and took a bite of Mrs. Talucci's fudge. When resettled, he said, "Scarth Krohn, I don't really know. We hear rumors. Over the years occasionally teenagers wander out this far. This is a remote corner of the lake, and we always have the most up-to-date protections. Now it's all computers that I don't understand very well. We've got radar and sonar and lasers."

Pierre said, "We have always had to be careful. Teenagers may grow older, but they are always replaced by another set of reckless fools."

"Thank god we were never reckless fools," Dominic said.

Mrs. Talucci said, "I have a list of times."

Dominic said, "It must be a very long list."

She said, "It takes up nearly the entire hard drive on my computer."

Pierre said, "As an attorney, I have made sure we are as protected as we need to be legally. The young men who guard us aren't here just because they are physically strong and pretty to look at. Phil is an attorney. The young man who brought the tea setting is also an investment banker."

"They stay here?" Paul said.

"We pay very well," Dominic said.

Turner asked, "What danger do the teenagers pose?"

"They've tried vandalism, petty crimes. The staff we hire is exceptionally well trained. When we were younger, we did most of the guard duty ourselves. Now we have our own little gay cordon of protectors."

"How'd you get them to stop?" Turner asked.

Pierre said, "A shotgun pointed at the side of your head is a persuasive argument. We used to have quite a reputation, but we live too far out. The memory of us is fading in the town's consciousness. We're off the tourist path and the fishing and hunting around here are awful."

"Really?" Turner asked. He looked around at the setting. "It looks pristine."

"We own several square miles along the lake and far into the woods. Bought it during the crash cycles when timber wasn't worth cutting. We manage to keep the word out that it's awful. Probably isn't. You saw the signs on the approaches on the lake. We also have signs posted inland, and during the hunting season we have guards posted."

"How long have you lived together?" Turner asked.

"Since we got back from World War II," Dominic said. "Back

then out here was too remote for anyone to notice. If Arnold or Blake Krohn ever suspected, they never said anything. Arnold was a greedy businessman, but he was no prude. He had seven kids with his wife here in Cathura, and at least another seven with various women in ports around the world."

"How do you know this?" Turner asked.

Dominic smiled. "I was his confidant. He didn't feel he could tell anybody else, but he was dying to confide in someone he knew about what a stud he was. Over time he came to realize I knew how to keep secrets."

Mrs. Talucci said, "He knew you were so far gone in the clutches of Satan that you wouldn't mind listening to his tales of sin and depravation."

"You never minded my tales," Dominic said.

Mrs. Talucci said, "Sin and I go a long way back."

Turner would love to hear those stories, but he doubted any would be forthcoming for the moment.

Dominic said, "For whatever reason, Arnold Krohn talked, and I listened. His son, Blake, was a wastrel and a fool. The poor woman he married was a dunderhead. His grandson, J.T., is a fool, but he's a mean and greedy fool. They doted on Scarth. Grandpa Blake supposedly set up some kind of trust for Scarth."

"It was complicated," Pierre said. "Scarth could begin withdrawing the money after he turned eighteen, but only with the approval of both his parents. Mom would always say yes. Dad always said no."

"Always?" Turner asked.

"Yep," Pierre said. "Lots of folks put in something in their trusts about the kid gets the loot when they turn a certain age or graduate from college."

"Aren't you breaking confidentiality to talk about this?" Turner asked.

Pierre said, "I worked for him for nearly fifty years. I know secrets upon secrets. I'm a lawyer and a good one, but I don't mind telling one thing about him. Not in a good cause. They can't take away my license. I haven't been near a court-room or a law book in years."

"There's absolutely no way Scarth could get the money?" Turner asked.

"If his mom and dad got divorced," Pierre said.

"Any prospect of that happening?" Turner asked.

Both men shrugged. Dominic said, "I've never heard of anything. She's got a very comfortable life."

Pierre added, "If we can get you information or help you make contacts, we will. The Krohn family owes us a great deal."

Dominic said, "We were faithful and loyal through good times and bad. They appreciated it. That's why I can get you in to see them. I can't guarantee what kind of answers you'll be getting to your questions. You're on your own there."

Turner said, "An introduction is a start. Do you have a notion of how serious the difficulties really are between the First Nations kids and Scarth's buddies?"

The two men looked at each other. "Tell him," Mrs. Talucci ordered.

Dominic said, "The problem's seriousness level relates to how bigoted and prejudiced the individuals involved are. Scarth was a bigoted jerk. Billy Morningsky's pride can be overweening. Billy's stayed out here a few times. We've kept him out of juvenile hall. We've harbored a few fugitives from both sides over the years. They were running for their lives."

234

"Has Billy committed real crimes?" Turner asked.

"The sheriff on occasion thought so."

"Billy told me they'd eventually try to pin the murder on him."

Pierre said, "If Schreppel has anything to do with it, yeah, he'd probably get hauled in. Schreppel has a history of bone-headed ploys. He's lucky he hasn't been fired. Probably will be. He's as prejudiced as Scarth, but he's learned to cover it up better."

Turner asked, "Do you know anything about the deaths of those other six kids?"

"No secrets that I know," Dominic said. "They were college kids. Everybody thought they got drunk and died."

Turner said, "Scarth was seen away from the waterfront after he'd been in the bar."

"He couldn't have just walked back?" Pierre asked.

"His car was not at the waterfront. He'd been driving that night." Turner paused and then said, "This next question is a little delicate." He looked from the men to Mrs. Talucci.

She said, "Precisely what do you think is too delicate for my ears?"

Turner's face got red. "We were told about a local porno-graphic organization."

Mrs. Talucci smiled. "I don't indulge myself, but I don't see why others shouldn't."

Dominic said, "I'm an old man and an old-fashioned man. I'm not sure we should discuss such things in front of—"

Mrs. Talucci said, "Oh, Dominic, sit on it and rotate. If we talk about pornography, what do you think is going to happen? I don't usually go shrieking about the countryside in rank terror if I acknowledge human anatomy."

"I do, sometimes," Dominic said.

"Now that," said Mrs. Talucci, "is actually information I do not want."

Pierre said, "Broder is the guy. As far as I know, it's fairly harmless. The young men, straight or gay, in this town have very few ways to make money. With the mill gone, they'll have even less. They'll leave. Most do nowadays."

Dominic said, "Do you think they were killed over pornography?"

Turner said, "Right now I'm mostly gathering information. I'll follow it where it leads."

Dominic looked at his watch. "It is time for my daily exercise." He looked at Turner. "Would you help me, young man? I must strictly stay off my feet except, of course, when I am to be taking my daily walk. I will need to lean against you."

Turner readily agreed. When Dominic rose to his feet, the dogs stood also. Mrs. Talucci and Pierre accompanied them. The four of them took a path into the woods. Dominic's arm clutched Turner's, and the older man leaned against him quite often. The dogs followed a few feet behind. Turner saw no obvious indications of commands being given to the pets. Pierre had Mrs. Talucci's arm. Turner thought it was more a gallant gesture than needed, although Pierre was nearly twenty years Mrs. Talucci's junior. It would not do for Mrs. Talucci, who was in her nineties, to take a fall on the forest path, no matter how well tended it looked to Turner. After a few minutes, the other two got ahead.

Dominic paused at a slight promontory, shaded his eyes, and looked out over the vast expanse of woods and lake. "So beautiful, so peaceful here."

Turner agreed. He felt a slight pressure on his arm. They

resumed their hesitant stroll up the hill. Dominic asked, "How is Kevin Yost?"

"He's a fabulous guide. He's a great kid. He's going to be a good man."

"He comes here now and then," Dominic said.

"He knows where this place is?" Turner asked. "Whenever we've speculated about where Mrs. Talucci goes, he's never said a word."

Dominic's eyes twinkled. "His grandfather brought him here years ago. I suspect his grandfather may have been a sister. Married to a woman, of course. His grandfather was a good and kind man. He helped us build this place. He helped us keep our secrets. Kevin comes here often. He says that sometimes he just has to get away."

"Has he told you he's gay?" Turner asked.

"No. I would never ask. He has also never asked us. He comes here on his own. He helps out. Sometimes he fishes. He even teachers Pierre a few things, and Pierre is a very good fisherman. Kevin refuses to accept payment. Many times he just sits on the dock and reads a book. He's a good boy. I'm glad he's your guide. Kevin never says much of anything. He talks about you once in a great while. He admires the kind of father you are, the kind of gay man you are, and the way you're calm and assured."

Turner blushed. "I do the best I can with my boys."

"I wish he could talk to you. I think it would make a difference." He sighed. "Waiting for an adolescent to realize it is okay to talk to you can be a strain." He smiled. "Rose talks about you, too." Turner had never addressed Mrs. Talucci by her first name. It was an odd but pleasant note. "She says you're a good man and a great father."

"I'll have to thank her for the compliment."

"She tells me about the old neighborhood. I barely remember it anymore. I'm glad she has you as a neighbor. At least you don't try to convince her to stop taking these absurd vacations." Mrs. Talucci was notorious for finding obscure vacations for the over-fifty set and then going to those places.

"She hasn't been hurt yet," Turner said.

Dominic laughed. "Not that she's told you about. That Mongolian trip was more for her than she'll ever admit to anyone except me. She is my favorite sister."

Turner said, "Your boat driver is armed."

"All the young men who work here are highly trained experts in firearms and martial arts. Along with having taut butts and tight muscles, the training is part of the job description. We aren't stupid. This might be so-called liberal Canada, but rural anywhere requires gay people to be cautious. We are well defended."

They came to a headland with well-cushioned outdoor furniture scattered under a magnificent spreading oak that might have been alive when Columbus first sailed. "Ah," Dominic said, "half done. This exercise crap is for the birds." He lowered himself into a chair. The dogs sat at his feet.

Mrs. Talucci and Pierre were already seated. For a while they listened to the birds, and the insects, and the breeze while they looked out on the magnificent view.

After pleasant minutes of delicious silence, Dominic said, "You should see this place in the middle of a storm."

"It's wet and dangerous," Pierre said.

"And it's beautiful," Dominic said. "I fell in love with this view and our place is the nearest land to it that's good for building on. We own this, if you can be said to own something that got this way all by itself." He sighed. "I want to be buried up here."

Mrs. Talucci patted his hand.

Dominic said, "There is a lot of prejudice in these towns. That sabotage may not stop. It isn't just Scarth. Zoll has more than a few fascist bones in his body."

"We've rented from him since I was a kid."

"I'm sorry," Dominic said.

"Should we rent from someone else?" Turner asked.

Pierre added, "You might consider it. It might be more than teenagers who tried to do you harm. You need to be careful. We always are. It's a sacrifice we make to live here as we wish. We can afford it."

"I'll be careful," Turner said.

Dominic added, "They'd be just as likely to go after your sons or your lover or your friends. Prejudice can come out at funny times. The wrong moment in the wrong place and we could have a Matthew Shepard–type tragedy."

"I knew that," Turner said, "but I never expected it here." He almost smiled to himself. Fenwick would have piped in with the old Monty Python line, "Nobody expects the Spanish Inquisition." He said, "I'll be extra careful. I'd rather not stop coming up here."

Pierre said, "I don't think you have to go that far. And I imagine you're always careful. Isn't it a second sense we all have?"

"Every gay person I know does it automatically," Turner said. "I'm curious, though: How come you're still here?"

Dominic said, "The view. Privacy. We've got more money than we can give away. Say what they like about the Krohn family, they were good to me."

Pierre said, "To us."

Dominic nodded. "Yes. We're not on anyone's radar. We've got wonderfully well-armed guards, well-trained attack dogs, and a marvelously up-to-date security system."

They sat for a while longer then made the slow journey back to the veranda. Paul thanked them profusely. He left Pierre and Dominic poring over another selection from the confection cart. He and Mrs. Talucci walked arm in arm down to the boat. About a quarter of the way to the pier, Turner heard Dominic say, "He's got a nice ass."

Pierre giggled and said, "Hush, he's your sister's friend."

Mrs. Talucci smiled. "That's what you get for having a great butt."

"I'm tough," Turner said. "I can handle it."

Phil was at the wheel of the boat. Mrs. Talucci hugged Turner. She said, "You can contact the Krohns as soon as you get back. Dominic will be faithful about making the contact. I hope you get this settled. As long as Buck Fenwick is around, I'm not too worried. Take care. Give my love to the boys." She hugged him again.

Paul climbed in the boat. As they pulled away, he waved good-bye.

30

It was just after six when Paul got back. Ben and Madge were waiting for him at the end of the dock. Ben said, "They came for Ian."

"What happened?"

Madge said, "That Schreppel guy showed up with official-looking people and papers. He said they had to question Ian. Ian protested and ranted, and they got a little rough with him. Buck went with him to the police station."

"Did they arrest him?" Turner asked.

"Nobody used those words," Madge said. "The Ontario Provincial Police officer, Bednars, was among them. She kept asking Schreppel questions. He looked pretty angry. She said they had Billy Morningsky in custody. She was pretty upset as well."

"Morningsky predicted he'd be arrested."

Ben said, "You should probably get down to the police station. The boys are helping with dinner. We'll be fine."

Turner checked on Brian and Jeff; then hopped in the SUV and took off for downtown Cathura.

At the station he found Fenwick, who said, "They won't tell me a thing."

A clerk, who seemed unusually distant, refused to answer their questions. They would have to talk to the chief. Turner and Fenwick were made to wait forty-five minutes to see Schreppel.

When the young cop finally ushered them into Schreppel's office, the chief did not rise to greet them. He squirmed in his chair as if he desperately needed surgery for his hemorrhoids.

Turner said, "I'd like to see my friend."

"I'd like to talk to all of you."

"About what?" Fenwick asked.

"What you've been doing around town."

Fenwick said, "Why would that be any of your business?"

Schreppel leaned over his desk. He planted his elbows on the top, clasped his hands together, then released both index fingers to point at Fenwick. "You may put up with that smart-ass crap in Chicago, but I don't. We are not in your jurisdiction. You are in mine."

"Did they repeal all the laws in Canada?" Fenwick asked. "Are you absolute dictator of the North Woods? I haven't committed a crime. Neither have my friends."

Turner said, "We've been trying to gather information. You have two homicides on your hands. We're concerned about what is happening to our friend."

Schreppel puffed out a large breath. "I'm concerned because you're friends of a suspect in a murder case. I'm wondering about your involvement."

"How is he a murder suspect?"

"I don't have to give that out."

"We'd like to see him," Turner said.

"I need answers to questions," Schreppel said.

"You've arrested Billy Morningsky," Fenwick said.

"We have not arrested him. I'm going to start hearing those goddamn accusations that I'm a racist, that the cops are racist, that we won't do anything about the racism in the police department. I am not a racist. You do anything but wipe the butt of one of these First Nations kids, and you're a racist."

"Is Ian under arrest?" Turner asked.

"Where were you from eight PM to midnight Monday?" Schreppel asked.

"Are we under arrest?" Turner asked.

"You're under suspicion."

"We barely knew the people who are dead."

"Suspicious things have been happening around you."

"The victim is guilty?" Fenwick asked.

"You had that alleged break-in—"

"Alleged?" Fenwick loaded the word with as much sneer and contempt as he could.

"We have only your word that it happened. And not really your word. It is only your friend Ian's word. He was the first one on the scene."

"He lives there," Fenwick said.

"You didn't call us about the so-called threats from the local young men outside the Naked Moose the other night."

Fenwick said, "We called about the attack on the lake."

"For which there is no proof."

"We're all lying?" Fenwick asked. "Why?"

"Murder's been done, maybe you're trying to cover up. Maybe a lot of things."

The detectives glared at him.

Bednars entered. She leaned against the door and smiled at Turner and Fenwick. "Did you get any information?"

Turner said, "It seemed kind of mixed bag with a strong lean toward Scarth as a mean-spirited bully. There is a small faction that liked him. His coach, some of his buddies, a few others."

"You've been busy."

Turner said, "We've talked to a lot of people, and we have no notion of who did it. Do you?"

Schreppel said, "I do. Billy Morningsky or your friend or both."

Turner said, "Have you charged them with murder? Are you saying there's a conspiracy? They didn't know each other."

"We had complaints about Mr. Hume."

"From whom?"

"I'm not answering your questions."

Bednars said, "Let these guys see them."

"You in charge now?"

"You going to be a bigger asshole than usual?"

Schreppel glared for a moment then slapped his hand down on the desk. "You want to see the nosy reporter? Go ahead. I don't care."

"How about Billy Morningsky?"

"The kid's got a lawyer coming. You'll have to wait on that."

A clean-shaven young cop escorted Turner and Fenwick to a plain cell in a reasonably clean jail.

Bednars accompanied them down the hall. She said, "Don't count too much on my beneficence. Schreppel is an asshole, but I've got to work with him."

"What is his problem?" Fenwick asked.

"The town can't afford the OPP contingent and the local police. They're threatening cutbacks. He sees us as rivals. He wants to make sure the contract with the OPP is canceled. Provincial funding was changed a few years ago. They no longer get as much money as they once did. The town has cut back on everything else. The mill is gone. The population is declining, but taxes are going up. The smallest OPP detachment allowed is eight. That costs money. That and he's a racist pig and an asshole."

"A tough combination to fight against," Fenwick said.

"Tougher than it should be in this day and age," Bednars said.

"Why did they bring Ian in for questioning?" Turner asked.

"They found his traveler's checks at the murder scene."

"Where exactly?" Turner asked.

"Half in and half out of Evon's front pocket."

"So Evon could have had them on her," Turner said.

"Or the killer could have put them there."

"Obviously someone stole them from our houseboat the night of the original break-in. Ian reported them missing at the time."

Bednars said, "I think your friend is going to be released soon, but it's the biggest anomaly we've had so far."

Fenwick asked, "How come you've taken in Billy Morningsky?"

Bednars said, "Schreppel believes in the round-up-the-usual-suspects method of police detection. We'll wait until his lawyer gets here. I'll bring you to your friend."

Ian was in a holding room with Howard Coates and a

woman who was introduced as Susan Rogers, a lawyer. Rogers said, "Do you wish to permit these two here during our discussion?"

"Yeah," Ian said.

"You okay?" Turner asked.

Ian said, "Good enough for now. The cops are morons."

Turner said, "Your traveler's checks were at the murder scene."

"I told them they were missing our first night here," Ian said. "I hid them in my toilet kit with my extra cash. I've told them that seventeen times."

"They don't believe you."

"That's not my problem."

"Actually, it is," Turner said.

Turner didn't add that it would have been easier just to use an ATM card. Ian didn't have one. He claimed he wasn't about to pay a fee to get his own money out of a bank. Turner had mentioned that they charged a fee for traveler's checks. Ian had ignored him.

Rogers said, "I'll have him out soon."

Ian said, "I'm in good hands."

Turner and Fenwick left.

In the SUV Fenwick said, "I think he'll be okay."

"I sure hope so."

"Who do we go talk to next?" Fenwick asked.

"If we can get in to talk to Scarth's mother and father, it would help. Dominic said he would make some calls. Trent said he would help out as well."

"Let's call."

Beth Krohn did not want to meet them at her home. She set up a meeting at Howard Coates's bar.

31

Beth Krohn wore sunglasses as she sat in the darkest corner of the Dangling Fisherman café on the waterfront. Phil, the driver of Mrs. Talucci's powerboat, sat next to her. He nodded to Paul, stood up, and said, "I'll be here when you're done."

Beth Krohn took off her sunglasses. She said, "Dominic Antonetti phoned me. He said you were a good person. Dominic has been my friend since before I married my husband. Trent spoke well of you. I don't see enough of Trent."

Turner said, "I'm sorry for your loss."

She wiped at a tear. "My husband is taking care of all the arrangements. He won't talk to me. It's as if he alone is allowed to grieve for my son."

"He sounds like a tough man," Turner said.

"I should have divorced him years ago."

"Why didn't you?" Turner asked.

"I don't know. Habit? He left me alone? We haven't slept

in the same room in years. Scarth wanted us to get a divorce. He begged me to do it. We fought about that."

"We were told he'd inherit a lot of money if you did."

"That stupid trust fund his grandfather set up. That family had a lot of sick men in it. Blake Krohn hated me. My husband wouldn't stand up to him. I was stuck. I doubt if any of the trust is left. I suspect my husband has spent it all."

"Can he do that without your permission?" Turner asked.

"He does everything without my permission. I have no job and I have no skills. Where would I go? What would I do? I'm not going to live in these woods by myself." She shivered. "My husband may have had hopes for Scarth and all that sports nonsense, but Scarth always promised me that when he started getting a professional hockey player's salary, he would take care of me. Alas! He was a good boy. You won't get me to say something bad about Scarth. I know people have said awful things about him his whole life. They aren't true."

Oh, my dear lady, Turner thought, they were probably all true. You're the one who didn't see them. Turner had listened to parents of killers for years. It was always society, always violent video games, always evil friends. It was never their kid's fault. It was never their poor parenting skills. It was always, always somebody else's fault.

"Scarth wanted you to get a a divorce?"

"Scarth was always urging me to get one. He'd pester me about it every holiday and birthday. He was after me for years. I know he'd get more money, but I just don't know what I'd do."

"Wouldn't you get a fantastic settlement in a divorce?" Fenwick asked.

"I signed a prenuptial agreement. I was a fool." She shook

her head. "It's all quite useless. Scarth was a fine boy. We brought him up right. We taught him to respect others and always go out of his way to help other people. He would never hurt a fly."

Turner said, "I wish there was something I could do to help. If I lost one of my children, I'd never get over it."

Beth Krohn whispered, "This will hurt for the rest of my life."

She pulled a tissue out of her purse and wiped at her tears. "My boy was not bad. When he misbehaved in school, it was the teachers' fault. He was bored. They never kept him interested. He was so bright as a little boy. They always wanted me to put him on medicine. I wasn't going to drug up my son to get him to obey their silly rules or to get him to do those stupid homework assignments."

Turner knew exactly where the school and social problem lay. Toxic parents. Turner wasn't about to lead a crusade saying who could be parents or not, but the right wing desperately wanted to blame everything that they thought was wrong with society on video games or the alignment of the stars or some angry deity that you'd pissed off, rather than starting at where the blame squarely belonged: the parents. It was the philosophy that said we're all good people, and it's the world that is evil and it is corrupting our children. It was never their poor pathetic selves with nonsensical beliefs in beings of vast superiority who control our lives or weird educational philosophies that all began and ended with "my kid is perfect, and I'm right, and even more perfect as a parent." And Scarth Krohn, in his early twenties, had been plenty old enough to begin taking responsibility for his own decisions, for his own mistakes. Turner kept all of this to himself. Why had he wanted to talk to her? Because her son was dead and you always talked to the family because in far more cases than anyone would care to admit, it was a family member who did the killing.

"We were told he was almost expelled from fifth grade."

"That's not true. Scarth was more active than most children. They never learned to adapt to his modalities of learning."

Turner thought, another crackpot educational theory used by some parents and educators to justify their own incompetence. Ian had said that Mrs. Krohn was a whack job, but she didn't seem further out of the norm than most clueless parents.

Mrs. Krohn said, "The problems seemed to disappear in high school. His coach said he was a good boy, just high-spirited. He won every trophy the school offered in any sport he tried."

Turner said, "We've talked to some people who are pretty angry at him."

"That's mostly jealousy of his father. They're still angry about that stupid paper mill closing. He had nothing to do with it. He sold the paper mill long before it closed. Those union thugs always had it in for my husband. Maybe they'd try to get back at him through his son. I hope someone's investigating that."

"Did you know Evon Gasple?" Turner asked.

"Scarth was always trying to help that girl. He had such a big heart. We knew she was from the poor side of town. He took pity on her. See. There. He was trying to help people. He gave her flowers and took her on dates."

Fenwick said, "We heard he was also dating Mrs. Gasple."

Mrs. Krohn's eyes flashed. She sat up straighter. "That woman corrupted my son. She came to me, you know." She shivered. "She tried to ruin my son."

"How was that?" Fenwick asked.

"She demanded money from me. From me!" Mrs. Krohn lowered her voice. "She claimed her daughter had to have an abortion. How sick. And that my son was the father. My son wouldn't do that. He was a good boy. I thought that woman was going to do something violent. Fortunately, we were in my home. I had the housekeeper show her the door. How dare she? She would say anything to sully his reputation."

Turner said, "We saw something the other night outside the Naked Moose restaurant."

She raised an eyebrow.

Turner continued, "Scarth and Evon seemed to be leading a group that was pestering some First Nations youngsters the other evening."

"I'm sure that wasn't true."

"I was there. I saw exactly what they did."

"I'm sure you're mistaken. Scarth would never do that."

Turner knew he wasn't mistaken, but it would be an even bigger mistake to try to get a reality she didn't want to believe through to this woman. He wasn't confident reality and Mrs. Krohn were very good friends.

Fenwick asked, "Why did you want to meet here instead of your home?"

"I'm not sure I'm ever going back there. I may just drive off to Vancouver. I'd go farther if there wasn't an ocean in the way. I never want to see that man again. You can go see him. I'm sure you're going to anyway. Dominic talked to him. It'll be a waste of time, but you might as well."

◣ 32 ◢

Turner and Fenwick approached the Krohn mansion. It looked like someone had taken the starship *Enterprise,* twisted it into several new configurations, and then plunked it in the middle of the forest. It was gleaming steel and aluminum with lots of saucer-shaped turrets and then phallic-shaped wings jutting at four different angles. Turner could imagine being beamed up into various parts of the house. They were met by a butler at the door. He said they were expected.

The interior was stark, the furniture mostly nonexistent. The few pieces in the hall were aluminum and leather chairs. Turner thought reclining on a cement slab might be more comfortable. They were led down several long corridors to a sitting room that was nearly as large as the entire ground floor of Turner's house. A solid concrete mass surrounded the low fireplace. Dark red coals spread over a bed of white provided a constantly even glow. The walls and furniture were oyster white. The chairs were the thick cushiony kind but with no arms. You never had any place to rest your elbows, a book, a television remote. Metallic coffee and end tables were bare of any ornament. Track lighting along the ceiling beamed conical bits of coldness from gray-plastic ovals at random intervals.

Mr. Krohn remained seated in his chair. He shook their hands. "My family and I owe Dominic Antonetti a great deal. That is the only reason I'm speaking with you."

Turner said, "We're sorry for your loss."

Krohn said, "Scarth was a good son."

Turner said, "We're hoping our efforts supplement the work of the local police."

"If you can help find who did this." He choked up for several moments, then said, "Dominic vouched for you. I hope you can help."

"Why would someone want to hurt Scarth?" Fenwick asked.

"People in this town hate me. They blame me for their own economic poor planning, and they don't have the courage to face me. You know how cowards are. They take it out on the most vulnerable. Those union people hate me. The do-gooders in town think I'm evil incarnate. They wanted the mill to stop polluting. That problem is solved. It's closed. Did that satisfy them? Of course not. Once the closing was announced, they joined the bandwagon of job-saving extremists. I work hard and make a profit. They can work just as hard and make money."

Fenwick said, "My guess is you started out with a bit more cash on hand than the average person in Cathura."

"I work hard."

254

Fenwick said, "I'm sure they do, too."

"I've heard that Coates asshole thinks Scarth's death is mixed up with those other six who drowned. That's nonsense. The others were accidents or maybe suicides. Scarth was murdered."

"You're convinced of that?"

"Yes. Scarth was an excellent swimmer. He could hold his liquor. He was seen around town after leaving the bar."

Fenwick said, "For someone to drown him, they'd have to be bigger and stronger."

"Or," Krohn said, "it could have been more than one. Maybe a group. Those union thugs threatened me and my family when this all started. My son didn't throw himself in the lake and drown. Somebody pushed him and held him under."

Fenwick said, "There were signs of violence on the body."

"The ME said he got caught in a propeller. No, my boy did not just fall off a pier."

Turner said, "We're sorry to bother you at such a moment, but if it was murder, we have to know who your son's enemies were."

Mr. Krohn said, "There are a few who openly hated Scarth. Oliver McBride, the kid who brought the gun to school to try and shoot him. There's that skinny First Nations kid, Billy Morningsky. Another is Ralph Bowers, who is out of control. That boy should be locked up. He is dangerous. He let his temper out on my boy. Those school people wouldn't do anything about it."

"How about his brother?" Fenwick said.

"Trent's a good boy."

Turner asked, "Could he have been jealous of Scarth?

Angry with him or you or his mother, maybe trying to get back at you?"

"For what? Trent has a good life. He's into that ecology, living-off-nature crap at the moment. He prefers the woods to a warm, soft bed. All kids go through that."

"Scarth didn't pick on him?"

"Scarth was three years older. He barely had time for his brother with all the activities he was in from a very early age."

Turner asked, "Could one of his friends have turned on him?"

"I don't know them that well."

"How about Evon Gasple?" Turner asked.

"She seemed nice enough. She went to his games and cheered for him."

Fenwick said, "We got the impression it was kind of an up-and-down relationship."

"What boy doesn't try and find himself and try to date all kinds of girls? Scarth was a healthy young man."

Turner said, "I'm not clear on their relationship. We heard she got an abortion, and we were told Scarth was the father."

"Impossible. I talked with Scarth in sixth grade. I told him everything. I stressed how important it was for him to use condoms. He told me the kid wasn't his."

"Did they do a DNA test?" Turner asked.

"Not that I know of."

Fenwick said, "It's a shame that one instant ruined his career."

"I hadn't given up yet. We were going to see more doctors in Toronto this winter. We had appointments. There were possibilities the leg could be rehabilitated, maybe operated on. He had so much ability. He had so much going for him." The man's tears welled up.

Turner did feel sorry for him. He'd lost his son. He couldn't imagine losing one of his.

Turner said, "We had some problems with sabotage on our boat. We were attacked by some kids in a charcoal gray cigarette boat. You have one of those."

"There are many of those on the lake. It could have been anyone."

Fenwick said, "We talked to Beverly Fleming."

"That bitch," Krohn said. "We tried to get him out of her class. The administrators insisted she was the only one who could handle him. Kids would make up stories about Scarth, and those fascists at the school believed the stories. Those people had it in for Scarth. Oh, sure, there were a few good teachers. Most were assholes. We thought of taking him out of that school, but it was hopeless. Scarth would have had to live in Toronto if he wanted a good enough hockey program. Coach Sterling was a good man. He knew his hockey. That Fleming woman started it. She ruined Scarth's reputation throughout all his school years. She spent years getting revenge on my kid. She made it a point to bad-mouth my boy to each of Scarth's teachers."

Neither Mr. Krohn nor his wife earlier seemed to be connecting to reality. Not a good sign, Turner thought.

Turner said, "We heard there were some oddities about his grandfather's will."

"My father was a bit eccentric."

Turner asked, "Were you and your wife planning on getting a divorce?"

"You're talking about that bullshit part of the will and us controlling his trust. My wife and I both had our son's best interests at heart. He trusted us."

Fenwick said, "I had a little bit of a different impression from Mrs. Krohn."

"I'm sure she's distraught. Probably she should be home where she wouldn't be distracted. When we got the news, I didn't think she'd ever calm down."

Fenwick said, "We were told Scarth pestered both of you to get a divorce."

"He never said such a thing to me."

Turner had heard a lot of the people he interviewed tell lies. Usually he could tell. He suspected a lie, but Krohn's eyes didn't waver. Maybe he was very good at it.

Fenwick said, "Did Scarth keep stuff here?"

"We kept his room as he left it. Once in a while he stayed here."

"Could we see it?" Turner asked.

Krohn hesitated.

Turner said, "It might give us some kind of clue as to who would hurt him."

Krohn still seemed reluctant, but they got a brief nod of acquiescence. He took them up a curving staircase.

Scarth's room was almost as stark as the rest of the house. Mr. Krohn stayed in the doorway. Fenwick asked, "Where was he living when he died?"

"In a trailer just outside of town. He was determined to earn money on his own. I taught him to be self-reliant."

Turner would rather the man had left them alone in the room, but Mr. Krohn remained rooted at the threshold. The bedroom was as big as the entire upstairs of Turner's house.

A huge trophy case covered one wall. Turner inspected a few of them. Most Valuable Player hockey trophies predominated. There was a scattering of others. The bed had military corners at the foot. Probably an efficient maid. There were no posters on the walls or books on any shelves. The desk was metallic gray. Turner opened the top middle drawer. When it was out as far as it would go, he felt under the top. He pulled out a plain white envelope. It was stuffed with American cash, nearly twenty thousand dollars in thousand-dollar denominations.

Fenwick turned to Krohn. "Your boy get a big allowance?"

Mr. Krohn walked over. "What have you found?"

Turner showed him.

"I have no idea where that came from," Krohn said.

"How would he have access to that kind of money?" Turner asked. Turner's first thought was illegal drugs. It was certainly a logical possibility.

"I don't know. His mother might have been supplying him."

"This much money?" Fenwick asked.

"I don't know. I just don't." Krohn sat his butt on the bed.

The detectives began examining the walk-in closet. Scarth had flannel shirts, T-shirts, and hockey jerseys. He had so many of them that Turner thought Scarth might have had one from every team in the NHL. He had eight pairs of hockey skates on the floor of the closet. They were all different. In the skate farthest to the left, he found a bag full of marijuana. The farthest one on the right had a freezer bag filled with white powder.

Turner brought them out. He showed them to Mr. Krohn. The man reached for them, and Turner gave them to him.

"What does this mean?" Krohn asked.

"Your son had a serious habit or he was dealing drugs or since he moved out, you or your wife have used this for your stash."

"Neither my wife nor I do drugs."

"Then it was your son," Fenwick said.

"Maybe his friends left them here."

"How would they do that without him knowing?" Fenwick asked. "Or you seeing them come into the house?"

"I don't know. Are you going to turn this over to the police?"

"No," Turner said. "We're not official police here. We don't want to bring trouble to your son. He's dead. I'd suggest you get rid of that so there are no accidents. The police may want to search the house."

"Not without my permission. I still have some say in this town."

33

They returned to the houseboats. Jeff and Ben were in a row-boat about a hundred yards out on the lake. Poles extended from the sides of the boat. Brian was nowhere to be seen. Madge told him he was fishing with the Fenwick girls.

Turner and Fenwick chatted on the top deck. They snacked on leftover Timbits.

A gray Volvo pulled up to the parking lot. Ian and Howard Coates emerged. They hustled to the houseboat. Ian grabbed a Timbit, sat down, and declared, "I was lost but now I'm found. I was delivered from evil by a kindly Canadian lawyer."

Coates said, "There was no case against Ian. Schreppel is a jerk, but he can't use Nazi tactics. At least not all the time. We also have news."

Ian said, "I don't like Canadian jails. I don't like Canadian chiefs of police. I don't like the lack of logic and sense. Vincent Schreppel is a first-degree moron."

"Tell us how you really feel," Fenwick said. "Try not to hold back."

"Although," Ian added, "the uniforms the police and guards wore were pretty natty."

Turner said, "Good to know you have your priorities straight."

Ian announced, "They officially arrested Billy Morningsky."

"For killing Scarth Krohn?" Turner asked.

"For killing all of them. They claim he killed Scarth, the girlfriend, and all the college kids who drowned."

Fenwick said, "That's nuts. Saying all those were murders and he did them all is a huge stretch."

Turner said, "How do they think he committed them?"

"They say he's got a motive," Ian said. "They say he hated Scarth Krohn."

"I'm lost," Fenwick said. "How does that translate into the other dead drowned kids?"

"They say he hated all white people and was on a crusade to exterminate them."

Turner said, "He's got to have alibis for some of the times of the murders."

"You'd think," Fenwick said.

"I'm just telling you what I heard," Ian said.

Coates said, "I have really hot news. I just found this out. It's gossip that I got about fifth hand."

Ian said, "That's almost better than truth."

Fenwick said, "So said the reporter famed for accuracy."

"No, listen," Coates said, "did you know Evon had an abortion?"

Turner said, "Mrs. Krohn said Evon's mother came to try and get money out of her for an abortion."

"No," Coates said, "the way I heard it is that Mrs. Gasple is the one who got the abortion, not her daughter."

Fenwick said, "Who was the father?"

"Scarth Krohn."

"I'm finding this hard to believe," Turner said. "He got both of them pregnant? And they both got abortions?"

"That's what I heard."

"Who told you this?" Fenwick asked.

"Christine Jenkins got it out of Marilyn Gwinn after you talked with us the other morning. Gwinn was told by Matalina McMahon."

"Evon's former best friend," Fenwick said. "We asked her if Scarth had gotten Mrs. Gasple pregnant and she said no."

"You were strangers," Coates said.

Madge said, "Maybe she trusted someone more her own age."

"He was boffing both of them," Ian said. "I thought I was a total slut but this kid could probably give me a run for my money."

"Does this information get us anywhere?" Turner asked.

Fenwick said, "I'm not sure it gives us more motives for murder. It certainly gives us no forensic proofs or eye-witness accounts."

Turner said, "We should try to talk to Morningsky and the cops."

Fenwick said, "We're in this deep already. We might as well get in deeper. Everybody's going to be uncooperative."

"Says sage predictor of the future," Ian said.

Turner told them about their recent interviews.

"Drugs?" Ian mused. "Got to be a connection. Maybe he sold drugs to those six kids. That would make sense. Or maybe they didn't pay their drug debts. That would be a good way to show any others that they better pay."

Turner said, "Maybe we can get some information from Bednars. We'll see if the autopsies said anything about drugs being found in their systems."

"Maybe they weren't looking," Ian said.

"We'll check it out," Turner said. "We should try to go to the jail to talk to Billy Morningsky."

Ian made to leave with them. "I'm going with," Ian said.

Turner held his gaze.

Ian said, "I'm in this."

"You'll get them more annoyed," Turner said. "Who got called in today for questioning? Who just got back?"

"They just wanted to pester me."

"I remember they did a pretty good job of it. You'll simply antagonize them."

"Maybe I like antagonizing them. Maybe they need antagonizing."

Fenwick said, "Maybe you should blow it out your ass."

Ian glowered.

Fenwick added, "I mean that in the best possible way."

Turner said, "No, Ian, sorry."

Ian gave it up. "I can mosey around town and see if I hear anything."

Turner said, "Mosey carefully."

The two detectives drove into town to the police station. They asked if they could visit Billy Morningsky.

Schreppel said, "I don't care who he talks to. He did it. He threw his lawyer out. He stopped talking to anyone. He's hopeless."

Fenwick said, "You wouldn't care to share your evidence with us? You know, as a professional courtesy."

"No. I don't like you."

Schreppel assigned someone to escort them to the prisoner.

To get to the jail they had to pass through the Ontario Provincial Police side of the building. Mavis Bednars saw them and hurried over. She said, "Are you going to visit him?"

"Yeah," Turner said.

"Tell him to get an attorney. He needs one."

"Do they have proof?" Turner asked.

"They've got his fingerprints inside Scarth's daddy's car. That's the car Scarth was using that night. It's an Austin Healy Sprite made back in the fifties. He drove it around town sometimes as if it was his own, trying to impress people."

"Did Morningsky say how his fingerprints got inside the car?" Fenwick asked.

Bednars said, "Well, that's the question. If there's an innocent explanation, Billy Morningsky is not giving it. He won't say anything to anybody." She glanced around then leaned forward and whispered, "Come see me when you're done."

34

Billy Morningsky was in a cell by himself. He was lying on a bare mattress. He had his hands behind his head. He was staring at the ceiling. He looked at the two detectives and got to his feet. He spoke very quietly. "I knew they were going to blame me."

"Why won't you talk to a lawyer?" Turner asked.

"What's the use? I'm probably never getting out of here. They keep asking where I was at the time of Scarth's and Evon's murders. I was home. I have no witnesses. How often can I say I was asleep? They hit at me about how much everybody knew we fought. That isn't news." He sighed. "Unfortunately, I did threaten him last Canada Day at the fireworks. Half the town saw us. Not much I can do but wait."

"What happened at the fireworks?" Turner asked.

"It was stupid. Their usual gang was down by the lakeside. We were in line for cotton candy. Then it was the same old crap: shoves, slurs, fists. Who started it?" He shrugged.

"It started when Columbus showed up on an island five hundred years ago, and it hasn't stopped yet.

"They kept Scarth and me apart, but barely. A couple of adults held us back. We were screaming. That's when I made the threats."

"What did you say?"

He shut his eyes. "That if I ever got the chance I'd kill him." He looked at the two detectives. "Not so good, huh?"

"Not so good," Fenwick agreed.

Turner said, "Why not talk to the lawyer?"

"I think I want to just sit here for a while."

"After that?" Turner asked.

"I guess."

"Did they tell you about any specific evidence they might have?"

"My fingerprints are in Scarth's car. I was buying drugs from Scarth that night. I'm not admitting I was doing drugs. My family would kill me, and I'd still go to jail. I didn't kill him, but I did commit a crime."

Fenwick said, "It wouldn't hurt to talk to a lawyer."

"Maybe soon. I appreciate you coming by."

"Why did you talk to us?"

"You're leaving. Trust is one thing. Knowing you'll be gone helps that."

Turner smiled and said, "We'll do what we can."

"Thanks." He gazed into each of their eyes for a moment then lowered his head. "Thanks," he murmured again. They left.

When Turner and Fenwick got to the hall outside Bednars's office, she spotted them and hurried over. "We need to get out of here," she said.

She followed them to their SUV. She hopped in back. "Drive down to the park."

Once again they were having a discussion at the fringe of the city park.

Turner said, "Morningsky didn't do it."

"I know that. Hell, I bet even Schreppel knows that." She had blond hair pulled back in a ponytail. She wore light makeup and small diamond studs in each ear. She wore a summer business suit as opposed to a uniform.

Turner asked, "Were the other six murders?"

"No, genuine accidents. We really did find Morningsky's fingerprints in the car. He won't tell us how they got there."

Turner and Fenwick didn't break confidence.

"What did the autopsies show on Scarth and Evon?" Fenwick asked.

"Scarth definitely drowned. Evon was beaten to death. It had to be after ten because that's when Scarth was last seen."

"She couldn't have been killed much earlier?"

"It's hard to fix the time of death exactly, but certainly the beating happened most likely between ten and twelve that night. She didn't die right away. She suffered. Her neck was broken, but she was conscious. She probably was conscious when animals started snacking on her."

Fenwick said, "Sometimes evil people get what's coming to them."

Bednars replied, "I didn't know her. I moved here when I got this job. I heard she was an awful person, but does anyone deserve that?"

Fenwick said, "Everybody says the people who do terrible things eventually get what is coming to them. That's a crock of wishful thinking. Sometimes the bad live on. Sometimes they die. Just like the good guys. Sometimes it's not clear how good or bad someone was. Evon was awful. I know nothing good about her. Maybe there was something. Maybe what I said was too harsh, but you know, that's what people feel. Satisfied when something bad happens to someone truly rotten. And that's how I feel."

Bednars said, "You are a unique man."

Turner said, "We've been meaning to talk to him about that."

Fenwick said, "Screw it. What else can you tell us?"

"Scarth probably died closer to eleven. It would take that long for the body to drift to your dock."

Turner said, "It's hard to imagine murder was going on that close to us."

Bednars said, "It is frightening."

"We examined his room at home."

"I've told Schreppel he should search the house and Scarth's trailer. He won't do it. J. T. Krohn is calling the shots there."

"You can't do it on your own?" Fenwick asked.

"The jurisdiction thing around here can be delicate. We want the OPP contract renewed. We depend on goodwill. No contract, no jobs. I can only push him so far. Did you find anything interesting?"

"He was a drug connection." They told her what they'd found out about Evon as a major dealer in the local drug market and the role Scarth and his friends played in it.

"Figures," Bednars said. "Wait a sec. That's what Morningsky was doing. Buying drugs. Got to be. That's why he won't talk. And Schreppel would lock him up for as long as he could no matter how minor the charge. No wonder the kid is scared."

Neither Turner nor Fenwick disputed her insight.

"Did they have drugs in their systems?" Fenwick asked.

"The test results aren't back yet."

Turner said, "Do you care if we check out his trailer?"

"If you find anything interesting, let me know." She gave Turner her card, then gave them directions to Scarth's trailer. She said, "You don't have a key."

Fenwick said, "We'll just look around."

Bednars smiled. "Good luck."

35

They found Scarth's trailer deep in the woods. Driving in, they hadn't seen another sign of human habitation for miles. They got out of their SUV. The trailer might have been new fifty years ago. The sides were rusted and shabby. Bits of the roof were warping away from the walls. It looked like the next winter storm might cause it to revert back to metallic and plastic kindling. They found no crime scene tape.

"You'd think he could have afforded a nicer place," Fenwick said.

"Maybe he needed that money from the trust more than anyone knew. Drug deals gone bad? Desperate for cash. Maybe that's why he did the porn."

Turner listened to the whine of insects and the rustle of leaves in the light breeze. The weather continued to be perfect after the storm.

A plastic awning covered the only portal. A trash bin,

half full of beer cans, stood to one side of the door. A black grill with large dents on the cover sat to the other side.

They tried the door. The knob didn't turn. Fenwick glanced around the woods and back down the driveway. He said, "Let someone with finesse and refinement handle this." There were two steps up to the door. Fenwick stood on the bottom, twisted his bulk slightly to the left, then rammed himself upward and to the right. His shoulder bashed into the door with all his weight behind it. The door opened with a rush and banged against the wall behind it. The noise rang through the woods. "See," Fenwick said, "it was open all along."

"I've always said you were a finesse kind of guy."

Fenwick looked back up the driveway and the surrounding woods. The noise had attracted no one.

They marched into the trailer. Since it was nearly barren of furniture, it seemed spacious despite the size.

"Scarth was reasonably neat," Fenwick said.

Turner glanced at the nearly empty interior. "How hard is it to keep practically nothing in order?"

In the living room they found a recliner with cracks and tears in its vinyl covering. A few of the larger rents had yarn stitching holding the two split ends together. A towel, originally white, now stained yellow and crusted on top, sat on the right armrest.

Fenwick said, "Looks like he liked to wipe up afterward."

Turner nodded. An ashtray on the floor had three cigarette butts in it. The only other piece of furniture was a forty-two-inch flat-screen television. It was attached to the front wall of the trailer. Under it was a stand with rows of DVDs.

Turner and Fenwick perused them. "Alphabetical order," Fenwick said.

Turner started on the bottom shelf. "These last few just have dates on them." Turner popped one in that had a date of the previous February. The remote was on top of the stand. He pressed On, then Play. The scene showed Scarth in a nondescript motel room. He was sitting in the middle of a bed staring off to the right of the camera. A voice said, "You can start whenever you want."

Scarth looked to the camera. "Do I look at you or what?"

"You can just watch the video and do like we talked about. Start with rubbing yourself through your jeans then do whatever turns you on the most."

"Okay." Scarth took a sip of beer then settled himself down.

Fenwick said, "He has copies of his porn tapes?"

Turner said, "Maybe this is his equivalent of family pictures." Turner flicked it off.

"Hey," Fenwick said, "I was getting into the plot and the dialogue had depth and meaning."

"He comes in the end."

"You ruined it for me."

"Trust me. That's how they all end."

"And you would know?"

"I know everything. Let's get on with this."

The kitchen cabinet had one pot, one pan, three forks, three knives, three teaspoons, three soupspoons, one bowl, one plate, one cup, one saucer.

Fenwick said, "I don't think he entertained a lot."

"Not formally," Turner said, "and not in here."

Arranged in straight rows under the sink were cleansers and soaps. They moved into the bedroom. The bed was neatly made. A pole lamp gave the only light. A nightstand had a small heap of condoms. Fenwick pointed to them. "He was prepared."

"No books to read," Turner said. "Nothing on the walls. Nothing that really gives this place personality." The closet had pairs of jeans and work shirts and work boots and boxes on their sides that contained neatly stacked underwear and socks.

They couldn't both fit into the bathroom at the same time. The shower was cramped, the toilet minimal. In the cabinet above the sink were shaving equipment, toothbrush, toothpaste, and aspirin.

"I wonder if he lived here much," Turner said when they were back in the living room.

"No clues to murder," Fenwick said.

The car was in the driveway. It was an Austin Healy.

Fenwick said, "Was this back here or did the cops bring it back?"

Turner shrugged.

"I gotta piss," Fenwick said. He repaired to the nearest edge of the clearing. Turner appreciated that he turned his back and was out of hearing range.

The car doors were unlocked. Turner popped the switch for the trunk. He walked back. The lid swung open to reveal a spare tire, tire iron, several rods and reels, a small tackle box, bits of cloth, and loose clothes. Turner moved a large blue hoodie sweatshirt. Under it was a dark blue T-shirt with lettering on the front that said FRODO LIVES.

The only person he knew who had such a shirt was his son Brian. He'd had it made at a Renaissance Fair in Wisconsin the summer before. He tucked the shirt in his belt next to his gun behind his back. His bulky shirt should cover both.

He looked back at the sweatshirt. Brian had one of those as well. It was size large. Same as his son. There were no marks on it. Fenwick still had his back to him. He tossed the sweatshirt into the far back of the SUV. He had questions to ask his son. He would not hide evidence from Fenwick, but this was his son. Turner was nearly sick to his stomach. He knew what the T-shirt implied.

Turner's mind tried to conjure possible scenarios. Could this stuff have been stolen the night of the break-in? Brian hadn't reported anything missing. How could the shirt have gotten here? Questions dinned in his head. What had his son been up to? What lies had been told? Had his son confronted Scarth Krohn and his buddies? He knew his son wasn't a killer. The boy would be unable to control the guilt over such a horrific act. But there had to be a reason for this shirt being here. Could Scarth have had one of his own? The odds against it being coincidental were astronomical.

Fenwick joined him. "Anything?"

He pointed to the interior trunk space. "Not much."

While Fenwick checked the front seat, Turner examined the back. They found a few beer cans, pop bottles, empty Fritos bags, a few hooks and lures, two condoms—one still in a wrapper, one used.

Turner wanted to talk to his son.

When they were back in the SUV, Fenwick said, "It's late. Let's get back to the boats and eat."

Turner nodded. He could feel the lump of the T-shirt pressing against his back next to his gun.

After they were on the road for a few minutes Fenwick looked at him. "You okay?" his partner asked.

"Yeah. Fine."

Fenwick glanced back at the road then to Turner.

"You sure?"

"Just a little hungry."

But Fenwick knew it wasn't that. You don't know somebody this many years and not have a sense when something is wrong. He respected the silence.

They returned to the boats. Brian was Jet Skiing on the other side of the bay. Jeff was fishing from the dock. Ben was cooking dinner. Ian was reading the collected speeches of Abraham Lincoln. Paul gave Ben a kiss, checked Jeff, nodded at Ian.

He went into the boys' room. He checked Brian's things. White athletic socks, T-shirts with the logos of rock bands Paul had never heard of, jeans, shorts, swimming suit. No hooded sweatshirt. No FRODO LIVES T-shirt. He sat on the bed. He pulled the T-shirt out of the back of his pants and put it on the dresser. He heard thumps on the dock, then Jeff calling to Brian. He heard the older son hop onto the deck and stride down the short hall to the room. Brian walked in. He was wearing board shorts and nothing else. He smiled at his dad. His skin was deeply tanned. Turner watched his son carefully. The boy's eyes went to the shirt.

Paul said, "I found this."

Brian leaned against the small dresser. His hands gripped the top edge.

"Where?" Brian asked.

"In the trunk of Scarth Krohn's car."

The boy looked genuinely confused.

"Do you know how it got there?" Paul asked.

Brian accompanied his "No" with a head shake.

"Did you have contact with him?"

"No, I swear."

"When was the last time you had the T-shirt?"

Eyes shifting, legs crossing at the ankle, uncrossing. "I went swimming the other day. I left it on the shore. It was gone when I got back." Paul didn't accuse his son of lying.

"You didn't mention it was gone."

"No. I guess I forgot."

"It was your favorite shirt."

"I figured I could get another one."

"Is there something you need to tell me?" Paul asked.

The boy hung his head.

"Where's your favorite blue hoodie sweatshirt?" Paul asked him.

"I lent it to Kevin. Why?"

"I haven't seen you wearing it and I don't see it here."

"He said he'd give it back."

"Why would you be lending shirts?"

"He was cold."

"He didn't have a shirt?"

"Is there a problem, Dad?"

This was murder, and Turner needed to know the truth.

Turner said, "Your sweatshirt and T-shirt were found in the trunk of Scarth Krohn's car."

"Is that important?"

"He's dead."

"Yeah."

"That T-shirt and sweatshirt are the only anomalies we've been able to find. I have no explanation for that. The official police don't know they're yours. They don't know you lent the hoodie to Kevin." Turner sighed. "On the first night we were here, I was rowing around the islands near here. You know I do that every year. I heard you and Kevin. I saw you making out with him. You said you were going to the movies. The movie didn't let out until after midnight. I didn't get started until late because I was playing chess with your brother. And don't bother with the nonsensical gambit that I was spying on you. You were there. You were loud. How could I not have noticed? I did not stop and take pictures. Nobody was putting you live on the Internet, but if you were trying to hide, an island in the wilderness with a campfire blazing is not a great choice."

"I'm not gay."

He said, "You know that's not what this is about."

The sounds of the others at the marina echoed and pattered outside the screened-in window. It was late afternoon. The wind was calm, the lake surface placid. Father and son sat down. Paul said, "You lent the T-shirt to Kevin."

"Yeah."

"What did he tell you when he didn't give it back?"

"I didn't think about it. We wear each other's stuff sometimes. You and Ben do that. Kevin was really depressed after that night. He wasn't scheduled to be with us full-time until the last two days."

This was true. Kevin usually spent the first two and last two days of their week with them.

Brian asked, "Why? What does it matter that he borrowed my shirts?"

Turner said, "Scarth and his girlfriend were killed that night. Your stuff was in Scarth's car. Kevin's the connection." He didn't say "or you are."

"Kevin wouldn't hurt anybody. You know him."

"Did he tell you anything?"

"No, I swear."

"I need to talk to Kevin."

"I want to go with."

"No, I'm going by myself."

"I think maybe he's going to hurt himself."

"What makes you think that?"

"He's really depressed."

"I'll find him."

"Are you taking Mr. Fenwick?"

"No, I'm going by myself."

36

Turner drove to Kevin's apartment. He'd dropped Kevin off a few times when the boy's grandfather had been alive. Kevin had lived with him there and had stayed on after his grandfather died.

Turner didn't see Kevin's car in the parking lot. He went up to knock on the door. It was open. All his cop senses hit high alert. He inched over the threshold, checking any corner or shadow for an enemy. The kitchen was on the right with a back door leading to a small patio. To the left was a small living room with a worn couch, a well-preserved easy chair, a pine footrest with a small stack of paperback books on it. Turner examined the bedroom from the doorway then stepped slowly in. He saw a small mound of clothes, a four-drawer brown dresser, and a twin bed. There were no signs of violence or of hasty packing as if someone were fleeing. The bathroom door was half open. He eased it the rest of the way with the tips of his fingers. Nothing. Clean, no mold on the shower curtain or between the tiles on the wall. White beach towels hung neatly from three racks on the wall. Turner breathed a sigh of relief. A small part of his mind had been expecting to find a dead body. He didn't think Kevin was suicidal, but the stress of watching a murder and possibly committing one might drive someone to almost anything. Safe so far. He returned to the front room. In the doorway were Doran, Nagel, Verinder, and Dunsmith.

Doran had a wicked grin on his face. "It's not easy to follow around a fag. You keep losing us."

"Why bother to follow me?"

"To get you alone."

"Was it you in the boat behind us the other day?"

"Yeah. We know there's some fags living far out on the lake. We wanted to get you and them."

Nagel said, "Kevin Yost is a fag. Scarth told us his butt was tighter than any girl."

"When was this?"

Nagel said, "Last weekend just before you came to town. He told us he'd share Kevin with us. That it would be fun to make him squeal and beg for more." He grabbed his crotch. "You'll get some of this before we're through with you."

"Scarth's having sex with Kevin didn't make you suspicious that Scarth was gay?"

Nagel said, "When you're tired of the same old crap from these twats up here, you figure a little recreation ain't bad. Scarth wasn't a fag."

Doran said, "You are, and you're here." He pumped his hips back and forth in a manner Turner presumed Doran thought looked sexy.

Turner remembered the back door was behind him. He

feinted toward them, picked up the vase with wilted flowers, threw it in their direction, then rushed for the back door. He slammed it behind him. Before they had time to react, he was in his car with the doors locked. Moments later they swarmed out of the apartment. He shoved the keys in the ignition, rammed the car into gear, and roared away.

What to do? He wanted to find Kevin before anyone else. He didn't know what the police would figure out. He needed to avoid the gay bashers. He looked in the rearview mirror. The flame red Mustang hurtled out of the parking lot and into the street then drove away in the opposite direction. He drove back to their dock.

He immediately called all the adults together and explained the incident at the apartment. Ian and Fenwick were for a frontal attack.

"Yes," Turner said. "That would be great. Better yet: stay here. Protect the kids. Call the Ontario Provincial Police and talk to Mavis Bednars. She'll send real help. I've got to find Kevin."

"Why?" Ian asked.

Turner said, "He might be in danger. I don't have time to explain now."

Fenwick nodded.

Turner found Brian and Jeff playing a computer game on the laptop they'd brought along. He said, "Brian, could I see you a minute?"

The boy accompanied him to the kitchen. "What's up?" Brian asked.

"I need to find Kevin."

"I don't know where he is."

"He's not at his apartment. Where would he go?"

"We were at his favorite spot the other night."

"I think I can find it in the daylight. I just happened upon it the other night."

Brian gave directions. He finished, "He'd be in his favorite boat—you know, that little blue one with the engine he souped up to go faster."

Turner took the houseboat and started out. He didn't want anyone else with him. Not yet. There must be a reason Kevin had done what he did. Had to be a reason. He wanted to hear that reason before he made a decision to turn him in. He wanted to hear that reason alone.

◣ 37 ◢

Paul Turner reached the island in about ten minutes. He saw no sign of a boat. After a moment's indecision, he landed and hurried inland. The fire was cold. There was no tent. No sign of Kevin. He stood on the water's edge and looked out on the surface of the lake. A fisherman drove by about thirty feet out. He was a portly gentleman with a white beard. Turner called to him, "Have you seen a small blue boat?"

The man cupped his hands around his face and called back, "About five minutes ago heading out." He pointed westward. "I think it was one of the guides."

Turner yelled thanks, got back into his boat, and started out in pursuit. For twenty minutes he headed west. He realized the impossibility of his task. The Lake of the Woods was far too vast for him to be able to hope to search every inch of it. Undoubtedly, Kevin knew it better than he did.

Then in the distance he spotted a pale speck caught in the last rays of the sun. It moved rapidly away from him. It was at least a chance. He took off in pursuit. In five minutes he realized the boat ahead was beginning to look bigger. For a few moments Turner thought this might be a hopeful sign. Minutes later, he realized there was no one sitting or standing up in the boat. When he got next to it and looked inside, it was empty. The sky was bright blue on the water. He noted ripples to his left. He turned his boat in that direction. He drove quickly. For a minute he thought he saw arms swimming, moving in the water. Then all movement stopped. Turner shut off the engine, threw out the anchor, and dove into the water. He reached the body in moments. He pulled the head out of the water. Kevin wasn't breathing, but his body was still warm. He couldn't have been in the water long.

Paul struck out for the houseboat about thirty feet away. He grabbed the ladder on the side of the boat and switched Kevin into a fireman's carry. He managed to clutch and climb and then gently place the boy on the deck.

Turner's CPR training kicked in automatically. Breathe into victim's mouth, hold, breathe in. In half a minute Kevin choked, coughed up water. The teen's body began to shake and shiver.

Turner hurried into a bedroom and pulled a blanket off the bed. He hurried back. Kevin accepted the blanket and clutched it to himself.

The teen was muttering, "I am so scared. I am so dead. I am so fucked. Why didn't you let me die?"

Paul knelt down next to him. He said, "You need to get out of those wet clothes." The boy nodded. Turner found a pair of Brian's jeans, a sweatshirt, and some socks. Kevin accepted them. The boy returned from the washroom in moments. He tossed his bundle of sodden clothes on the floor. The boy sat in a chair, looked up at Paul, out the window, down at the floor. Paul sat on the kitchen chair opposite him.

"Why were you in the water?"

Kevin spoke to the floor. "I was trying to kill myself. I was going to keep going farther and farther out into the lake. When I was a mile out, I changed my mind. I didn't make it back."

"Why were you going to kill yourself?"

"You know." Kevin met his eyes. "You know."

"You killed Scarth Krohn."

"Yes."

"Why?"

"You know what he was like."

"Tell me."

"Since I was eleven I've had to—" The kid hesitated. He looked at Turner. The boy was pale and frightened. He continued to shiver. Turner was in the presence of a killer. He didn't think he had to keep his guard up, but the boy had killed at least once. He'd tried to commit suicide. He could help prepare a moose or bear for being pulled into parts. The boy was used to violence. Was he used to murder?

"Since I was six he made fun of me. He was always the one in the school who led the viciousness. The other kids knew I was different from before I knew I was different. Sissy, gay boy, fag boy, faggot, and a million names a million times a day. He was the first to call me names. Always the first. Always the loudest. Always the meanest. I told the teacher. I told the principal. I told my parents. I did what I was supposed to. I tried to ignore it. I tried to be bigger than the other kids. I tried to brush it off. I tried to ignore it and let it roll off my back. Does anyone actually think that helps with bullies? The adults did nothing. Nothing." Kevin began to cry. Turner handed him a tissue. "Scarth Krohn never stopped. Never let up. Never let go. I learned my lesson. I stopped complaining. The adults didn't care about a gay kid. Scarth was sacred around this town. The summer I turned ten, he made me blow him. He was four years older than I was. He was an athlete. He was so strong." Unfettered tears escaped the boy's eyes, but he continued on. "For all these years, he's made me have sex. Sometimes he'd hit me. A couple times he pissed on me. As I got older, I tried to fight back. It was useless. This year on my seventeenth birthday, he fucked me for the first time. I tried to hide. Do you know how small this community is? And if I hid one day, he'd find me the next. He was so popular with everyone. Everyone wanted to be his friend, except me. I wanted him dead. Dead. I'm glad he's dead. I'm glad I killed him. The torment is over. No matter what happens to me, the pain is going to be less." He wiped at his eyes. "You know, he never used a condom. Never. I'm petrified to go to a doctor."

"Do you feel ill?"

"No, but I think I should be checked just in case."

Turner understood the fears and terrors of being a gay kid. As a kid, Paul had managed to hide his sexuality, but the fear of discovery was real. He had no concept of what six years of incessant torture must have felt like.

"What happened that night?"

"He was drunk. Usually when he found me, he was drunk. I liked it better when he was sober. He'd come faster, and he wasn't as mean. Drunk, sometimes he'd beat me senseless."

"But you're a strong kid."

"He's more than six inches taller, and he's been an athlete all his life. I'm strong, but I learned long ago not to put up a fight. I would always lose, and he would always be more violent after I couldn't fight back anymore."

"You couldn't show a doctor the bruises?"

"And admit I was gay or that I was getting fucked?"

"Was Scarth the only one?"

"What?"

"Did he bring his buddies around to abuse you?"

"Never for the sex. Just to be abusive. You must know what it was like to be picked on."

Turner nodded. He knew. Much as he had tried to hide his sexual orientation, he knew the pain of being picked on. Most gay kids did. He remembered the pain, the sharp memories coming back unbidden.

"Do you have any proof that he did this?"

"I kept a diary. On my computer. I'll show it to you if you want."

"What happened the night of the murder?"

"He was driving around town looking for me. I'd been out with Brian, who had lent me a sweatshirt and his T-shirt, the one with FRODO LIVES on the front. I was wearing them. I was heading back to the dock to give them back when Scarth drove up. I ran. He ran faster. He was so drunk. He's so big. We were at the dock. He had me trapped. He was drunk. He was a mean drunk, but I don't know if I've ever seen him drunker. I'd heard about the other guys who'd fallen in and drowned. Everybody had. I wished he'd fall in and die. At the end of the pier, I dodged and darted and tried to get around him." By this point the kid was speaking through sobs. "He caught me and dragged me to the car. He took off my clothes and made me ride next to him naked. I was humiliated." He rolled up his sleeves. "Why do you think I always wear long-sleeved shirts?" Scars of attempted suicide decorated both wrists. "I never had the nerve to make a deep enough cut. I dreamt of being brave enough to kill myself or kill him."

Paul had to ask. "How did Evon Gasple get involved that night?"

Kevin hung his head. Paul saw tears, but this time there were no heart-wrenching sobs. Turner waited. He wanted all the truth. Kevin didn't look up when he finally began to talk. "She pulled up next to us at an intersection while we were in town. She started screeching at him. They drove to the park and had this big fight. No one was around. He'd taken my clothes. I was going to run, but he could still catch me. He could run faster. I'd tried that before."

He hiccupped and gulped. Turner handed him another tissue. Kevin wiped his nose and continued. "She began screaming that he was a fag. That I was his fag boy. They were fighting, fists, kicking, everything. Finally he knocked her out. He dragged her to the backseat. We went to the boathouse at his father's mansion. He picked one of the boats, threw her on the deck, grabbed me, and started off."

"You still didn't have your clothes?"

"He gave me my jeans. That's all. It was cool that night on the lake but not cold, but I shivered every second. On the way Scarth bragged that he was going to show me what a real man could do. We drove to that little cove. He dragged her out of the boat. I thought maybe she was dead already, but I did finally see her breathing. As we got there, she started to come around. When she came fully around, she went nuts. I've never heard anyone scream and carry on like she did. She kept making fun of him for wanting me along. She called him 'fag' over and over. I think they'd both done some drugs besides being drunk. He went nuts. She tried to run. He chased her into the woods. He dragged me behind. She probably would have gotten away, but she kept turning back to screech at him. He finally caught up to her. Maybe she let him catch up. I don't know. He tried to have sex with her, but she didn't like it that I was there. I tried to run while he was busy, but he grabbed me and knocked me silly. I couldn't see straight."

Turner said, "Supposedly she'd had sex in public with others."

"She wasn't in the mood that night. His pants and shorts were around his knees. He had his dick out, but he couldn't stay hard. She added laughter to her screeches. Then she told him she'd seen the two of us one night when he was screwing me. She threatened to tell everyone. He went crazy. In seconds he bashed her, and she was on her knees. He tottered and weaved around a few seconds then went after her again. She stayed on her knees and refused to go down. One time I got up and tried to protect her. I tackled him around the legs. He rammed me into a tree. She'd managed to get to her feet and stagger toward the boat. All this time she kept screaming at him, taunting him, and laughing at him. He tackled her. Her head banged against a tree. I think he must have knocked her unconscious at that moment. I never heard a word from her after that. I don't think he realized what was wrong with her because he was screaming and beating on her. She didn't lift a hand to help herself. I got to my feet, but I was nearly unconscious myself. I thought I was next. Scarth was insane. He saw me getting up. He pulled up his pants. He chased me for a few paces. If I'd gotten a little bit more away, I'd have been able to lose him in the dark. I was thinking maybe Evon needed help. She sure wasn't a friend of mine, but hey, she looked hurt. He caught me."

Kevin was crying again. "This time he did get it up. He fucked me and fucked me. I hated him." He sobbed and sobbed. Finally, after a terrific snuffle, he wiped his tears with the back of his hands. "When he was done he yanked me to my feet. He went over to her and knelt down. I guess he shook her to wake her up, but she didn't move. He swore at her. He looked more pissed than ever. Then he looked at me, and I got really scared. The lake is only about twenty yards north of there. He began dragging me toward it. I knew what he was going to try to do. He was having a hard time because of the booze and drugs, but I knew if I didn't do something, I was going to die. I was a witness to what he'd done. I had to be gotten out of the way."

"Why not just beat you to death or hit you against a tree?"

"He was shoving me, laughing, wrestling, trying to turn me around to hunch up against me, hitting, grabbing. We got to the water's edge. I went nuts. I managed to break away. I'm a good swimmer. I thought maybe I could get away by swimming far out in the lake and coming up far from him. After a few strokes, he jumped in the water and caught me. We wrestled for a few minutes in the water. He was trying to hold my head down. I was lucky. I managed to get behind him and hold him under. I'm not sure he knew what was going on at first. He probably hadn't drawn a large breath as he went in. He'd been laughing and snarling and swinging those big fists. I dunked him once, and he came up enraged. He

294

screamed, 'Die, faggot, die.' If I didn't do something, I knew I was going to die in the next few minutes. Over the years I'd gotten stronger. I dove down. He must have been exhaling when I managed to grab his feet from under him and tip him over. I held on to his ankles as if my life depended on it. I held him upside down by the ankles. He fought like mad, but he couldn't grab me and my shoulders and my chest muscles are strong. I held him under. He didn't thrash all that long. He was too drunk maybe to figure it out before it was too late. I don't know how long it took. One instant he was struggling. The next he stopped. I watched him drift away. I felt free. For the first time since I was eleven, I was free. I killed him. I would do it again in a heartbeat. If he'd been sober, I'd be dead." The boy's tears and snuffling turned to sobs. The teenager's frame was wracked with weeping. Paul sat next to him and gathered the boy in his arms. The kid's tears and snot soaked through the shoulder of his flannel shirt. Paul patted the boy's head. He held him until the emotional storm eased.

"What did you do with the boat?" Turner asked.

"I ran it into some rocks not too far from the shore near Kenora. I swam ashore. I didn't know what to do. I couldn't report Evon because I'd have had to admit that I'd killed Scarth."

"Did you go back for Evon that night?"

"Yes. She may have been as rotten as Scarth, but I was worried about her. I couldn't find her. It was dark. I tried going back the next day. Even for me the woods can be confusing at night. It would have taken search parties maybe weeks to find her."

Turner said, "The medical examiner told us that the best medicine in the world couldn't have saved her."

"I hope that's true," Kevin said.

Paul met Kevin's eyes. He saw tears. Kevin said, "I've never been so confused. So frightened and so scared. I wanted to kill myself. I didn't see any other option."

"Maybe I can help you find some options," Paul said.

Kevin looked at him and then hung his head. They were silent for several moments.

Paul asked, "Were you dating my son?"

"What?"

"I saw you and Brian necking in the woods when he told me he was going to the movies."

"Brian is nice. He's kind to me. He's never violent. He would hold me and wouldn't make demands on me. He was gentle. I don't think he's gay. He comforted me."

"Did you tell him about Scarth abusing you?"

"No. I couldn't. People didn't bully me when Brian was around. Even Scarth wouldn't come around when you guys were here. That's why I was always hanging around. I liked helping you guys. I liked feeling safe."

"You could have checked on the Internet. There are groups who help. There are kids who have won cases against school administrators who did nothing."

"They're far away and this is a small town."

Turner said, "Does Brian know you killed him?"

"No. No one does. Just you. What's going to happen to me? Are you going to turn me in?"

"Right now, we're going to get you someplace safe. Then I'm going to discuss options with you."

. 38 .

Kevin gave him directions to the nearest marina. Even Kevin
couldn't find the way to Mrs. Talucci's brothers at night. Paul
called the number. An hour later the silver cigarette boat arrived with Phil at the helm.

Before leaving the houseboat, Paul gave Kevin one of
Brian's letterman's jackets for warmth. They climbed
aboard. The teenager sat close to him as they drove but neither spoke. The full moon gleamed ahead of them as they
started out.

Paul was thinking. The boy had certainly acted in self-
defense. He doubted if Schreppel would see it that way. The
chief of police was a problem. Not turning the boy in was another. Paul had little doubt that in Chicago, he'd be forced to
turn the teenager in. He was a cop. It was his job. He'd be be-
traying his profession and his principles if he didn't turn him
in. Here, now, in Canada, he had no standing, as he'd been reminded and warned about several times, by a rude, officious

twit who seemed far more concerned with his own ego than with accomplishing the task at hand. It went against his grain not to turn a criminal in. He thought of discussing it with Fenwick, but if he was going to condone a felony, the decision would be his. He didn't think Fenwick would disagree, but Paul Turner was not about to make a decision for which he could go to jail and then involve a friend. Well, at least not his friend Fenwick. Not yet, anyway. He needed to make decisions first.

Mrs. Talucci was another matter. She was someone he could discuss all the parameters with. He also had to decide what he would tell his sons. Neither boy was stupid. And if he was going to cover up the crime, was he going to simply let it continue to be unsolved and risk the local idiot sheriff wouldn't figure it out, or that the moron would accuse someone innocent? Turner had to make sure the wrong person wouldn't be convicted.

Or would he take an active role in covering up who did it? If he were to do so, where was Kevin to go? How would the teenager deal with what he had done? He'd just attempted to commit suicide. That wasn't the option Paul wanted, either. He wasn't sure what would bring the boy back to health. Would Scarth Krohn's father use his money to try to find his son's killer?

At some later point, Kevin said, "Brian and I never had unsafe sex. Mostly he was passive and gentle. He held me like you did. I felt so safe with him."

And what if the boy was lying about this? Or the murder? What if Brian had had some role in the murder? Had he helped? His teenager hadn't been caught in a major deception until now. Having sex with someone instead of going to the movies, in the pantheon of evil, was pretty far down on the going-to-hell-for-that list.

It wasn't hard to believe the slight figure of Kevin had successfully held the much larger and stronger Scarth Krohn under. He'd seen Kevin lift heavy objects more easily than Brian could, and Brian was extremely strong. Still, two against one was even better. Paul Turner needed absolute forensic proof or reassurances or a video. Or something.

As for the other question, did Brian need to be tested? Did other partners Brian had need to be tested? Had Brian had other partners male and/or female? How long had the two boys engaged in a sexual relationship? Paul didn't really want to know. He wanted the answers about Brian to be that he was safe and healthy. He would need to have a discussion with his son.

Fifteen minutes out, Phil slowed. The boat's running lights illuminated a half-moon path ahead. Turner looked behind. He saw a pinpoint of light following.

Phil said, "We're being followed again."

"Same guys?"

"Can't tell so far."

"One boat or two?"

"There's only one light. This is more dangerous. I know these waters but there are rocks. We hit one at any speed, we could have trouble. We have to assume these guys mean business. I won't take any chances. This needs to stop."

Turner said, "It's not just someone on the lake?"

"No. They're following."

"How far behind are they?" Turner asked.

"Half a mile."

"You're slowing down."

"I want them to catch up a little more."

The light behind them grew: a quarter, a half-dollar, a sun rising. The light bobbed in the waves. Soon he could see the outline of the boat. The moonlight helped cast their shadows on the water.

Phil jammed the throttle down. Their boat leapt away. Turner barely saw the rocks they zigzagged between. The boat was at full speed. The wind whipped his jacket. Kevin stood next to Phil. He saw them shout to each other. Turner realized that Kevin must know these waters as well.

Through the black night they raced. The boat behind fell slightly farther behind. Turner felt their craft slow almost imperceptibly. The distance remained constant for ten minutes.

He saw flashes of light on the other boat. He knew what they were. Gunshots. One thudded into the seat in front of which he was standing. He pointed this out to Phil, who nodded. Turner looked back. More flashes.

Half a minute later, he saw Kevin point. Phil moved the wheel slightly. The boat rocked a trifle sideways. Turner thought he heard a rough scrape through the noise. Then they were speeding on.

It was over in seconds. The boat behind them held on true. One second the light was following them, the next it veered toward the sky. A terrific explosion was followed by a billow of red and yellow flames.

Phil slowed immediately. In the quiet Phil said, "We've got to see if there are any survivors."

Turner nodded.

It took a minute for the boat to make the arc through the water back to where remnants of the explosion flamed, sizzled, or sank. Phil cut the motor down to nearly idle. They inched as close as they could to the scene. The three of them scanned the water for survivors.

The nose of the attacking boat pointed straight up. The midsection was caught on a rock. Patches of oil still burned on top of the water. Turner could feel the heat from the burning wreckage as it smoldered and flickered. They motored slowly around the perimeter of the flaming debris.

Three minutes later the remnants of the boat slipped off the rock and into the lake.

The three of them took flashlights from the storage container near the back of the boat. They shone them on the water. They circled again. Nothing so far. They started around again.

Turner looked back the way they had come. "There's someone else," he said.

Phil and Kevin looked. The boat was not coming as fast. Phil touched the gun in the holster under his arm.

In a few minutes the new arrival showed up. No shots were directed at them. Phil stood ready to jam the throttle down.

"It's Ralph Bowers," Turner said. Was this a second wave of attackers? Ralph drove a much simpler craft with an outboard motor. Ralph pulled alongside their boat. Since theirs was much larger, Turner eased himself down into it.

"We had some problems," Turner said.

Ralph nodded. "I was trying to help. I knew they were after you. I tried to keep track of them. I can't go as fast."

"We're looking for survivors."

"I'll help."

Turner stayed with Ralph's boat. If possible, he didn't

want Kevin to be seen. The two boats shone lights down onto the surface. He and Ralph found three bodies drifting with the current. They hoisted them onto Ralph's boat. The bodies were badly charred and burned.

Ralph said, "It's Doran, Nagel, and Verinder."

"They're dead," Turner said.

They heard a noise on the port side. A hand reached up over the gunwale. Ralph and Turner rushed over. They helped Dunsmith into the boat. The back of his skull looked crushed. One arm hung at an odd angle. His clothes were burned. His flesh had been seared. He gasped for breath. They eased him into the bottom of the boat so he could stretch out. Dunsmith alternately shivered and screamed.

The larger boat pulled close. Phil came over with a medicine kit. Turner looked up. Kevin was at the helm of the other boat. There was little they could do about him being seen, but Ralph seemed to pay no attention.

Turner said, "We have to get him to a doctor."

"I don't think he'll live that long," Phil said, "but we can try."

Dunsmith screamed, "Help me!"

Turner held the man's hand. Dunsmith said, "I told them not to. I told them not to."

"Told them not to what?" Turner said.

Dunsmith spoke between gasps. "Not to follow you. They wanted to kill you. I couldn't say no. I had to go along. They'd have attacked me, too. They hated you. They were going to hurt your kids, but there were too many people around. We saw you leave."

"The other three are dead," Turner said.

Dunsmith raised his arm and grabbed Turner's sleeve.

He clutched at him. His back arched in agony. He slumped back. He stopped breathing. He died.

Phil, Ralph, and Turner stood up. The four corpses and the three of them made the smaller boat feel cramped.

Phil said, "We'll have to take them back to town."

"I will," Ralph said. "You've got business."

Phil said, "There's a marina only a few minutes to our south."

"I know where everything is," Ralph said. "I'm fine. I'll contact the police. You go on. It was an accident. They happen."

Phil and Turner returned to their boat. They watched Ralph's craft motor away.

"Did he see you?" Turner asked Kevin.

"He didn't look this way," Kevin said.

On the dock at Mrs. Talucci's brother's, one of the hunky help was showing Mrs. Talucci a Jet Ski. She had on a life jacket. Turner nearly smiled. It would be like Mrs. Talucci to want to ride one of the machines, at night no less. He wasn't sure she was strong enough to control the machine. He was not about to tell her that she wasn't. Two powerful flood-lights illumined the scene.

Mrs. Talucci approached his boat as they docked. She waved and smiled. Then she saw that something was wrong.

Paul and Kevin stepped onto the pier.

Mrs. Talucci said, "Come up to the house."

She led them away. She asked no questions.

Once on the veranda, Kevin said, "I need to use the washroom." He left them.

Mrs. Talucci sat on the two-seater swing. She patted the spot next to her.

Paul sat down. He gazed at the lake and the trees.

Mrs. Talucci said, "You're okay? The boys are okay? Ben is okay?"

Paul nodded. He listened to the birds and the leaves and the breeze. If he listened hard enough, Turner thought he might be able to hear the moonlight on the lake. He shook his head. "I've got a decision to make."

It was Mrs. Talucci's turn to nod. "How can I help?"

"I have information the police could use."

Mrs. Talucci looked toward the door through which Kevin had entered the house and then looked back at Paul. Her shrewd eyes had a knowing look.

"You're not going to tell them, are you?"

"No."

"Of course not."

"It's not that I don't know what to do, it's that what I know is the right thing to do is hard."

"It usually is," Mrs. Talucci said.

The silence built between them. Paul heard voices inside the house. Dominic was gushing about how happy he was to have a surprise visit from Kevin. Dominic shuffled onto the veranda. He was leaning on Kevin's arm. He smiled at Paul. "So good of you to come back," he said. He saw the look on their faces. He let himself be led into a chair. After he plopped down, he sighed.

Kevin said, "I'm going down to the pier."

Turner caught his gaze and stood up.

Kevin said, "I'm not going to do anything foolish." For an instant he hugged Turner fiercely. Paul returned the embrace.

In a moment it was over and Kevin left. At the pier the teenager began helping Phil scrub down the boat. Pierre came out and sat next to Dominic.

Dominic looked at Turner then at his sister. "Something is wrong," he stated.

Turner said, "I've solved Scarth Krohn's murder."

Dominic nodded. He did not look out at where Kevin was standing knee-deep in the water next to the boat. He kept his eyes on Paul's. Dominic said, "They weren't connected with the other six drownings?"

"No. Those were genuine accidents," Turner said.

Dominic said, "You aren't going to tell the police."

"No," Paul said.

"But that's not your problem," Dominic said.

"What is?" Mrs. Talucci asked.

"I have to be able to tell my sons something. Brian knows or at least can make some good guesses. Jeff is not stupid. I don't want something this big to hang between us."

Dominic said, "Parents keep secrets. Sometimes it is necessary to protect the children from the truth."

"Brian is old enough to handle the truth most of the time."

"Will he understand the truth this time?" Dominic asked.

"I think so. I hope so."

Mrs. Talucci said, "If you know, Fenwick will have guessed."

"He doesn't have a crucial piece of evidence, but yes, he'll probably guess. If he doesn't already know."

"Tell him," Mrs. Talucci said. "Just tell him. And tell Brian."

Paul smiled at his old friend. He said, "At the moment I

have the burden of truth. Do I have a right to inflict that on them? If I tell, one secret of mine is traded for theirs and mine."

Dominic said, "Brian will know?"

Paul said, "I think he does already. I will have to talk to him. Another question is what happens to—"

Dominic said, "We can make a place for Kevin here. He'll be safe. He can earn money and go to college. We have more money than we ever dreamed of. Pierre inherited quite a bit, and, as I said earlier, we saved and scrimped for years. We've earned a few comforts. We've earned the right to be generous."

"He should also be tested for diseases," Paul said. "Scarth never used a condom. Most likely he'll need psychological help."

Pierre said, "We will make sure he gets everything he needs."

Paul said, "I'm also worried about someone being falsely accused of the murder. Billy Morningsky is still in jail. I'm not going to turn Kevin in, but I don't want someone innocent to suffer."

Dominic said, "I will take care of it. Billy will be out of jail before you return."

Turner looked at him. "You have that much influence?"

"I have enough. Pierre and Phil are attorneys. They will make sure everything is taken care of legally. Legal mechanisms will be in place, both for while we are alive, and after we die, so that every contingency is covered. There will be no threat to Kevin. There will be no threat to anyone who is innocent."

"Thank you," Turner said.

Mrs. Talucci said, "Can you tell us why Scarth died?"

"Because a young gay man finally said, 'Enough is enough, I am not going to take it anymore.' Because the Matthew Shepards of this world have taught every gay person a lesson. All the lawsuits filed by gay kids in schools about being harassed have taught us a lesson. Because we learned from Stonewall that we must fight back. Because we have learned that if we do not fight back, we will be victims forever. Because the constant punishment hurts too much. Somebody finally put an end to an enemy capable of enormous evil. I wish Kevin had made a different choice, but . . ."

"What choice was there?" Mrs. Talucci asked.

Paul thought a long time. He gazed at the trees, the lake. He shut his eyes and listened to the world of the forest. "None," Paul said. "None. Absolutely none."

Dominic said, "It was self-defense."

Pierre said, "Very much so."

"Then your questions are answered," Mrs. Talucci said.

The silence built again. Dominic and Pierre rocked. Finally, Dominic said, "I'd better get Kevin settled in."

"He has no family left in Cathura," Turner said.

"All the easier," Dominic said. "We will take care of him." He eased himself out of his chair. Turner offered to help. "No," Dominic said. "I think I'll walk down to the lake and see what Kevin is up to." He began his slow shuffle toward the pier. Pierre joined him. Kevin spotted them and hurried forward. Dominic leaned heavily on Kevin's arm.

Mrs. Talucci said, "Are you all right?"

"Not yet."

She nodded and said, "You will be."

"I suspect so. I'm not going to turn him in." He let out a deep breath. "It feels so right to say that."

Mrs. Talucci said, "It's the right decision."

"I have to talk to Brian."

"If I can help with anything, let me know."

39

Phil led Turner and the houseboat back through the night. Turner arrived back about four in the morning. Glimmers of dawn crept around the branches of the trees. A few birds were calling. The humidity was back, as was the warmth.

Ben hurried out of the Fenwicks' houseboat. Turner saw Fenwick and Madge appear at the door.

After docking Paul pulled Ben into a powerful embrace. He felt the warmth and assurance of his lover's arms. When they unclenched a bit, Ben asked, "Are you okay?"

"It's been a hell of a night. I need to talk to everybody."

They returned to the Fenwicks' houseboat. Buck and Madge expressed their concern. Paul said, "We'll talk as soon as I check on the kids."

Brian was asleep in a chair in the small living room. A book was open on his chest. Paul looked in on Jeff, who was asleep on the Fenwicks' bed. He ruffled his son's hair and kissed his forehead. Brian awoke as Paul passed back from the bedroom.

"What's going on, Dad?" Brian asked.

"I'd like you to come up on the top deck with everyone else."

Ian was stretched out between two lawn chairs on the screened-in area of the top deck. He awoke as the others shuffled in.

"What's up?" he asked.

Brian asked, "What's happened to Kevin?"

Turner said, "I need to tell all of you what has happened."

Paul sat with his back to the rising sun. Brian sat next to him. Madge sat across. Fenwick stood behind her. Ian and Ben were near the door. It was a comfortably close atmosphere.

He told the story. When he finished, Fenwick said, "The other four are dead."

Paul nodded.

Madge said, "You must have been terrified."

Paul said, "When I have time to think about it, I might be." He turned to Buck Fenwick. "I'm sorry I didn't show you what I found in the car."

"No need for an apology," he said. "I would have done the same."

"I'm not going to tell the police what I know. I'm not going to turn him in. I couldn't live my life not having told the five of you. It's a huge secret that would come between us. Buck, because we share a profession. Madge, because you are a dear friend. Ben, because we share a life. Brian, you're my son."

"What will happen to him?" Brian asked.

"He'll live with Mrs. Talucci's brother for a while. It may take him some time to sort out his feelings. There's no

310

question it was self-defense. Maybe he could have stopped after Scarth passed out when he was holding him down. Maybe. And I think Scarth would have killed him sometime."

Fenwick said, "As Watson said to Holmes in *The Abbey Grange,* 'I trust your judgment.'"

Turner felt a smile tug at his lips. He didn't remember when he'd smiled last.

Paul turned to Brian. He said, "Can you possibly understand why I'm not turning him in?"

"Yeah," Brian said. "Like Mr. Finch at the end of *To Kill a Mockingbird.* Kevin told me sometimes how bad it got. I'm sorry I couldn't have done more."

The sun was nearly full up and the world was brighter than it had been.

"You've had a rough night," Madge said.

Ian said, "I couldn't be gladder of a story I'm never going to get to write." He patted Paul on the shoulder.

Ben said, "It's the right decision."

Everyone nodded.

"Thanks, everybody," Paul said. "I think I want to eat something and then sleep for a while."

He stood up. Brian put his arms around him. Paul hugged back. Brian said, "I love you, Dad."

"I love you, too," Paul said.

It was a hugging moment. Ian finally said, "If this gets any sappier, I'd think I was at a group hug at the end of a *Golden Girls* episode."

"You watch those?" Fenwick asked.

"Every rerun I can," Ian said. "I thought you'd love them. It's your kind of humor."

"I do love them," Fenwick said.

Paul waited for the others to trudge out. Everyone was tired with the all-night vigil. Fenwick nudged Paul's sleeve. The two paused for a moment at the edge of the deck and looked out at the dawn.

After several minutes Fenwick said, "You see the problem?"

"Yeah. Oh, yeah." Fenwick waited. Turner finally said, "I only have Kevin's word for what happened. I have no proof his story is true."

"What are you going to do?"

"I trust my gut instinct. I believe the kid. I'm also a cop."

"I'd trust your gut instinct more than a mountain of facts."

"Thanks. I'm sure, but . . ."

Fenwick nodded. They watched the dawn for a few more minutes then Fenwick said, "You know what I liked about this case?"

"Plenty of Timbits?" Turner said.

"That, too. No, no paperwork, no bosses, no Carruthers, no cute cop talk with other detectives." Back in Chicago Carruthers was the insecure nebbish on their squad. From what Turner could figure out, every squad and indeed every profession was cursed with at least one such.

Turner said, "I thought you liked cute cop talk."

"I do, mostly, but it's a strain being that witty all the time."

"If it was a real strain, you'd have died from the stress years ago."

They stood in companionable silence for some time, enjoying the Canadian morning.

Fenwick said, "This is why I take vacations."

Moments later Paul touched Buck's shoulder. "I've got to get some sleep."

312

Fenwick said, "I'm glad you're my friend."

"Same here," Paul said.

When Paul and Ben were alone in their bedroom, Ben asked, "Are you going to tell Jeff?"

"I'm not sure I have much choice. He's old enough to understand."

"Is he old enough to not talk about it?"

"I'll have to find a way."

Turner lay down and shut his eyes. The events of the evening ran through his mind. The ghastly hand reaching over the side of the boat replayed over and over. Kevin's story sounded absolutely true. He knew the boy. Paul trusted his own instincts.

40

Very late that afternoon all the Fenwicks and Turners, except Paul, headed out for a last bit of fishing. As prearranged, Paul was at the Naked Moose restaurant with Mavis Bednars.

Bednars said, "Ralph Bowers came back with a passel of dead bodies. He said there was an accident on the lake. Looks like four drunken teenagers died."

"They were drunk?" Turner asked.

"We're waiting for tests. They were seen earlier drinking. They must have been racing around on the lake. None of them were wearing life jackets."

Turner said, "Stupid to race around at night."

"Lucky Ralph was there."

"Or unlucky."

"Ralph's a good man. He says he was out there alone."

"Why would Ralph lie?" Turner asked.

"I saw Ralph earlier. He said he was looking for you."

Paul said, "I hope we run into him before we leave."

Bednars said, "Billy Morningsky was released."

"Schreppel has seen the light?"

"The Crown Attorney refused to press charges. He laughed at Schreppel."

"What's going to happen?" Turner asked.

"Scarth Krohn killed his girlfriend, Evon Gasple, while drunk and on drugs."

"The tests came back?"

"Yes. He was both. Bits of one of his dad's boats have been surfacing. He must have taken it out on the lake, run into a rock, and drowned."

"That's the final official story?"

"That's the final official story. Mr. and Mrs. Krohn were in at the same time. I wouldn't say 'together.' Mr. Krohn insisted that the case be closed. That he was going through enough grief. That he didn't want his son's name dragged through the headlines. Schreppel might not have believed anybody. He might want to defy the Crown Attorney, but he listened to the Krohns. It is officially over, right?"

"Right."

Her eyes searched his. "Because if you knew anything else, you'd tell us."

He gazed back evenly. "If I had found out anything the police needed to know, I would want to do that."

She smiled. "You're a good cop. I hope you and your family and friends come back." She left.

, 41 ,

The next morning amid a flurry of packing and last-day fishing rituals, Ian stomped on deck and strode up to Paul. He lifted his arm to point at Paul when his feet slipped from under him. He landed on the same pile of rods and reels as he'd done the other day. Ian swore. The St. Croix reel started tipping off the boat.

"Get it," Paul yelled.

Ian snatched at it. He went halfway off the boat. The line swung out as the rod dipped halfway into the water.

"Don't let go," Jeff said.

Ian yanked at the rod with all his might. He flopped back on to the deck. With him came rod, reel, line, and a fish.

Paul grabbed the rod. Jeff grabbed the fish. Brian rushed to help him.

"Goddamn stupid fish," Ian said.

Jeff said, "It's a big damn fish."

Paul said, "Language."

"Sorry," Jeff said. "Look at it, Dad. It's the biggest fish anyone's caught all week."

Ian said, "I hate fish."

Fenwick leaned over from his boat. "What's the excitement?"

Jeff held up the fish. "Ian caught it."

Brian said, "More like it caught him."

Madge came up beside Fenwick. She saw the fish and the looks on their faces. She began to laugh.

"It's not funny," Ian said. "I'm soaked."

"You'll dry," Paul said, "but we're going to have to live with the fact that you caught the biggest damn fish."

"Language," Jeff said.

Ian exited mumbling. The others returned to whatever they could salvage of a day of fishing.

About nine, Ralph Bowers appeared at the end of the dock. He approached Turner. "May I talk to you?" he asked.

"Sure," Turner said. They strolled toward the woods. Turner waited for Ralph to say what was on his mind.

At the beginning of the woods, Ralph handed Turner a package. Inside was a miniature carving of a muskie. It was as beautiful as the one he'd seen at Beverly Fleming's. Ralph said, "I want you to have this."

"Why?"

"Kevin is my friend."

"Thank you," Paul said.

This time Ralph's eyes met Paul's and they did not waver. Ralph said, "I was there. That night. I had my boat in the lake. I watch when I can. I didn't see what happened to Evon. I heard Kevin and Scarth in the water. I would have saved Kevin. Scarth was going to kill him. He said, 'Die, faggot, die.'

Who cares if someone is gay? Kevin was lucky. Afterward Kevin cried a lot. I heard him. I didn't know what to do. I didn't go to him. Kevin is a friend. I'll never tell. Scarth is dead. I'm glad. I wish I had done it."

Paul thought, Kevin had a witness. The amount of relief he felt surprised him. One less thing to worry about. The last major thing was would all these people keep silent? He would have to trust that to the future. Ralph patted Paul's shoulder and said, "You are a good man to worry so much and to take such care." He gave an awkward smile then offered his hand. Paul shook it. Ralph said, "I gotta get to work."

42

One of the final rituals they went through on their last day was that Paul and Jeff spent time alone. He directed Jeff's motorized wheelchair on the most level path to a small beach half a mile into the woods. Once they arrived Paul picked up some pebbles. He handed a few to Jeff. Father and son pitched them into the water seeing who could make the stones skip the most.

After a few minutes, Paul said, "I'm a little worried about you."

"I'm okay. I guess." He met his dad's eyes.

Paul said, "Some of this stuff's been a little scary?"

"Yeah, I guess." The boy got misty-eyed. He reached his hands out for his dad. The boy said, "I don't want that ever to happen again."

Paul said, "We'll protect you."

"I know."

The boy unclenched. Jeff asked, "Is Kevin okay?"

"Yes," Paul said.

Jeff said, "I hate bullies. A few kids pick on me because of my wheelchair so I understand."

"Did you want me to talk to the teachers or the principal?"

"No, when they realize Brian is my big brother, they back off."

"You'll let me know if there's a problem."

"I will." Father and son watched the sun rise higher and felt the heat increase until Jeff said, "I'm glad you're not going to turn him in."

"How did you figure it out?"

"You went tearing out of here looking for him with a whole houseboat. You don't do that unless it's serious. What's the most serious thing that's happened? It had to be connected to Scarth Krohn. And I listen to what you guys say. It wasn't hard to follow."

Paul was reasonably sure he was happy he had bright children, and Jeff showed every evidence of being very bright. Sometimes he worried. Now, he smiled. He was proud of his sons.

Halfway back to the houseboat, Jeff demanded, "How come Ian caught the biggest fish?"

"Dumbest luck I've ever seen."

"He doesn't even know how important it is."

"I won't tell him."

"Me neither."

A few miles past Duluth, Paul heard Jeff and Brian wrangling in the backseat over who had used the best bait to catch the

322

biggest fish. Both boys were adamant in their annoyance at Ian's luck. The reporter had refused to return in his chartered plane. He took a bus from Kenora.

The time for fishing had been far more limited than Paul had wished, but the amount of wrangling over useless issues his kids could do was about the same. That felt normal. So did Mrs. Talucci's presence, far in the back, rereading *The Princess Bride*. She still claimed it was the funniest book she'd ever read.

43

Paul Turner was in his son Jeff's bedroom. They'd gotten back to Chicago that afternoon. The boy had been quieter than usual on the drive back. He'd had only one helping of his favorite dessert at dinner. After going to bed, he had fallen asleep quickly.

Paul saw his son's copy of the book *Freddy the Detective* on his nightstand. Paul knew his son read numerous books over and over again. He also knew which ones the boy tended to read when he was upset. *Freddy the Detective* was always one of these. He sat for a while next to the sleeping child, kissed his forehead, and eased out of the room.

Brian was in the living room watching their DVD of *Casablanca*.

Paul sat next to him. Bogart was just refusing to help the Peter Lorre character. The last few pieces of a heaping plate of Mrs. Talucci's fudge sat in front of him. The family had been gulping it down all day. Mrs. Talucci had many old-fashioned remedies for many things, but she always said chocolate was one of her greatest and most sure cures. Paul was not about to dispute such wisdom.

Paul said, "Can we talk?"

Brian hit Pause. "Sure." He leaned back on the couch, shut his eyes for a moment, then looked at his dad.

Paul said, "Are you okay?"

"Mostly, I think. I've never known somebody who committed murder. He was a friend. Is a friend. I worry about what's going to happen to him."

"They will do the best they can for him. Right now I'm worried about you."

"I've got a lot of stuff to think about. You know, I'm glad I made out with him. It wasn't icky or anything. I'm straight, but I'm okay with what I did. It felt warm and friendly. Was I wrong? Did he think we'd have some kind of relationship? Did I screw up?"

"You were kind to a person who needed kindness. If things had gone differently, you'd have had to discuss his and your feelings. It would be like the girls you've dated the longest and broken up with. You discuss your feelings. You work things out or don't work things out. Sometimes friendships or relationships don't work out. Kevin is a good man. So are you. You did your best. Kevin couldn't help his past and neither could you your past. Sometimes events outside of us can be overwhelming."

"Will we still go fishing up there? I'd like to see him."

"That's next year's decision." Paul added, "I got a call from Canada. Kevin was tested for STDs. He's clean."

Brian smiled. "Without going into details, I can say that

326

we were very safe. I like Kevin, and it felt good, but it wasn't, you know . . ."

"Passionate?"

"More friendly and very safe. I do actually listen to you."

This confirmed what Kevin had told him.

Brian shook his head. "The thing is, I wish I could have done something sooner, or maybe if he'd told me, we could have . . ." His voice trailed off.

"Being abused is one of the hardest things to deal with. Kevin's been pretty independent for a long time. You did your best. You did nothing wrong. I'm proud of you."

"Thanks," Brian said. He gave his dad a quick, fierce hug.

Paul pointed to the television. "Why this tonight?"

"Kind of puts my problems in perspective."

Paul sat down to watch with his son.